Ghost in the Brew

Ghost in the Brew

A Kami White
Para(normal)legal Mystery

E.L. Oakes

CAVEL
PRESS

Kenmore, WA

A Camel Press book published by Epicenter Press

Epicenter Press
6524 NE 181st St.
Suite 2
Kenmore, WA 98028

For more information go to:
www.Camelpress.com
www.Coffeetownpress.com
www.Epicenterpress.com
www.eloakes.com

Design by Scott Book and Melissa Vail Coffman

Ghost in the Brew
Copyright © 2025 by E.L. Oakes

Library of Congress Control Number: 2024940170

ISBN: 978-1-68492-228-4 (Trade Paper)
ISBN: 978-1-68492-229-1 (eBook)

CHAPTER 1

Monday Morning: Marin Ave

I WOKE TO ANOTHER TYPICAL MONDAY MORNING at White Legal Services. A hairless cat, a suit of French Crusader armor, a cheap folding desk, and a couple of secondhand chairs greeted me. There were no messages in my email, no blinking light on the office phone. I took a quick shower in the tiny bathroom at the back of the office and slipped into a pair of clean jeans and a pink t-shirt. I tucked my messy blond curls under a grey military cap, stuffed poor naked Hoover into his San Francisco 49'rs sweatshirt and his harness, and headed for the door. "I need coffee. And you need a walk."

He didn't seem eager about coffee or a walk, but it was a beautiful April morning of the sort that was rare in the Bay Area. The sky was clear and bright blue, a faint breeze carried a heady spring perfume of daffodils and bottle-brush blooms. We needed to get out of the office for a bit. I tucked him under my arm for the walk over to Reese's Café. Before I even made it across the street, I spotted Morri Morrimont and Mallory Kent, along with Reese Calhoun, standing in the doorway of the cafe, looking down the street.

"Morning, gang. What are we doing?"

"Hatin'," Reese replied. Her tone was casual but there was fire in her eyes.

I followed her gaze. What I saw ripped a gasp from my throat that startled Hoover and he abandoned my arms for Morri's shoulder. The formerly empty and dilapidated pharmacy had been getting a facelift for weeks, and there'd been much speculation and gossip about what was going to happen with the old place. Now we knew. The banner hanging in front, in bright green and red, read CAFÉ FANTASTIQUE: ORGANIC FAIR-TRADE COFFEE.

Morri turned his bright blue eyes towards me, a faint frown on his weary, wrinkled face. "Mornin', poppet. Though not a good one, I daresay."

Morri could daresay whatever he liked. He was a retired war correspondent and lifelong cruciverbalist who was spending his retirement in the office above mine writing crosswords and those find-a-word puzzles you see in magazines. He had a vocabulary that dwarfed *Webster's Universal Unabridged Dictionary* and was tough, smart, funny and wonderful by turns. I had a real grandfather, Grandpa Dan, and I adored him, but Morri was my adopted grandparent. I've always believed that we get to choose our real family, and I chose Morri.

Mallory Kent adjusted his bright fuchsia tie that made his round, ruddy face look even ruddier. He had matched it with a pale blue shirt today, and it looked quite stylish. "I get that organic is supposed to be better for you, but does it really taste any better? I mean, coffee is coffee, right?"

"You drink instant Folgers out of a Styrofoam cup," I reminded Mallory kindly as Hoover purred on Morri's shoulder and rubbed his hairless chin over Morri's grey-stubbled head affectionately. They were old friends. "Do you seriously think this will hurt your business, Reese?"

The owner of Reese's Coffee and More fluttered her hands over the front of her brown, coffee-stained apron, the sunlight highlighting her tattoo of braided roses. "Of course it will! Two coffee shops on the same street? There's not enough business for two shops. Kami, there has to be something we can do to stop them. How did this get past the planning commission?"

"The coruscating lure of a new café won't change your coffee clientele." Morri pointed to the row of morning-break taxis on the street. "Concern is warranted, but let's not get carried away."

"Let me guess," I played my usual game with Morri. "This week's puzzle is 'c' themed?"

"Ah! You've conceived my creative contrivance!" Morri crowed at me, reaching out to fluff my curls. "Consider yourself the conquering champion!"

"I don't feel like a champion." I didn't. I felt terrible. "Reese, what can I do?"

She sighed, pushing her black braids back over her shoulder. "Find a way to shut them down. I don't care how. Start with the planning commission. Check licensing, health and safety . . . anything. Everything. It doesn't matter how we do it, we just have to do it."

"I'll look into it," I agreed, but I didn't feel hopeful. "Does anyone know if there's a non-compete written into the downtown business association charter?"

Morri and Mallory shook their heads. No one competed with a cruciverbalist, and Mallory was the only insurance broker in the neighborhood. As for my business, there was another law office over on Main, but they specialized in bilingual criminal cases, nothing that competed with my business.

"It would be like someone opening an Irish pub right across from Magillies on Main, wouldn't it?" Reese continued as if she hadn't heard us. "They can't just come trotting in and open a new coffee shop. We worked like crazy to keep the big chain places out of downtown, and then the city allows this?"

"We don't even know if they're any good," I reminded my friends. "They haven't opened yet. You know most of these new small businesses crash within the first year, and with the way the economy has been . . ."

"Exactly!" Reese interrupted. "With the economy how it's been, with rising ingredient prices and operating costs, we're still turning a profit, but only because I'm well established. If we lose business, I'm shut down. Dammit!" She slammed her right fist into her left palm. "I've worked too hard for this to lose it now!"

"You're going to give yourself a heart attack, Reese," Mallory said in his usual placid tone. "Let's all go inside, get a nice hot cup of something, and stop making a spectacle on the street."

Reese looked ready to punch Mallory, but she nodded and turned inside. I handed off Hoover's leash to Morri and let him and Mallory go ahead of me. I was about to follow them when I heard my name called from across the street by an all-too-familiar voice. *Could today get any worse?* I groaned as I turned to face my caller.

Irvin Zetttlemeyer looks like a frightened small dog most of the time. He's taller than I am, but his anemic complexion and slumped posture make him seem much smaller. The geeky, thick-framed glasses he wears make his sad, round eyes appear even sadder and rounder. Don't get me wrong. He's an absolute sweetheart when he isn't accusing my cat of being an alien or introducing me to serial killers. And if you need someone to architect a software project, the word in the industry is that there is no one better with a tech design. With him on the sidewalk was a heavyset young woman dressed entirely in black. Her shoulder-length hair was dyed blue-black, her lipstick and eyeshadow were black, even her necklace and earrings were black. She was wearing a black velvet skirt, black t-shirt, and black combat boots.

"Hey, Irvin." His traveling companion had piqued my curiosity. They jogged across the street to me, not even checking for traffic.

"Kami!" Irvin gave me a quick hug. "We need you."

I returned the hug and backed away, taking in the unlikely pair before me. They were polar opposites, one completely light and the other completely dark, and both completely at odds with the gorgeous spring day. "For what, exactly?"

Irvin lowered his voice. "For, you know . . . what you do."

"I do many things, Irvin." Now I knew for sure what he was going to ask, but I wasn't going to make it easy for him.

"It's a . . . well . . . it's weird . . . and it's . . ."

The woman cut off his stammering. "I think there's some of kind of demon haunting my house and Irvin said you could help."

"Demon?" I looked back and forth between them. "I don't do demons. I only do ghosts."

Irvin opened the door to the café. "I'll buy you coffee if you just listen."

Well, how was I supposed to say no to that?

I led the way to a table towards the back of the first floor, and Irvin broke away to place his order at the front counter.

"I'm Prue," the woman put her hand out. "Prue Amber. Thanks for talking to us."

I gave her hand a shake, noting that she had a good confident grip and met my eye directly. "I'm always happy to meet a friend of Irvin's."

She glanced towards the counter and a hint of a smile tugged at the corner of her mouth. "He's . . . different. That's why I like him."

She liked Irvin? As in *like* liked Irvin? Okay then. I gave a glance around to see where Mallory and Morri and my miscreant cat were. My cat and Irvin have a bit of a history. Mallory and Morri were sitting with one of the other regulars, and Hoover was settled on Morri's knee lapping up what appeared to be a cappuccino cup filled with whipped cream. I just hoped Irvin didn't see him. That could go badly for everyone involved.

Irvin returned with a caramel latte for me, a pot of jasmine tea for Prue, and an orange smoothie for himself. How do you come to Reese's and not get coffee? Or at least tea? "No coffee, Irvin?"

"Doctor said I should probably lay off the stuff. I've been kinda nervous since . . . Well, you know."

I did know, all too well. I felt a stab of sympathy for the guy. "Yeah, I've been a bit more jumpy since then, too." I shifted back to the subject at hand. "Okay, tell me what's going on."

Prue and Irvin exchanged glances, and then Irvin spoke up. "We think there's something in Prue's house. She moved in about a month ago, and it's been getting worse ever since."

"What is 'it,' exactly?"

"I thought it was my imagination at first, but now," Prue paused, her head tilted. "I think it's not good. As in, it's bad energy. Bad juju. Whatever you want to call it. It's just bad."

"I think it's a demon," Irvin stated, his pale blue eyes staring at me behind his thick lenses.

"A demon?" *Oh, Irvin, you always bring me the craziest stuff.* I sipped my coffee to hide my disbelief.

"I didn't want to say it," Prue admitted, "but I've read a thing or two, and I don't know what else it could be. It's evil."

"So, Prue," I started with a deep breath. "I'm going to be straight with you. I don't usually deal with demonics. There are more experienced groups in the area for that kind of thing." And people more patient and more willing to suspend belief than me.

"I don't know who else to go to," Prue's voice was barely above a whisper.

"I can vouch for how bad things are," Irvin spoke up.

"Irvin . . ." I tried to think of the nicest way to say what was on my mind, but tact has never been my strong point. "The last job you called me about was nothing more than a leaky toilet. The job before that, your friend was suffering from mental illness and thought his real-life sister was a ghost."

"His sister was really pale. She could have been dead," Irvin persisted. "Please? Just come take a look."

"Who's paying for it?"

"I'll pay for the initial consultation. Please? I don't know anyone else. You're our mage, remember?"

Right. I was the mage. At least, I was in the eyes of Irvin and his former roommates. Except for the serial killer one, but since he was in a coma, I didn't think he counted very much. "Okay. Here's how it goes, Prue. In my day job, I'm a paralegal, studying to become a lawyer. I do everything by the book. I look at all the evidence, and then I present my findings. What you do with that is up to you. If you think you can work with that, we can continue. If it's truly something beyond my experience, I'll call in reinforcements who have more experience than I do with this kind of thing."

"Father Joe?" Irvin asked.

"Father Joe," I confirmed. "So, does that sound okay?"

Prue nodded. "No one else believes me. I'm getting seriously freaked out. I'm not even sleeping at home whenever I can help it. I only go back to shower and change clothes."

That sounded serious. "Why don't you tell me what's happening?"

"It started with scratching in the walls. I thought it was mice or something. Nanna was in a care home, so the house was vacant for about a year before I moved in. So I set mousetraps, but I never caught anything." Prue took a hesitant sip of her tea. "And then the growling started. It seems to come from everywhere. And there's knocking and tapping. It's not a mouse!"

I don't do demonics because I don't believe in them, but I do know a bit of what to watch for. Growling, scratching, knocking. Check. "Have you noticed more activity at certain times or when you're doing certain activities?"

Prue's eyes rolled towards the ceiling as she thought about the question.

"Tell her about the smell," Irvin suggested.

"Oh, yeah. That happens mostly when I'm showering. Sometimes I can hear the growling over the water, but it's the smell . . . nasty, like a garbage dump."

I felt a shiver crawl up my spine. "Like sulfur, or rotting meat?"

"Like rotting *everything*," Prue nodded. Irvin pushed his smoothie away.

Darn! That was nearly everything on the might-be-a-demon list. "What makes you afraid to be in the house? Has something specific happened to frighten you or make you think you're in danger?"

Prue paused, her tea held in front of her mouth in a guarding position. "Nothing specific. I just feel like I'm being watched all the time. It's really freaking me out. Sometimes when I come back, things are knocked over: shampoo bottles in the bathtub, or soda cans on the floor. I have cats, but they stay in their room when I'm not home. I've stopped leaving things on the coffee table or side tables. I don't even like going in the house anymore. I inherited it from my Nanna and I love it, or I'd have sold it already." Tears welled in her eyes and spilled over, tracking black mascara down her cheeks. "I just want my home back."

The tears had me. She needed help. "I'll tell you what. If you'd like, I'll come over and do a preliminary examination. That's where I come to your house, set up cameras and sound equipment, and see if we can catch any of this activity on tape."

"Like you did at my house?" Irvin asked, his pale watery gaze meeting mine, and I knew we were both remembering the spectral screams we'd captured on the recording of his preliminary investigation.

"That's right." I turned my attention back to Prue. "Look, the activity you described could be a regular haunting, or it could have a simple explanation like bad plumbing or someone trying to prank you. So, we'll do the prelim and if I think you actually have something demonic, I'll call in Father Joe, and if necessary, refer you to a group that specializes in this kind of thing. If you're agreeable, I'll draw up a contract for you, including my privacy clause, and we can set up a time and date for the preliminary."

"Tonight? Can you come tonight?"

It was Monday. I had a paper due on Friday, and I wanted to figure out how to help Reese. "Is tomorrow soon enough?"

"I'll pay for the preliminary investigation," Irvin spoke up. "I'll pay for anything if we can help Prue."

Prue's eyes glowed as she looked at Irvin.

"Demon activity is usually highest between midnight and 3 am. Why don't we plan for 10:00 pm to 12:30 tonight. I really can't do later than that on a work night. What about your schedules?"

"I'm on sabbatical writing a book about software development," Irvin shrugged. "I have work to do on my book, but I can do that any time."

Prue added, "I'm a freelancer, and mostly I've been working from Irvin's."

"What kind of freelancing?" I didn't really care, but I had a prurient curiosity about her relationship with Irvin.

"Front-end development. Mostly for corporate websites."

"Will Nicky be helping you?" Irvin asked.

"Nicky is in Hawaii." I sighed with regret. My best friend would have loved to be there for a demonic. The whole paranormal research thing was her fault anyway. How dare she get me into this and then fly off to Hawaii? "Ryan qualified for Waikiki Classic, so she went to cheer him on."

"Too bad. I think she'd like this one."

He wasn't wrong, but it was hard to admit when Irvin was right, so I just nodded my agreement. "Okay. I'll see you tomorrow, then."

"Just figure out what it is and get rid of it." If Prue's house wasn't haunted, her eyes certainly were. She texted me her address and I checked to make sure it showed up in my map app.

"Don't worry. We'll figure this out," I reassured her, even though I had no idea whether or not we would.

SOMEHOW, IRVIN MADE IT OUT OF THE CAFÉ without spotting Hoover, who was now lounging across Morri's lap, being petted and pampered. Spoiled little beast. I headed over to their table, latte in hand.

Mallory waved for me to take a seat with an urgency that made me worry about what else had happened while my back was turned. "We've been coming up with a plan!"

I settled in, Morri slid a napkin covered in notes to me, and they filled me in. It was an entire marketing plan, focused on social media and public awareness. "I like it! I'm in."

CHAPTER 2

———— ❦ ————

Monday Afternoon

T HE PLAN MORRI AND MALLORY HAD hatched was solid. I gathered up Hoover and headed back to my office to enact my part of the plan. I couldn't help but look down the street to the new coffee shop going in on the corner. Organic, fair trade. Well, the price of that kind of quality alone would keep Reese's customers coming to her instead of going down the block. The taxi drivers and the office-worker lunch crowd knew value when they tasted it.

As I watched, a tall, younger man carrying a clipboard came out of the building, stepping around the cones and the debris dumpster. He looked my way, paused, and for a moment, I watched him and he watched me, then he waved politely and went back to studying his clipboard. The new owner, I wondered? Or just someone managing the remodel? None of my business anyway, I decided. If there was going to be a battle of the bean on our street, I would be on Reese's side, for better or worse.

Reese's Café had a Facebook page and a website, but they were sorely neglected. Fortunately, I had access to both. I had barely logged in when I spotted Mallory coming across the street. I thought he would go open his office for the day, but instead, he came into mine.

"I just recorded these videos," he held up his phone. "I'll work on the Youtube and Tiktok accounts. Max just gave me the passwords."

"You use TikTok?"

"My daughter showed me." Mallory shrugged his broad shoulders. "When you have a sixteen-year-old, you have to know these things."

"I'll cross-link everything and put out the appeal to Reese's fans to post their own videos." I'd just finished updating my own basic website, so the café website was a breeze. "The website has a page where you can list events and take reservations. We should line up some events," I suggested. "Any ideas?"

"What about live music? That coffee shop over in Mountain View has live jazz most weekends."

"Do you know any jazz musicians?"

"Uh. No." Mallory shook his head, his tie waving. He held up his phone. "What do you think of this?"

The video was a close-up of Hoover's wrinkly face with a drop of whipped cream on his chin as he lapped up his treat. Mallory had added bouncy music and captioned it with a play on the café's tagline. "Kittehs luv Coffee and More at Reese's!"

"I love it! But what if people don't like cats?"

"You're right, we'll have to get a dog video, too." Mallory heaved his large frame from my small office chair and stretched. "I should go open the office, but I'll keep working on these. Morri is loving his secret mission. I don't think he's had this much fun in years."

I glanced out the window to see Morri standing at the corner near the café, pen and pad in hand and camera around his neck, talking to the cab drivers and business lunch folks as they arrived. "He does seem to be having fun."

"I guess once a journalist, always a journalist." Mallory headed back to his office and left me alone with Hoover and Evrett to get on with my own work.

WITH THE SOLUTION TO REESE'S PROBLEMS UNDERWAY, I turned to Irvin Zettlemeyer's problem and dug into my favorite paranormal research site for advice on demon hunting. From my quick bit of research, it seemed that those who believe in demons are vehement in their insistence that demons exist. Those who don't believe are mocking and derisive of those who do. I was neither mocking nor derisive, but I was doubtful. The only demons I'd ever seen were very much human both in body and soul. I was tempted to call Irvin back and tell him to call someone else, but a look at my calendar reminded me that I didn't have any other contracts this month for paralegal work or document preparation. The last tag on my career list was Notary of the Public, but that doesn't really pay anything. It's just a good thing to have when you're a document preparer. So I needed the work, even if it was just a preliminary evaluation.

"I dunno, Evrett." I shifted my gaze to the suit of armor in the corner. "What do you think? Does Irvin have a demon?"

There was no response from the French Crusader. He'd been inactive for a few weeks, and I wasn't sure if he was bored, or just doing whatever it was ghosts do when they're content. I was sure that he wasn't gone. He'd gotten a message across that he was staying until he'd fulfilled his life's purpose. I didn't know what that was, but if it included driving the infidels out, he was going to be here a long time. I kicked back and put my tennis-shoed feet up on the cheap folding desk that was my only real office furniture, everything else having been swept away in the great hurricane called Juliet Hanford. "No demons? Nah, I don't think so, either."

The visor on Evrett's sallet helm slammed shut loudly, the ringing echoing through the office.

Egads! I snapped upright and grabbed my cellphone. I found Father Talbon's contact information and gave him a call, which he answered with a cheerful, "Good morning, Kamera. How are you this fine day?"

"I'm well, Father Talbon," I replied, instantly feeling cheered by his greeting. Hardly anyone called me Kamera anymore. "I was hoping I could ask a favor."

"Does it involve Happy Cookie?" He named Morri's wife's cookie shop with more than a little hope in his voice.

"Yes, it does," I improvised. "There's a whole specialty box of Happy Cookie with your name on it if I can keep you on standby tonight for an investigation." I filled him in on the details of Irvin's potential demon haunting and he agreed instantly.

"I'll be up late tonight anyway working on Wednesday night's sermon."

"I'll call you if I need you, but I think I should be fine. You know how many of these things turn out to be nothing at all."

Father Joe Talbon paused, then asked, "Will Nicky or Morri be with you?"

"Not this time. It's for Irvin Zettlemeyer. You remember him, right? It should be fine."

"I think it would greatly set my mind at ease if you would text me at one a.m. to let me know everything is well."

"I would hate to have your mind at any unease, Father Joe," I agreed. "If you don't hear from me by 1:30, you can send reinforcements."

My office door swung open with a ring of the bell. I signed off with Father Talbon and turned with a smile and a friendly, "Hi. Welcome!" before realizing it was the young man with the clipboard from down the street.

He was in his mid-twenties, with dark green eyes and a shock of unkempt black hair, a goatee beard and tidy mustache, and tribal tattoos down the exposed areas of his neck and arms. "Hi. I'm Wyatt Halden from down the street. Your sign says you're a notary?"

"I am." I smiled a little less politely. "I'm not allowed to help you, though." I pointed across the street. "You see, you're the enemy. I'm a Reese's girl."

"Oh." His face fell. "I don't suppose you could make an exception? I need these papers notarized and submitted before five, and I'm running behind on everything. It's going to take me an hour just to get down to the county planning office."

I glanced towards Reese's. Notary Publics can only charge a nominal fee, and *that* wasn't worth getting eaten alive by Reese. But I couldn't afford to alienate customers either. "So, you're a partner in the new coffee shop?"

"Yeah. Me, my uncle and his friend. I do the managing part, Uncle Grady does the food (he's a chef), and Thomas is the coffee expert. He's been in Central America up until now, negotiating with the coffee trade organizations. His company, Coffee Imports LTD, is really kind of our backer. You'll see them listed in the paperwork." He showed me the stack of papers on his clipboard.

"And you just manage the cafe?"

"Well, eventually I'll be able to just manage the cafe. Right now, I have to oversee all the renovations, make sure all the permits are in order, get all the equipment and furnishings, and everything else." Wyatt sighed. "I managed a chain store before. I thought I knew what I was getting into, but starting from scratch is a lot harder than I thought it would be.

"You know, you're going to have a tough time of it in this neighborhood." I insinuated, trying to be sly. (Subtlety is not my strong point. In fact, it's not really a point with me at all, but I just keep trying for some reason.) "People are really loyal to Reese."

He laughed. "We're trying to attract a totally different market segment. I mean, look at Reese's, with those cabs and delivery vans parked out front all day? We're all organic, all fair trade, and vegan friendly. We're going to bring in the pedestrians and bicyclists off Main Street. You'll see! We're going to bring a whole new life to this street. Walk-by traffic will increase, and that will be good for everyone. Including this place."

Hoover leaped to the top of the desk and glared at the coffee guy, clearly maintaining his loyalty to Reese. But I had to admit that increased walk-through traffic sounded good. I didn't believe it for a second, but it sounded good.

"All right, Mister Wyatt Halden," I reached for my Notary book and stamp. "I'll notarize. But I'm warning you beforehand that I'm not changing loyalties or switching sides. I'm on Reese's side."

"Great! Thank you! I owe you a coffee anytime you want!"

It turned out to be worth my time since he had several documents to notarize. I caught an error and was able to do a correction on the spot, and I charged him for that, too. I promised myself I'd pass on the love by spending some of the money at Reese's later.

With a little coffee money in my spare cash jar, I was able to focus on other things. I pulled up the address of Prue's house and looked at the street-view. It was an older house in the Cherryland district of San Lorenzo and one of the many single-story, two-bedroom, one-bath homes that had appeared in the 1950s to house the returning soldiers of WWII. The street was tree-lined and the lawns were mowed, but there was a shabby feel to the neighborhood. Sidewalks were cracked, houses were in need of paint, and old picket fences were gapped and tilted. Settling into my research, I looked up the sales history on the house, which showed that it had changed hands after the original owner—Prue's grandmother, from what Prue said—passed away. I tried running a background check on Prue, but working with just her name, and probably not her full name at that, it was unsuccessful. I didn't find any recorded deaths at the house. In fact, I didn't find much information on that address at all. It was just a quiet old neighborhood in a quiet old district.

HAVING DONE ALL I COULD I DO ON THAT FRONT, I started on my paper that was due Friday. I was only taking one class this semester because it was a hard topic for me and I wanted to do well. I barely got started before my door jangled again. "Hi, welcome in." I greeted before looking up.

"It's me again."

Me was Wyatt Holden. "More paperwork?"

"No . . ." he hesitated, looking side to side.

Uh oh. He wasn't going to ask me out was he? If he asked me out, I was probably going to have to throw him out on his ear or something. What little love life I have is complicated enough.

"Is your sign serious?"

I glanced at my hand-stenciled window sign. "It's a very serious sign. I've never heard it tell a single joke."

In the corner of my eye, Everett's gauntlet shifted a fraction of an inch. The knight was not amused. Hoover strolled in from the back room and hopped up on the desk, eyeing our newest client with a jaded gaze.

"I mean the 'paranormal research' part. You really do paranormal research?"

Was he having second thoughts about my legal work? "Yes, I do. I also do legal and topical research. The paranormal work is a, well, I'd call it a side gig. It beats driving for Uber."

"So how does it work?" There was no sign of ridicule on his face, and though I searched for some sign that this was a put-on, I didn't find one.

"Every case is different. I try to take an open-minded approach, evaluate any claims, find logical explanations for any activity, and if that fails, I do a full investigation using cameras, sound, and electronic equipment to gather evidence." I kept my gaze on Wyatt's face, but his expression was completely passive. "If there's sufficient evidence of haunting, then I work with my colleagues to resolve the situation to the satisfaction of the client."

I left out that my biggest case had been a genuine haunting that had resulted in my nearly being killed, and not by the disembodied, fortunately. I'd discovered the hard way that just working in an office with a haunted suit of armor didn't qualify me to hunt ghosts, even when they were struggling desperately to be found.

"How much do you charge?"

"That depends, but initial consultation is a hundred. I know a lot of research groups work for free, but my work comes with written contracts, including confidentiality statements and damage waivers. I make no claims that I cannot substantiate, and I act as your advocate every step of the way."

"I see." Wyatt was gnawing his lip. Did he need convincing? Did I even want to convince him?

"Why don't you tell me what you have going on? I don't charge anything for asking questions."

"My uncle thinks we have ghost activity in the new shop."

"But you don't think so?" My mind strayed back to that old drugstore robbery. That kind of shooting could easily have left an imprint of violence on the premises, and it was possible that a spirit who suffered a violent death might be hanging around.

There was a long silence but I waited it out.

"I don't know what to think. At first, I thought someone was screwing with stuff, but now that the remodeling is almost done, there are only three of us with keys. Look," Wyatt hesitated again. "It's not that I think that hauntings don't happen, but I don't believe that every abandoned building is full of them. I don't really believe in ghosts. I believe in logical, reasonable explanations."

"I believe in both. It's when we can't find logical explanations that we have to look beyond the normal and into the paranormal." I smiled in what I hoped was a reassuring manner. "Tell you what. If you want me to investigate it, I won't charge anything for the consultation, and I'll cut you a very good deal on any research into the property I do. If you need a full investigation and I have to bring in my teammates, I'll only charge you costs. Good neighbors deserve good deals." Okay, so I wouldn't make much on the job, if it even turned into a job, but it would give me a chance to scout Reese's competition from the inside. If I could use the job to give Reese the edge over Café Fantastique, I'd take it.

"Are you sure?" Wyatt looked skeptical. That was promising. Skepticism was necessary for good ghost-hunting.

"Absolutely. When's a good time to come by and talk to you and your partners?" Remembering previous problems, I added with hurricane speed, "You should know that everyone involved has to be onboard with the investigation. If anyone has a problem with it, I won't do it. My reputation is very important to me, and I've had issues with bad faith in the past." Specifically a murderer who thought I was creating evidence to frame him, but that was kind of beside the point. "I don't want that to happen again."

"It won't. Uncle Grady and Thomas are both believers in this kind of thing."

"But you aren't."

"Like I said, it's not that I don't believe in ghosts, but I haven't seen any evidence that convinces me. That is, until now."

"You saw something that persuaded you?" I tried to keep my tone curious and encouraging. "What did you experience?"

"I installed a new industrial mixer last night. I set the whole thing up, plugged it in, tested it, turned it off, unplugged it, and headed home. When I got in this morning, Uncle Grady read me the riot act, asking why I'd gone off and left the mixer on all night. I unplugged it, I'm sure of it. And the more I think of it, there's been other things. Things misplaced, not where I left them. Water turned on in the sink. Just little things that I attributed to the chaos of the remodel at the time, but the more I think about them, the more I'm . . ."

"Haunted by them?"

"Yeah. You could say that."

He was obviously disconcerted. I could relate. Evrett and I haven't always had the most amiable relationship. When he first arrived, I steadfastly refused to believe the suit of armor was haunted, and the old knight worked overtime to change my mind. One too many tipped cups of tea and an infamous incident involving a misplaced legal brief, and I eventually came around. Now I considered him a friend and ally. "When is a good time for me to come by and meet your partners? I can do a preliminary walk-through and see if I think it warrants more attention."

"Tonight? Can you come tonight?"

I considered that for a second. It would get me inside the new shop and give me a chance to snoop around for Reese. I wasn't going to make beans off this job, which would be a fine reason for refusing, but I wasn't doing this for me. I was doing it for Reese. "I have plans, but I can probably squeeze down there between five and six, if that's not too late? Otherwise, it will have to be Wednesday or Thursday."

"We're planning to open on Wednesday. We really want this resolved before then. Uncle Grady and I will be working late all week, so five tonight would be okay, I think. Come around the back and knock and I'll let you in."

I sent him on his way, stuck my tongue out at Evrett, and started collecting my cameras and recorders and checking my batteries. The process reminded me of what happened the last time I went on a ghost-hunting job alone and I wished Nicky was with me. I texted her. "Wish you were here, Nickydoodle!"

She texted back almost immediately. "KamiLambi! You wish you were HERE!" with five wave emojis and five surfboard emojis.

She was right. I wished I was there. I didn't surf anymore, but Hawaii sounded far better than the possibly haunted old building down the street.

CHAPTER 3

Monday Evening

I FINISHED THE ROUGH DRAFT OF MY STATISTICS analysis paper just in time to gobble down a yogurt before walking down to the new café. There was a man in coveralls peeling the paper off the front windows. He had a stenciling set laid out and I'm ashamed to admit that I was sad to see that he wasn't our usual neighborhood sign painter. Our local guy does a lovely job with the lettering but isn't big on spelling. Mallory Kent's office still read *Malroy Kent Insruance.* After three repaints, Mallory finally gave up and left it. I saved my precious pennies and painted my window sign myself. You can only see the smudges if you look closely. Or if the sun's shining directly on it, which is only most afternoons between two and four. Too bad the new café hired a professional. It might have done Reese's some good if they'd had the usual guy do it. Or paid me to smudge it up for them.

Following Wyatt's instructions, I walked around to the back of the shop where a heavy-duty security door, similar to the one at the back of my office, was propped open a few inches to emit chemical odors that even my non-handy-man nose could recognize as paint and glue. I rapped my knuckles on the doorframe and announced myself with a cheery, "Hullo? Anyone home?"

There was a moment's hesitation and then the door swept the

rest of the way open. "Wyatt told me you were coming. I'm Grady Halden." Grady looked like an older, stockier version of Wyatt, sans tattoos. He waved a flour-dusted hand at me.

I decided I liked him. "I'm Kami White, paralegal at large, paranormal investigator at least." I smiled. "Wyatt told me you have a situation you'd like me to look into?"

Grady ran a hand through his salt and pepper hair. Or maybe that was flour, not grey hair. "I'm surprised he came to you. We're not entirely sure what's going on, but he's been pretty adamant that there are logical explanations, up until the last day or two."

Wyatt came in through a swinging door that opened to the front dining room and hung his clipboard on a hook by the door. I half-smiled to myself. That door was darn shiny, without a single scuff or scrape on it. That wouldn't last long once it was getting kicked open by busy kitchen staff a hundred times a day.

I let my gaze stray around the back room of the café. There were two gleaming stainless steel commercial ovens and an industrial stove-top similar to Reese's but about five models newer. The requisite three-sink system and powerful commercial dishwasher were seamless stainless steel, straight out of a restaurant supply catalogue. There were solid worktables and specialized equipment, some of which I recognized from my mother's herb business. The floor was red-brick tile. Compared to Reese's kitchen, this was beautiful. It made me want to cook something, and I don't even like to cook. I gave it a jaded, "This is pretty nice."

"Give it a few days. We haven't opened yet." Grady said cheerfully as he opened the oven and removed a tray of what looked and smelled like snickerdoodle cookies. He scraped one from the tray and slid it onto a small plate, waving a hand over it to cool it down. "Try this and tell me what you think."

It was hot and tasted boldly of cinnamon, and it was sweet enough, but it didn't have the melt-in-your mouth quality of Reese's cookies, and it certainly didn't hold a candle to Happy Cookie over on Second Street. I'm no chef, and what little I do know about commercial baking, I learned in the heat of summer afternoons working at Reese's Café. But a glance at the ingredients lining the shelves told me exactly what I needed to know. "This is pretty good. I take it you use shortening for the oil?"

"Pure soybean shortening. It's vegan," Grady agreed proudly. "All organic. Non-GMO."

"Ah. It's tasty," I said enthusiastically. *But it could use some butter.* I finished the cookie and promised myself I'd get an extra special dessert at Reese's later. I'd choked down enough of my mother's healthy, cardboard-textured cookies that I no longer felt guilty about splurging on desserts made with real sugar, milk, and eggs. "Please don't tell me that it's the cookies you think are haunted?"

Wyatt and Grady exchanged worried glances, and finally Grady just shrugged. "Not so much. We've had strange things happening. Things moving from place to place, equipment turning on by itself. The other day the faucet turned itself on and the sink overflowed while I was talking to the carpet layers."

I pulled out my EMF detector, digital recorder, and notebook. "Okay, give me the grand tour and show me everywhere you've had problems."

"I watch Ghost Seekers! That's an EMF detector!" Grady seemed quite proud of himself. "You really know what you're doing."

I tried to make my smile friendly, but I was guarded. "I'm a professional, sir. Those reality ghosthunter shows have very little bearing on what I do. Where's your other partner? Thomas something? Will he be joining us?"

Wyatt waved his hand. "His flight was delayed. He won't be back until late. We can wait for him if you want?"

I didn't want to wait. I wanted to get this over with. I also really wanted to know what else they didn't do as well as Reese's. They showed me around the small dining room with its stylish stainless steel and wood dining chairs and tables. The walls were dark grey and hung with prints of famous art pieces featuring food and dining. Degas' *L'Absinthe* shared a wall with Kalf's *Still Life with Ewer*. There were more, but those were just the ones I knew the names of, thanks to an elective in art history. It was all very stylish, but I had to wonder how long it would be before those bright metal frames and the protective glass would be covered with whipped cream splashes and oily fingerprints. Did soybean oil leave the same smudgy fingerprints as butter? Unless they wanted to spend all their time polishing, it wasn't going to age well. Not my problem, though. I was ghost-hunting, not writing a restaurant critique. I turned back to Grady. "You're sure your partner is okay with this? I don't want to have any conflict."

"He's fine with it," Grady shrugged again, something I was beginning to realize was characteristic for him. "He's a bit superstitious."

"A bit?" Wyatt cried out incredulously. "He's insisting we open this Wednesday because next Friday is the 13th. He made me fire the painters because their logo had a black cat on it. And one time, he threw salt over the kitchen because he knocked over a bag of sea salt."

"Okay, maybe more than a bit," Grady agreed. "He's afraid we've got bad juju. I think he lived in the Caribbean too long."

Another Zettlemeyer? I was going to need a blessing from Father Talbon myself if all my clients were like this. I let them show me through the rest of the building, taking digital photos and jotting down EMF readings. All the EMF numbers were well within normal margins, probably because the whole building had new electrical work.

I showed them the numbers I'd recorded and explained how high EMF readings could affect some people. "If the normal operating EMF levels are low, or only spike when certain equipment is turned on, I can count out the natural effects of electromagnetic frequencies on the human body as a factor that might be affecting perception of haunting. Looking at these readings, I don't believe a 'fear cage' response is a factor in what you've experienced."

"In other words, we aren't crazy?" Grady cheerfully interjected, then added more somberly, "I think the jury is still out regarding our sanity. We have to be crazy to try to open this place, right?"

Wyatt laughed. "This place is driving *me* crazy. I was perfectly sane before I got here."

"I research haunted houses for a living. I'm not sure I'm on the sanity bandwagon myself." I continued quickly before they could start debating my sanity instead of their own. "In some hauntings, a spirit can produce high electromagnetic frequencies. A sudden spike in EMF readings that can't be explained by electrical issues might be an indication of haunting. If you hire me to do a full investigation, we'll be able to compare the readings I took today with any anomalous readings we might get during the investigation. Right now, all the readings are well within comfortable range, so any high readings we get at other times might indicate an active spirit."

"By spirit you mean ghost?"

"They prefer the term disembodied human," I joked, but when they exchanged glances, I felt compelled to shake my head. "Sorry, bad time for humor. Yes, I mean ghost, or spirit. One thing I have to warn you about is that sometimes people who die violently don't understand that they're dead. That's why they can't move on. They exist in a state of confusion, and don't understand what's happened to them."

"Die violently?" Grady asked, firing Wyatt a perplexed glance.

Uh oh. The old robbery was practically legend in San Amoro. How did they buy the building and not even know about it? I took a deep breath while they stared at me in puzzlement. "You do know there was a shooting here? About ten years ago? A pharmacy robbery gone wrong?"

They obviously didn't know. Grady's eyes were wide and his jaw muscles were twitching. Wyatt started rubbing his eyes and let out a pained groan. "I thought they had to disclose that kind of thing at purchase?"

"Only if there was a death on the premises within three years," I explained. These poor guys had no idea what they'd purchased. If they hadn't been the enemy, I would have felt sorry for them. Who am I kidding? I felt terrible for them. "No matter. If there's still some lost soul hanging around, we'll sort it out, but so far I'm not seeing anything that can't be explained by human actions. Water left on. Lights not turned off. Equipment running. Those sound more like accidents than anything else."

"It's not," Grady assured me swiftly. "We aren't so senile or overworked that we'd forget to turn the water off or unplug the mixer."

"Okay. If you'd like, I'll do an overnight investigation. You're welcome to join me, but we'd need to stay together during the investigation to prevent contamination. If you agree, I'll draw up the contract and disclaimers and bring them by tomorrow."

"Tonight would be better," Wyatt gestured around him. "Tomorrow is going to be crazy. I've just got too much to do if we're going to open on Wednesday."

I already had Prue and her demonic scheduled. "I'm sorry. I have an investigation tonight."

"We can't keep working like this. I'm going crazy." Grady insisted, his eyes narrowing. "If you can't do it, maybe we'll have to find someone else."

"Know a lot of paranormal researchers, Uncle?" It was clear that Wyatt's patience was wearing thin. He looked back at me hopefully. "Maybe you can come after your other investigation?"

I sighed. My head was starting to hurt. "Let me see if I can shift my other job. Demonics are most active between midnight and three. I can come here earlier, but I really need to be on the other job when . . ."

"Did you say demonic?" Was it my imagination, or did Grady just turn a wicked shade of pale green. Maybe Grady was the ghost.

"Sure. Although it's probably not a demon. They're extremely rare. More likely it's a mouse, or maybe a plumbing problem." I continued. "Here's what I can do. Let me see if I can push that job out an hour or two. That way, I can do a small preliminary here before going over there."

"We wouldn't have to do it at 3 a.m., would we?" Grady looked tired. I felt a bit sorry for him. If he was doing all the chef work and baking, and they didn't have a crew hired yet, the pace would be killer. Maybe they'd be so tired and overwhelmed that they'd give up and go out of business. Then I wouldn't have to figure out if the place was really haunted at all, and Reese could be happy.

"No, you don't have a demonic. If there's a ghost, it probably stems from the robbery shooting. Maybe it's the old shop-owner just trying to put things back the way they were, or it's the robber that the police shot and he's just lost or confused. But so far, I haven't seen anything to indicate that you really have a haunting at all." I smiled and put out my hand. "Let me get some dinner, gather my gear, and I'll come back at eight to set up. We'll go until ten thirty or so, and you can both be home in bed by midnight."

They shook my hand in turn, Wyatt's grip business-like and affirming, Grady's strong from kneading dough and manual labor. I promised I'd be back soon and made my escape out the back door.

A delivery truck was pulling up as I slipped out, and I stopped to watch. The driver came around and opened the back, unloading burlap sacks that wafted the scent of freshly roasted coffee bean in my direction. Extremely familiar smelling fresh coffee bean scent. Organic, fair trade, and house roasted? Those rats! The sacks of Whole Bean Arabica Dark Roast that he was unloading were exactly the same as Reese's house bean and were roasted in a warehouse in Oakland! Oh, I couldn't wait to tell Reese about this. I scuttled back to the office before I busted up laughing where the two of café owners could hear me.

CHAPTER 4

Monday Night

TWO INVESTIGATIONS IN ONE NIGHT. I was insane for even trying it. I texted Nicky again, telling her she was missing all the
fun. Her response was a photo of surfers riding huge blue waves
with perfect curls. Okay, so she was having more fun than I was. I
put all the batteries I had on the chargers, put some crunchies in
Hoover's dish, and crossed the street for some dinner and a dose
of caffeine.

"Have you seen this?" Twila Genae was working the counter, her bright, orange-dyed hair springing from her ponytail
like a sparkler fountain. The ad she pushed under my nose was a
half-page spread in the local weekly newspaper. The top proudly
proclaimed, "Bringing Real Coffee to Marin Street for the First
Time" and in the center was a faux ink sketch of the front of the
new café. Twila bared her teeth savagely. "Real coffee? Seriously?
Reese has been here for over a decade! Can we sue them for libel
or something?"

I snickered. "Real coffee. Hah! I was down there today, and the
truck was unloading the exact same coffee beans Reese buys. And
they're charging nine bucks for a double latte!"

Twila growled a little. "If they put me out of a job, they're gonna
pay."

"I don't think we can sue them for lost wages," I said sadly. "But I'll tip extra if you make me a tuna salad and a Black Bottom."

"A B and B? At this hour?" Twila raised her drawn-on eyebrows and cocked her head at me. "Girl, you be crazy!"

The Reese's Black Bottom is a cup of Reese's dark roast with two pumps of hot fudge in the bottom, a shot of espresso in the middle, and a top layer of cream. Lack of care in consumption could cause heart palpitations, eye twitches, and reckless endangerment of self or others. I shrugged. "I'll take it slow. I've got a long night ahead."

"It's your kidneys," Twila shrugged back and rang up my meal.

I headed upstairs and grabbed an empty table by the window where I had the opportunity to look over my building. I could see Morri at his computer in the office directly across from Reese's, probably working on his secret assignment. Downstairs, Mallory came out and locked his office door, closing shop for the day.

"Hey."

I looked up to see Reese approaching with my tuna salad and coffee. She also had a fruit cup on the tray, which she plunked down unceremoniously in front of me.

"Since when are you delivering food? Do you need a waitress?" A while back, when I found myself in financial trouble, I'd begged Reese to let me come back and work for her, and she'd told me no, but I'd continued to pick up the odd shift here and there. "Where's Tobiana?"

"Downstairs delivering food." Reese answered curtly. "I wanted to talk to you."

Uh oh. "Please don't tell me you have a demonic presence in the walk-in cooler."

Reese's pursed lips didn't crack. She crossed her arms over her coffee-stained brown apron. "Twila showed you that *ad*." The word had never sounded more like an epithet. "It's an abomination."

Reese is a tough gal, street-smart and wicked sharp, and a self-made businesswoman out of Oakland. Abomination wasn't just harsh, it wasn't in her vocabulary. I pointed to the chair opposite me. "Have a seat."

"*Real coffee*?! Real coffee for the first time?" Reese spun the chair around and straddled it. "Do you think anyone's gonna believe that?"

"You're the cornerstone of this neighborhood, Reese. No one wants froo-froo organic at twice the price. Besides, you've got the best tuna salad on the block." I shoved a huge bite of food into my mouth to prove my point. And to shut myself up before I said the wrong thing.

She rubbed the knuckles of her fisted hands together. "I just wish there was something we could do. I don't suppose you've had any luck with the planning commission?"

"They aren't doing anything wrong, Reese. We don't have any grounds to protest." I waved at the stream of customers coming and going below. "It's not like you're hurting for business, is it? I mean, half the time, you're running silly, right? So what if a few people decide to get organic fair trade instead of driving another three blocks to Starbucks? That could be a good thing for the neighborhood."

"Oh crap." Reese uttered.

"I already updated your website, and Mallory's been posting videos online all day. I've been thinking we should organize some events to bring people in, too." My mind was already racing ahead. "You can get my mom to come talk about fresh herbs and demonstrate how you use them in your ingredients, like this dill in your tuna salad. And what about Writer Rick? He'd love to do an author signing or three."

"Oh, no."

"No? But everyone loves Writer Rick. He's popular and fun . . . ny . . ." I belatedly realized that Reese wasn't looking at me. And she wasn't looking at the new café. She was looking down at a man on the sidewalk. He was middle-aged, soft around the middle, dressed in polo shirt and rumpled black slacks, with black curly hair cropped close to his head. He stopped and looked up at the building, but at the wrong angle to see us through the balcony windows. I looked back at Reese and her expression was still, her eyes wide, and her lips pursed and pale.

"Reese? What? What is it? Who is that guy?"

She seemed frozen, her eyes fixed on the stranger as he walked through the doors below us, disappearing from our line of vision.

"Reese? You want me to do something here? What's going on?"

"Got your phone?"

"Of course."

"Dial nine one, and wait. If this goes bad, dial the other one." Reese pushed out of her chair and strode towards the stairs. She was wearing her kick-ass-first-and-take-names-later expression. I pulled out my cell and hovered my thumb over the 911 emergency contact as I snuck down the stairs behind Reese. There was no way I was gonna miss this, whatever it was.

The next words I heard Reese say were, "Get the hell out of here."

I couldn't hear what the man said in reply, but his tone was conciliatory, and soon cut off by Reese.

"I got nothin' to say to you! Nothing! This is my place now, and you better high on outta here before I do something you're gonna regret!"

Reese was ready to swing, but the man stood his ground, his voice low and his tone reasonable. Reese cut him off. "I told you. I'm not talking to you. You wanna talk to someone? Kami? Come on down here and tell this jack-off that you're my legal representative and unless he wants charges pressed, he will get the hell out of here!"

I wasn't technically her legal representative. My bar exam was still a good two years away, and until then I was still just a paralegal without attorney supervision. And I wasn't dressed to impress. Unless you were into the couch potato look. As couch potatoes go, I was the height of fashion. But I took a few steps down and stood on the last stair to bring my five feet of height into better alignment with his six plus. He was over forty, a little soft around the middle, with a round face and oval eyes. A faded barbed wire tattoo laced his bicep. He might have been handsome once upon a time, but life hadn't been kind to him. "Sir, I'm prepared to call the authorities. As a privately owned establishment, this restaurant has the right to refuse service to anyone. You have been asked to leave, so you are now trespassing."

He stared at me like I was an insect. Clearly no skinny, frizzle-haired white chick was going to tell him what to do.

I raised the cellphone higher. "I believe you've been asked to leave."

"I only came to talk," he growled at me. "This isn't your business."

"Legally, it is if Reese says it is." I hoped I sounded more confident than I felt.

He looked from me to Reese, who was standing with her hands on her hips, her glare set to shred him from head to toe. His tone turned derisive, "You let her speak for you?"

For a second I thought Reese would let him get to her, but instead she shook her head. "No one speaks for me. But my lawyer is authorized to speak on my behalf when I say so. What the hell do you want, Tivon?"

Tivon. This, then, was Tivon Shuman. Reese's ex-husband. That explained everything.

"I just want to talk to you, babe." He waved a conciliatory hand around the café. A few of the cab drivers looked ready to bite it off. "Look, you're making a scene. Is that what you want?"

"No. I want you to get out of my life and never come back."

Tivon's frown reminded me of Hoover in his starved-kitten pose, but what works for hungry cats doesn't have the same impact for middle aged men. "Why you gotta be like this?"

"Just get out."

"Look, baby, it's over between me and J.J. I just want . . ."

Reese's head snapped sidewise as she spat out, "Do I look like I give a rat's ass what you want, Tivon?

I spoke up before Reese did something drastic. "I'm dialing the cops right now . . ." My fingers started to tap the screen, but a movement outside caught my eye and I stayed my hand. "Never mind. Here comes the local force right now. Good afternoon, Detectives!"

Detective Ron Brittle and his partner, Detective Dortman, swung through the door, Brittle's hand half-raised to greet me. They

both sensed the tense atmosphere and froze in place. The customers, mostly the after-work meet-up crowd, were stalled with their
drinks halfway to their mouths, their eyes darting around the dining room as they assessed their escape options. Reese was standing
cross-armed and stiff with fury-glazed eyes. Dortman's hand slid
under his jacket towards his weapon. I waved my phone at Brittle.
"I was just about to call you guys."

Tivon bailed, pushing past the plain-clothed detectives, forcing
Dortman to swivel aside to let him pass. I wondered if Tivon real-
ized how close he was to the business end of Dortman's weapon.
Dortman was a shoot first, face the music later kind of cop.

As soon as Tivon slammed the door and pulled away from the
curb in the beat-up-looking old Ford Focus he was driving, I started
laughing. I couldn't help it. Laughter is my coping mechanism.

Reese had a far more reasonable reaction and started swearing.
"That jerk! That absolute ass! How can he just walk back in that
door like he never left? Who the hell does he think he is? Takes off
with that hussy and just leaves me here, and then waltzes right in
thinkin' I'm gonna take his scrawny butt back . . ."

Detective Brittle . . . Okay, confession time. These days, to me,
he was just Ron, not Detective anything, and he calls me Kami,
not Miss White. We have a standing Thursday night dessert
meet-up at Reese's. Don't ask. It's complicated. Ron took Reese's
arm and steered her towards a back corner. Dortman (Out of
respect for Ron, I'd promised to try to stop calling him things like
Doorknob, no matter how fitting they were) went straight to the
counter and ordered from a bewildered looking Twila as though
nothing had happened.

"So, who was he?" Ron looked back and forth between me and
Reese. "Was he starting trouble? Do we need to get a uniform unit
down here?"

"He's her ex," I explained as Reese tried to quell her snarling
rage. "The one who ran away to Costa Rica . . ."

"With the rap singer?"

"Uh huh." I cringed. The entire East Bay music scene knew
the story. While Reese was busy establishing their corner of the

coffee empire, Tivon was trying to break into the music scene by DJing at some of the hottest clubs in Oakland. A bright, young, rising-star rapper caught his eye, and suddenly he was gone. He sent a postcard from Costa Rica, telling Reese that he needed to "be free and live the life" with his barely legal lady singer. Reese was left holding payments on a fancy house and yacht, along with a business loan and a struggling coffee shop. She sold the house and the boat, kept the café and built it into a business institution beloved by all of San Amoro.

"And he was looking to talk to you? And you told him that he needed to leave?" Ron's calm, measured tones were contagious, and I felt my shoulders ease as he continued. "I understand. Did he say what he wanted from you?"

Reese studied Ron with a steely, determined gaze. "As long as he never comes back, I couldn't care less."

Detective Dortman came over with cups of coffee for himself and Ron. I caught Ron's eye and shook my head slightly, warning him to give Reese time to cool down. I helped by changing the subject. "What brings you two down here so late? I thought you were nine-to-five guys?"

I didn't mean that last bit. It was just a dig at Dortman, who looked like every donut-laden, ill-fitted-suit-wearing cop you see on every TV show and then some. A rounded gut launched over his belted Dockers and his standard black tie looked like it was choking his bullish neck. I politely averted my eyes before I said something truly rude. After all, I'd promised Ron that I'd try to behave myself.

Ron held up a stack of flyers and handed one to Reese. "Community outreach. We're distributing these to local businesses and asking that they post them. We decided to start here because, well . . ." He held up his steaming latte as explanation. I have mentioned that Reese makes the best lattes on the planet, right? "It's the best place to start."

The flyer was a basic information-wanted law enforcement notice regarding a series of break-ins around town. They were mostly after-hours smash-and-grabs; so far there hadn't been any physical threats. The poster announced that anyone with information about the break-ins could call anonymously. Reese's anger seemed to fade a bit as she over the flyer and nodded, "Sure, I'll put it up. Glad we haven't had any trouble on our street."

"That's probably because Kami sleeps with all the lights on." Dortman snorted. Ron rolled his eyes and Reese smirked.

I glared. No one was supposed to know I was living in the office. Technically, I was in violation of zoning codes, but no one I knew seemed to care. And I owned the building, so who was going to turn me in? And if Dortman had been kidnapped and locked in the dark, he'd leave the lights on, too! And, in the end, he was probably right that having someone on our street twenty-four hours a day kept it more secure. I forced a teasing smile. "Only when I sleep alone."

"So, every night then?" Dortman probably meant it as a joke.

"As a matter of fact, last night I slept with the most handsome guy in the neighborhood." I gestured across the street where Hoover was in the front window of the office, grooming his hairless tail. "Doesn't hog the covers, and doesn't snore, either."

Reese smiled, but it was tight, like a dress that didn't quite fit. "I have to get back to work. If there's anything else I can do for you gentlemen . . .?"

"No, thanks." Ron touched her arm lightly, pausing her motion. "And if there's anything we can do for you, Kami has my number."

Let's just announce that to the whole world, shall we? I managed not to groan. It wasn't like we were dating. Our weekly evening dessert meet-ups at Reese's weren't dates. I had a sneaking suspicion that that negation wouldn't hold up under scrutiny in court. I managed not to smile. "I need to finish my dinner. I've got a local job followed by a demonic possession in Cherryland."

"You're still ghostbusting?" Ron asked with a raised eyebrow. He was half-smiling, but I could see the conflict racing behind his eyes. He wanted to tell me not to go in alone. To be safe. To stay clear of clients who might be serial killers. Instead, he just waved his hand in a what-can-I-do-about-it gesture. Dortman snickered and Ron slapped his shoulder.

"That's what I do, buddy. Coffee, ghost hunting and term papers are my life." I turned to Reese. "I'll dig up your divorce paperwork, too. There might at least be grounds to get a restraining order against him."

I waved farewell with a finger wave, gave Reese a good strong hug of the sort my mother would approve of, and jogged back up the stairs to my table.

Switching focus to the café haunting, I opened my laptop and looked up the history of the location that was now Café Fantastique. (Café Mediocre was more like it. Soybean shortening cookies. Blech.) Wyatt had to get planning commission approval for the café, so all the building plans were online. I perused them on my laptop, but there wasn't anything unusual. The first haunted house I'd researched been a big house on the hill with hidden spaces behind the walls, massive heating conduits, and an elaborate intercom system. Café Fantastique was a former drugstore renovated into an eatery. There was nothing special or strange or unexpected. I'd checked the EMF readings myself that afternoon. It was just an average commercial building from the mid-70s, renovated in the late 90s and again by the new owners. Nothing special.

I turned to the robbery. The one news article that I found was pretty much what I remembered. Two gunmen had gone into the pharmacy just before closing, taken customers hostage and demanded all the money and drugs. When the owner's son took too long to open the safe, they shot him. The police arrived and killed one gunman in a shootout, but the other was taken into custody. I groaned in near physical pain when I saw the name of the arresting officer who gave the reporter a police quote. Junior Detective Raymond Dortman. Oh god, someone shoot me. Oops. Better not say that too loudly if Dortman was who I had to talk to. He would probably call it a mercy killing.

It seemed like a wild long shot that Dortman might be able to tell me much about the robbery. Twelve years is a long time. The old pharmacy was ancient news in the fast-moving Bay Area crime scene. But the only other lead I had was the original robber that had survived, and the only information I could find about him was that he was eligible for parole, but it had been denied two years running. Presumably someone still remembered what happened back then and was determined to keep him in prison. With Dortman on the line as an eyewitness, I hurried back down the stairs. Ron and Dortman were nowhere to be seen, but when I asked Twila, she said they were headed down the street with their fliers. I ran to the door and saw them just leaving the watch repair shop. I trotted towards them, waving my arms yelling, "Detective Dortman! Wait up."

He drew up on the sidewalk and turned back towards me. "Miss White? You called?" Amazingly, he sounded almost friendly!

"I did!" I caught up to them and paused to catch my breath. I needed to do more cardio.

Both detectives looked a little bewildered.

"This is going to sound really out of left field, but . . ." I paused, searching for a way to be tactful, but finally just spewed it out. "I was wondering if you remembered the shooting that took place in the old pharmacy? Where the new café is opening. Ten years or so ago?"

"Yeah. I remember." Dortman's voice was instantly guarded. Try as I might, my brain called him Detective Doberman. I instantly chided myself. That was no way to think of someone from whom I needed help. "Why are you bringing that up?"

"I just read the news article about it. One Tribune article was all I could find online, and I was just a kid at the time, so I really don't remember it. There were two people killed, right? The son of the owner and one of the robbers?"

"Yeah. That's right." Dortman said shortly. He obviously didn't want to talk about it.

"Can you remember anything else about it? Do you know what they were like, the victim and the criminal that were shot?"

There was a long pause as he stared at a crack in the sidewalk at his feet. Finally, he looked back at me, and his gaze was shrewd and gauging. The Doberman was in full force. "Why are you diggin' all this up now?"

I glanced between him and Ron and gave him my best

hopeful pleading smile. "Well, you know I sometimes do para-normal research for people who think they might have a ghost problem?"

There was another long pause and Dortman crossed his arms. Finally, he nodded at me in sudden comprehension. "Does this have to do with that medieval helmet from the Cheshire case?"

I sucked in a deep breath and admitted, "Kind of, yeah. It's haunted by its previous owner, so I sometimes take it along on investigations."

"Uh huh." Dortman glanced at Ron, and I imagined he was mentally twirling his finger at his temple, indicating how nuts he thought I was. "So, what's going on?"

"Well, the new owners of the café think they might have a prob-lem of the paranormal kind, so they asked for my help. The only deaths I could find attached to the café were from that robbery. You were the one who gave a quote to the press after the arrests, so I thought maybe you remembered something about the victims that wasn't in that article." I hesitated, then continued hopefully. "I'm not asking for anything confidential about the case, just anything you might remember about it that might help me. I'd really owe you."

"You want to know what I remember about that case?" Dortman's voice dropped half an octave, his body leaning back from me and his heavy-lidded eyes narrowing. "What I remem-ber? What I remember is this. What you said about the victim and the criminal being killed? Well, the only victims in that building that night were the hostages."

"What? I don't understand."

"That's all I've got for you. Sorry. Have a good evening." And Dortman spun on his heel and strode away before I could inquire further, or even say goodbye. It was the most civilized conversation we'd ever had.

Ron paused a moment longer. "That was a dark time in the department's history. There aren't many left who are still around from back then. If you want, I can look into it."

"Thanks, but no." I smiled at him. "I'm not sure it matters to my case at all, and I don't want to stir up anything."

Ron looked at Dortman's departing back. "Might be too late for that."

I WENT BACK TO THE OFFECE AND GATHERED MY LAPTOP and bag. Going on the only solid information I had, there were two obvious suspects to explain any spirit activity at the café; a college-age young man or a twenty-nine-year-old hardened gang-banger criminal. I could only hope that if there was a ghost, that it was the owner's son, and not the criminal. Armed with that hope, I got to work. Before heading down to the not-so-Fantastique café for the investigation, I gathered my gear and made sure everything was in order. There were two pieces of advice that I'd gleaned early on from other researchers: always keep tons of spare batteries, and don't get emotional. The first was easy. I had a good supply of high-quality rechargeables and two chargers that I cycled through constantly. The second, after the rush of the day and the conversation with Detective Dortman, wasn't so easy. I took on a series of yoga stretches and pushed myself to hold the more difficult positions until my breathing slowed and I felt centered. A quick shower washed away the rest of the day and left me clear-headed and focused. I put on what I had decided was my ghost-hunting gear; blue denim jeans, black t-shirt, black denim jacket (with internal pockets for extra batteries, compact camera and recorder), and my grey military-style cap. The low flat visor made a perfect perch for my headlamp light and GoPro camera.

I grabbed my black duffle bag and packed it with all my cameras, audio recorders, and other gear. As an afterthought, I threw in a yogurt and some trail mix. Finally, I collected Evrett's helmet. I used to wrap him in a silk scarf that I had laying around, but I'd found a velvet lined purse at the thrift store for three dollars, and that seemed like a classier way to carry around an antique artifact. "Sorry, Evrett. I don't expect this will take too long, though. It's possible there's a haunting, but I have my doubts."

The rest of the armor was silent, and I didn't feel like trying him on to see if he had anything to say. It was just past eight when I decided that I was ready enough.

The wind off the Bay had picked up and a chill breeze was sweeping across San Amoro. I was glad I'd grabbed my jacket. With my duffle bag over my shoulder and my now lukewarm coffee in hand, I walked down to the new café and knocked on the back door.

Wyatt greeted me. He looked beyond weary.

"Heya!" I greeted. "How's it going?"

"How's it going?" Wyatt gestured towards his laptop, propped against a cutting board on the kitchen table. "It's not. We've had exactly two applicants for jobs. One was an admitted alcoholic who refuses to work before noon because they're always hungover and the other was an ex-con who only applied because his parole officer ordered him to get a job. We can't do this with just the three of us. We open on Wednesday and honestly, I'm not even sure we're going to be able to do that. If we don't, we risk losing everything."

"How so?" I set my duffle bag on the table next to his laptop and started laying out my gear.

"We need to meet projection for the first week. The numbers Thomas and his company put together looked good on paper, but it's just been one little problem after another. We've got everything invested in this. If it doesn't meet projected income, we just won't make it. There's the mortgage on the building, the insurance, the cost of the remodel and repairs . . ." He sighed and rubbed his eyes and I almost felt sorry for him. He registered Reese's logo on my coffee cup and his eyebrows arched as he glanced up at my face.

"Hey, I told you not to expect a change in loyalty. This brew has been my personal fuel for so long it's in my blood stream." I thought back to my discussion with Reese earlier. "Maybe you need a special grand opening event or something. Though I suppose if you don't have the labor force, that would be hard to pull off."

"Grand opening event? Like what? Some kind of giveaway?" Wyatt ran his palm over his eyes again and gave a sad laugh. "We can give away one-third partnership in the café to the first customer. They can have mine."

"I was thinking something more like a raffle, maybe call the local radio station and see if they want to send a DJ down for an hour or two." I didn't feel guilty about offering the suggestion. No one even listened to radio DJs anymore, did they? Besides, Reese was going to be doing the really cool events, way better than any raffle.

Wyatt nodded. "Yeah, maybe I could pull off something like that. Hey, do you do events?"

I blinked. "Me? No. What would I do? Workshops to teach people how to file small claims?"

"Ghost hunting, of course." Wyatt leaned across the table on his elbows, chin propped on his fists. "If this place is really haunted, you could lead ghost-hunting events where people can come and actually participate. That would be so awesome! Just think of how much we could charge! Fifty or sixty a head for a two-hour ghost hunt? You could show 'em the EMF meters and this thermometer thing and stuff. Let them try it themselves. Customers would eat it up!"

"Whoa! Now, whoa. Hold up. There's nothing yet to even say this place is haunted." And there was no way under the official International Orange color of the Golden Gate Bridge that I was going to make an ass out of myself to help promote Café Mediocre! "You're getting way ahead of yourself. And even if it is haunted, using troubled souls as a show attraction is immoral and I wouldn't take part in that. Ghosts are *people*, Wyatt. They're spirits, and if they're reaching out it's because they need help."

Wyatt straightened and held both hands up in a gesture of surrender. "Okay, okay. I just thought . . . A lot of places make money on that kind of thing."

"If you're talking about *places* like the Stanley Hotel, the Stanleys stay there because they loved it in life and still love it in death. They're proud of the hotel and enjoy having guests. If you've got ghosts here, they most likely died miserable, violent deaths in that robbery . . ." I hesitated, wondering again about what Detective Dortman had told me earlier about the only victims being the hostages, but managed to go on. "Exploiting them would be wrong, Wyatt. It's just as bad as making money exploiting the misery of living people."

Grady came through the swinging doors from the dining room. He looked tired, too, but he was smiling. "The dishes are all washed and the espresso machines tested. The shelves are up in the walk-in fridge, so we're ready to start taking deliveries of perishables. I think it's all coming together."

Wyatt nodded, "Then I guess we're ready to get this show on the road."

I looked around. "Where's Thomas? Won't he be joining us?"

"Yeah, he'll be here later. He had to run to Oakland Restaurant Supply. Apparently, we need a lot more forks than we budgeted for." Grady chuckled. "I don't see why people can't just eat cake with their fingers, but Thomas informs me that that's gauche."

"Don't look at me." I shrugged and pulled out my camera cables and laptop. "I eat everything with my fingers. Well, we can get the cameras and recording equipment set up while we wait. Can we pull the shades over the windows?"

"Why?"

"Darkness. With most hauntings, there's activity going on all the time, but you may only experience it at night because there are too many shadows and lights during the day already. The shades will also help muffle any sounds or voices from the street. We want as little contamination of the investigation as possible."

By the time I had everything set up, and we'd turned off the breakers to everything that wasn't critical, like the icemaker and the refrigeration unit, the mystery partner had returned. Thomas Griggs was tall and lanky, with greying brown hair and a narrow nose and pale grey eyes. He reminded me of a grey marble rolling pin. He was juggling an armload of boxes of cutlery and cases of paper napkins, which he dropped on the kitchen floor. His gaze strayed over the gear on the table and he asked without preamble, "So, are we haunted?"

"Don't know yet. And may not know tonight, either." I tried to be as honest as possible. "Ghosts don't perform on command. We may not have any experiences tonight at all."

"Are we supposed to light candles? Sit in a circle or something?"

I fired Wyatt a glance, but Thomas didn't appear to be joking. "No. I'm a researcher, not a psychic. I'm not a medium and this isn't the nineteenth century. Candles and holding hands won't do anything more than we can accomplish with the K2 meter, and we can do it without attracting negative influences from outside."

"Negative influence sounds pretty nineteenth century hocus pocus to me," Wyatt stated, but before I could rebut, he continued, "But I'll go with the flow."

"Great. Can you set this up over there?" I handed him a digital IR camera with a mounting clip and pointed to the shelf over the sink. I wanted to get a FLIR as well, but those were still out of my budget for the occasional paranormal gigs that I was reporting on my taxes as hobby income. The IR night cameras would have to do for now. "It's important for all of us to turn off our phones. Also, if the café has a PA system, we should switch it off. I'll put out the radio frequency detector, too, and that should help eliminate any false positives."

"No P.A. system," Thomas answered, "But the security system has infra-red detectors. Should we turn that off?"

I was grateful that this man who I'd only just met seemed ready to leap in with sensible suggestions.

"It's not on," Grady said good-naturedly. "It's set to automatically switch on at nine, but I didn't see the point if we're all here."

"I'm assuming it includes cameras and audio?" I pulled out the RF and K2 and tested them on both the motion sensors and the alarm box itself. "I think we're good there. And it might be good to have it on to pick up things we miss. Is there anything else that puts out a signal?"

Wyatt sheepishly pulled out a second smart phone and switched it off.

I hooked up my laptop to the cameras and set my new software to record, glancing around at the cameras that would provide a real-time view of the entire café, including the office and storage closet. When comparing it to my first real investigation, I realized that my equipment was absolutely primitive compared to what I was running now. Back then, I had one camera and a single digital sound recorder, and Nicky as backup. I missed Nicky. I hoped she was having fun in Hawaii.

I gestured to the kitchen. "Since most of the activity takes place here, I think that's where we should start." I didn't mention that it was also, as far as I knew, where the cops had shot the hostage-taking robber. I indicated that we should stand around the worktable, with our backs to the table, looking outward in different directions from each other. I set the K2 and the IR monitor on the counter and kept my digital thermometer in my hand to do frequent monitoring of the immediate temperature around me.

"So, what now? Do we call the spirits or something?"

"First, we wait a bit. Be very quiet and mention any changes you experience. In the darkness, your eyes will play tricks on you, but if you see shadows or moving lights, mention it out loud so that when we sync the recordings we can see if the camera catches it." Gee, if I kept teaching my clients how to do this, I'd be out of business. This business, at least. One day, I was going to be a lawyer, and leave all of this behind.

We waited in silence for close to twenty minutes without any movement or even so much as a stray noise. It was so silent that when the ice-machine cycled its tray with a loud clatter we all jumped and I'm afraid I may have squealed, just a bit. Wyatt laughed, and I joined him.

"You don't realize how loud that damned thing is with all the other noise." Grady sounded a little embarrassed in the darkness. "I'm back here with it all day and I swear I just jumped out of my skin."

Adrenalin combined with the Reese's Black Bottom had my heart racing. I took a few deep breaths. "Temp is the same comfortable sixty-seven degrees that it was when we started." I circled the room, pausing to show the readings to the cameras as I passed them. The only change was a bump in the warmth near the oven, still cooling from a hard day's work. Ovens don't get overtime or hazard pay, do they? If I was running at four-hundred degrees with cookies going in and out all day, I'd want hazard pay. "Let's move to the office. We can leave the camera and recorders going in here just in case."

"In case the ghosts are shy?" Wyatt laughed.

"Or in case they just don't like you," I quipped with a smile. "If there's activity now, it's for a reason. They might not like what you've done to the place."

"They're dead, why should they care?" Thomas sounded genuinely interested. I thought he was the superstitious one?

"One of the shooting victims was the former owner's son," I explained. "He may have liked things the way they were. Or maybe he just doesn't like coffee."

None of them seemed to care for that answer.

By 9:30, WE STILL HADN'T HAD ANY SORT OF ACTIVITY in the office or the storeroom or the kitchen or the dining area. I tried question and answer with the K2 meter, and also encouraged any spirits to try turning on the mixer as they had in the past. There was no response. I only had one trick left up my sleeve. I left the three partners in the dining room asking questions with the K2 meter, which remained conspicuously dark. "I'm going back to the kitchen to check the cameras. Keep going."

I wasn't checking the cameras. I was going to the best last resource that I had for dealing with the disembodied. I gently extricated Evrett's helmet from its bag and gave him a friendly squeeze. "I don't know, Evrett. This place seems as quiet as graves ought to be. What do you think?" He was still and silent, cold steel in my hands. "Okay, let's see what we can see."

I lowered his helmet over my head, as always impressed as always by how roomy it was inside. I gently lowered the visor and peered into the shadowed space through the slits. Pivoting slowly on my heel, I took in a three-hundred-sixty-degree view of the kitchen, then I walked over and to the storeroom. There was nothing. The office, too, appeared unchanged. Through the steel, I could hear the hum of the ice machine and the faint buzz of the oven's exhaust fan. Only a slight chill at the back of my neck told me that Evrett was with me. "This is a total bust," I muttered to him as I pulled him off and tucked him back into his bag. "I owe you an oiling when we get done here."

In order to make sure it wasn't a total waste of time, I took a quick look in the stock-room, and what I saw there made me snicker. Boxed cake mixes. They didn't even make their cupcakes and coffee cakes from scratch. They used boxed mix! And not fancy gluten-free high-fiber organic boxes either. Just standard generic cake-mixes from the restaurant suppliers.

I tried not to roll my eyes as I rejoined the others. "I think it's time to wrap this up. I'll go through all the sound and video over the next couple of days." In between doing a second investigation with far more promise than this one, helping save Reese's café, and finishing my classwork. "I'll let you know if I find anything."

"That's it?" Thomas looked around the new dining room with concern. "Is the weird stuff going to keep happening? You can't just stop it?"

"That's not how it works, unfortunately." Seeing the crestfallen look on Wyatt's face gave me second thoughts about helping them. "Well, there's one thing I can do to help right now, without knowing what kind haunting, if it even *is* a haunting, that you're dealing with."

"Then do it!" Grady encouraged with a wave of his hands. "Whatever it is, do it."

"If it's really an active haunting with an intelligent haunt, this could help." I shrugged, then added in warning, "Or it could make it a lot worse."

"Worse?" Grady stopped flashing his 'get-on-with-it' motion. "How worse?"

"Angry spirits don't like being told what to do." With that warning, I turned and raised my voice, addressing the room at large. "Okay, listen up. Grady, Thomas and Wyatt are the owners of this business now, and you don't have any right to interfere or tell them what to do. If you want to stay here, that's fine, but you have to start being helpful and stop messing with equipment and the lights. You can stay, but stop interfering, okay?"

I dusted off my hands and returned to packing up my cameras. "That's it?"

"Sure. You may have to tell them yourselves." I glanced up and made sure they were all listening. "Remember. It's important not to say it in anger or fear, because some spirits can feed on that. Just calmly assert that you own the building now, and they can only stay if they're polite and not rude. Usually does the trick, and sometimes opens a whole new ability to communicate." I said it like I had a lot of experience with that, but most of my knowledge came from Evrett, and he was uniquely friendly and helpful as far as ghosts go. Only rarely did we come to conflict, but in my mind, Evrett was family and what family didn't squabble from time to time?

They were all watching expectantly as I packed my gear neatly back into my duffle bags. Finally, feeling a little uncomfortable, I felt I had to say something. "Like I said, I'll review everything, and if you have an actual haunting on your hands, I'll call in my associate. Father Talbon is a priest, and he can do a cleansing blessing and help them move on."

"What if they don't want to go?"

"Father Talbon can be very persuasive." I headed for the door. "And if you have any activity before you hear from me, give me a call. Heck, if you really need me, I'm just a few doors down. I could probably hear you if you scream."

They let me out and locked the door behind me. I walked back down to the office. Remembering the break-in flier, the detectives had brought to Reese's, I took a good look up and down the quiet street, but all was quiet. I swapped the memory cards from the cameras and sound recorders, put the gear bag in my pickup and went inside to lock up my evidence and feed Hoover. I thought he'd be starved for attention, but he just rubbed his head on my hand for a second, then completely ignored me.

"Okay, be good. I'm going to go see Irvin and look for demons."

Hoover didn't even look up from his plate of gushy food. That's how much he loves me.

CHAPTER 5

After Midnight

P RUE'S HOME WAS IN THE CHERRYLAND DISTRICT, a community
built in the post-war boom. Most of what I knew about it came
from childhood school field trips to the Meek Mansion, the his-
toric mansion of the plantation that had once existed there. Back
then, the land had been covered with hundreds of acres of cherry
orchards. Now it was well worn-in suburbs. New in the late 1950's,
most of the houses looked old and tired by today's standards. Most
of them were similar in shape and build, with fenced-in yards and
neglected looking lawns. There were a few old well-established
camphor trees lining the streets, and the cars parked alongside
them were older models, or affordable newer models of practical sedans, SUVs, and mini vans. My little grey Nissan pickup felt
right at home. It was usually completely outclassed by everything
in the Bay Area.

Though the glowing streetlamps generated plenty of light, Prue
had left the porch light on for me, and she opened the door when
she saw me pull up. She appraised my all-black ghost-hunting garb
with a nod of approval, "Nice."

"Thanks. You too." She was in all black, too, but in a black high-
collared button-up blouse and black cotton pants. Irvin was in
khaki slacks and white button down. If the shirt had fit properly on

his too-thin frame, I might have considered him sharply dressed. "Okay. Why don't you give me a short tour and then we can get the cameras set up. Irvin, you're familiar enough with my gear, so I trust you to know where it should go."

Hopefully giving him something useful and technical to do would take the look of nervous terror from his eyes and give him some focus. Whether we had a demonic on our hands, or just a malicious spirit haunt, I didn't need it feeding off Irvin's freestyle panic. Prue had inherited her house from her grandmother, and it was a typical post-war two-bedroom, one bath, with a small kitchen and dining room that opened to an enclosed porch and, beyond that, a brick patio. Three cats were out in the porch area, looking in through the sliding glass door. I did a small double take. They all had hair, which, after living with a hairless cat for so long, just looked a little weird. There was a yellow tabby, a grey and white, and an all-black shorthair. I stooped down to greet them. "Hi, kitty kitties. Are you being good?"

"They have a cat door," Prue pointed to a cat flap set into the wall. "But I closed the catch so they don't mess stuff up during the investigation. They can come in after we're done."

Hoover was an all-indoor cat. I couldn't imagine leaving him outside for any length of time by himself. But we also lived on a busy street, not in a quiet suburb with a fenced-in backyard. "Probably a good idea. Besides, my cat wouldn't like me coming home smelling like strangers."

"I swear, cats are worse than boyfriends." Prue laughed. Irvin was setting up a camera on the kitchen counter and glanced over at us.

"I wouldn't know." he deadpanned. "I don't have a cat. Or a boyfriend,"

Dear god! Had Irvin Zettlemeyer just made a joke? I glanced between him and Prue in disbelief. Maybe Prue with her dark goth attitude was just what stiff and strange Irvin needed in his life.

The bedrooms were at either end of an open hallway. The whole house was a small space, easy to cover with the equipment that I'd brought. Since the bathroom was where Prue had noted the strange bad smell, I put the K2 and IR detector on the bathroom counter and my mini-DVR cam where it could record both pieces of equipment and the rest of the bathroom.

It was nearly midnight. I slammed the last of my coffee drink and checked the camera feed to my laptop. "Okay, let's shut off the power and see what we get."

With the power shut off and the drapes closed, all was dark and quiet. This was a working neighborhood, and on a Tuesday night, it was perfectly still. No cars trailed past the front windows, no porch lights or music drifted over the back fence from the neighbors. For paranormal research, the conditions were ideal. I settled in a dining room chair facing the corridor, with the living room to my right and the kitchen to my left.

"Did you hear that?" Irvin whispered suddenly.

"Hear what?"

"A kind of . . . squeak!" His voice was practically a squeak.

"I didn't hear anything." I glanced at Prue, who nodded that she'd heard it, too.

We all listened for a moment, but it was silent. As we started to relax back in our chairs, I could hear the faintest creaking sound.

"What is that?" Irvin's eyes looked like giant white ping-pong balls behind his thick glasses.

"Irvin . . ." I pointed at his arm. "Take your elbow off the corner of the table."

"Why? Is it here? Is the demon here?"

Before he panicked and freaked out, I shook my head. "No, it's not the demon. Put your elbow back on the table and lean your weight on it like before." The second he did, the table leg of the vintage metal and Formica table let out a faint groan and Irvin yanked his arm back up. I sighed. "Is that what you heard before?"

Somewhat sheepishly, Irvin put his arm back on the table and leaned. Squeak. He picked it up again, then pressed back down. Squeak. Then he reached out and jiggled the corner of the table. Squeaksqueaksqueak.

Prue burst into giggles, but I managed to keep a straight face. "Nice debunk, Irvin. Remember what I told you when we investigated your house?"

"Always look for the logical explanation first?"

"Yup, that's it. Also, remember that even if this is a demonic haunting, the chance of harm coming to us from a few hours of exposure is really zero to nothing. It's going to look for the weak and exploit their fears. Show it no fear, and it will have nothing to work with." Or so the demon research sites said. I really had my doubts about . . .

"Grrrgggh." The faint growl seemed to come from under the table.

I sat up straight and looked at Prue and Irvin. Irvin chuckled. "Was that your stomach, Prue? I told you not to get tacos from that place on the corner."

Her black-rimmed eyes were saucer-shaped in the darkness and her voice was a hushed whisper. "That wasn't me."

I slowly panned my light under the table, and then around to the patio door to see if one of the cats had managed to slip in. All three cats were coiled up in a sleeping pile on the doormat, completely relaxed.

What the holey donut . . .? I pushed slowly to my feet and clicked the trigger on my digital thermometer, taking a full set of readings around, above and under the table, but the temperature remained a comfortable seventy-one degrees no matter what direction I pointed.

Irvin was taking EMF readings and chanting them out loud. "Zero point two except directly at the refrigerator. Fridge is one point five."

I felt a shiver run down my spine and reached for the digital recorder and played back the last few minutes. The growl was on the tape, but there was no hidden EVP, at least not in the frequencies we could hear with our naked ears.

"Resuming investigation," I told the recorder and gave the time before I set it back on the table.

"That's what I've been hearing." Prue's voice was calm, but her eyes were wide and unblinking, and her hand was clenched on the edge of the table. "Now do you believe me?"

"I never *dis*believed you, Prue," I reassured her. "If I did, I wouldn't be here. But sometimes there are explanations that we haven't considered yet. Do the cats have toys that make noise? Things that squeak or click? Any electronic toys that make noise?"

"All their toys are organic. I make them myself, mostly out of burlap and yarn, stuffed with straw and catnip and that kind of thing." She retrieved a toy from the bookshelf and handed it to me. It was an adorable hand-stitched burlap mouse with a yarn tail that smelled faintly of catnip. I wondered if Hoover would like something like that. He eschewed expensive pet-store toys, preferring his rubber ball from the discount store and crumpled pieces of paper.

"What about you? Do you collect any toys that make noise? Dolls, stuffed animals, or action figures? Things that might make noise that you've forgotten about? An old radio with batteries running down?"

"I'm more of an art and music girl."

I could see that. And the sound had seemed to come from inside the dining room with us, not a closet or storage box.

Scritchscratch scritchscratch.

This time all three of us jumped out of our chairs. The sound seemed to come from under the table again and I flashed my light underneath. Then I snapped a dozen still shots with the digital camera while turning slowly in a circle. "Okay, let's see if we can't get some reaction going on." I handed the still camera to Irvin. "When you hear a noise, don't think, just snap a photo in that direction. Don't think," I reiterated, "Just push the shutter button."

Irvin nodded and held the camera comfortably in his left hand, right forefinger over the trigger button. I'd learned on his investigation that he was something of a camera nut and hoped that giving him something to focus on would keep him from getting worked up. Well, more worked up than he already was.

"Starting EVP test. Dining room. Prue, Irvin and Kami." I reeled off to the recorder. "If there is someone here, making that scratching noise, can you make it again?"

We all strained our ears in the silence, listening closely, but heard nothing. "We also heard a growling noise. If that was you, can you do it again?"

"Grrpfff."

It came from directly behind me. I heard Irvin's finger clicking the camera in rapid sequence. Kind of close to how fast my heart was beating. I swallowed a deep breath to calm myself before continuing. "That was really good. Can you do it again?"

Scrabble scrabble scratch.

"It's running from us." Prue stood up and pointed towards the retreating sound.

"Sure sounds like it." I pushed cautiously to my feet, leaving the recorder running on the table. "Irvin, just keep snapping . . ." I held up the EMF detector and thermometer briefly in front of the video camera on the kitchen counter to document the numbers. Then, comically tiptoeing in single file, we went in the direction the sound seemed to have gone. It was dead silent except for our feet shuffling one after the other. I was in the lead followed by Irvin and then Prue.

We moved into the hallway. "Which way? Do you hear it?"

I was standing directly in front of the bathroom and could also see into both bedrooms. I had a perfect view of the camera and meters on the bathroom counter, but everything was silent. The monitors didn't flash. I could see our reflections in the vanity mirror over the sink. We were all poised, alert and listening, every nerve on edge, Irvin's pale face peeping from behind my back and outlined against Prue's body. His all-white shirt, outlined against our all-black clothing, made him stand out like a ghost himself. I almost giggled aloud. Sometimes, it felt that I'd been haunted by Irvin since the day I first met him.

I was just about to turn the line around and move us back into the kitchen when I heard the growl again, this time so close we all jumped. Prue let out a nervous laugh and I glanced her way. Was this all an elaborate prank? No, I could tell from her expression that she was genuinely scared.

"I'm just so glad you guys are here for this! I thought I was going nuts."

"We still don't have evidence that it's a demonic." I thought for a second. "You said you can smell it mostly when you're in the shower?"

"I am not going to shower with you guys! No way." Prue snickered again and this time I joined her.

"No, I'm just going to turn the water on . . . Maybe it doesn't like clean people."

"Or maybe it's a perv and wants to shower with you . . ." Irvin might have thought he was being helpful. Still, I had to struggle to resist the urge to smack him upside the head.

I reached around into the shower and turned the water knob. Cold spray echoed on classic 1950's style teal tile. We wouldn't be able to hear growls over that. All I could smell was chlorinated water and the faint scent of soap. The water warmed, and turned hot, steam billowing around us and fogging the mirror. One thing you learn during paranormal investigations is that fresh steam can reveal marks on mirrors and windows that are months old . I checked just in case "murder" or "Get Out" had appeared on the mirror, but there were only old fingerprints.

"This is a bust, I think." I reached into the shower to turn off the water and simultaneously three things happened. My nose was assaulted with the stench of rotten garbage. The linen closet door flew open. Irvin screamed like a Japanese anime schoolgirl and started running.

I spun towards the bathroom door, but my shoe caught on the black thick-pile bathmat and I fell backwards, slamming into the bathtub under the steaming shower. Prue screamed and ran after Irvin. Hot water poured over me, soaking through to the skin, and I'm afraid I might have taken the low road by expelling a scream of my own when the headlamp on my hat flooded with water and went out. In pitch darkness, I slipped and scrambled on all fours, trying to get out of the wet bathtub.

I finally gained purchase with my feet, but my flailing hand grabbed the shower-curtain. It tore free and landed on top of me as I pulled myself over the edge of the bathtub and tumbled out of the pouring water and onto the bathmat on my hands and knees . . . and came face to face with a demon!

GLOWING RED EYES! SHARP, SNARLING WHITE TEETH! "DEMON!" I screamed. It screamed back. Then it attacked. Claws raked down my arm and I whacked it with the EMF detector before trying to flee, but I was tangled in the shower curtain, which flipped over the demon, trapping it under the curtain with me. In a chaos of growls and screeches, some of which were mine, I managed to launch myself over the monster and scrabble for the bathroom door on hands and knees. The door slammed shut just as I reached it. My feet were tangled in the slippery wet shower curtain, with the demon! It grabbed the hem of my jeans, shaking my leg left and right as my slick hands failed to twist the doorknob. Morri's words raced back to me: stay calm. Stay calm! It feeds off fear, I tried to remind myself, right before I started screaming at the top of my lungs in full blown panic, pounding on the door with one hand and twisting the old glass knob with the other. "Help! Let me out! IRVIN! Get me out of here!"

The door latch finally caught, and the door flew open so quickly that I fell into the hallway. I heaved myself over, kicking my leg free of my attacker and the entangling shower curtain, before slamming the door in the demon's face. Leaving a trail of water behind, I launched to my feet, slipping and sliding on the hardwood floor until I tripped on the lip of the living room carpet and went down again. Where were Prue and Irvin? Oh, god! Did it eat Irvin? "Irvin! Where are you?"

Rolling over, I looked back, but the bathroom door was closed . . . Had I done that? The front door of the house was open and outside I could see Prue waving at flashing blue and red lights that were approaching. How had the cops gotten here so fast?

The living room lights came on, and I realized that Irvin had run to the kitchen and flipped the breakers back on. The guy was off his rocker in a lot of ways, but technology was his thing. Prue was on the porch, screaming at the cops that there was no way she was going back into the house.

My arm was striped with bloody streaks and hurt like a demon slash, and I was leaving a full-body wet spot on the nineteen-seventies aqua-green shag rug. I could barely hear, let alone think, over the pounding of my heart and Prue's panicked wails, but as I lay there, the adrenaline started to recede and my over-worked brain suddenly made sense of what I'd seen in the bathroom. And it wasn't a demon. I collapsed into hysterical laughter that didn't stop until I was choking.

"Ma'am? Are you Kamera White?" A strong hand landed on my shoulder and I looked up to find a uniform cop standing over me. I registered the Hayward Police Department badge on his chest and managed to stop laughing as he stared at me with a worried frown. "We were asked to check on this address? A friend was concerned?"

Oh, God! In this case, quite literally. I'd forgotten to message Father Talbon! "Yeah. I'm okay. I think. Um, can you call animal control?"

"You're bleeding." The cop pointed to my arm, then looked back at me. "Animal control?"

"There's a possum in the bathroom . . ." My brain cells managed to all work in unison for a moment and I pieced together the evidence from my little investigation. "Actually, it's probably back under the house by now."

"A possum?" The cop helped me to my feet and then looked at my bloodied arm in real concern. "Did it bite you?"

"I don't think so . . . I think it's just a scratch." Then I remembered my leg and looked down. My jeans were in bloody tatters around my ankle. I pulled up my pants-leg and dropped it again immediately. "Oh."

"You need to have that checked out at the ER. You'll probably need a tetanus shot, and maybe rabies vaccination."

"It's a demon! With giant teeth!" Prue was standing on the porch, arms crossed, trying to explain to the officer's partner. "I saw it!"

"No, Prue. It's a possum." I pointed to the bathroom and the officer snapped on his flashlight and nudged the bathroom door open with his foot, one hand hovering over his gun.

I followed at a judiciously safe distance, dripping rapidly cooling water from every inch of my body. Water poured out of my now-dead headlamp and off the brim of my cap. I made a mental note to stop buying paranormal research gear from the Dollar Store. The cop's light swept the bathroom. Then he stepped over the remains of the shower curtain and shut off the water. The linen closet door was still open and he dropped down to shine the light inside. Under the bottom shelf was a small hatch that was missing the door.

"Probably a plumbing access hatch that leads under the house. And phew, you're right. Something's living down there." The cop grabbed a hand towel out of the linen closet shelf and handed it to me to wrap my arm. Then he gestured me out into the living room while he radioed for animal control.

Now that the panic was wearing off, my arm hurt. Really hurt. My wet clothes were cold, and I was starting to shiver.

The cop's partner had convinced Prue to come inside, and they showed her the hatch and pointed out what was probably opossum scat in the back of the closet.

Irvin came up and carefully wrapped the towel around my scratched-up arm. "You okay?"

"I don't know." I answered as honestly as I could. "Are you?"

"Yeah." He ducked his head, a blush creasing his narrow boney cheeks. "That was . . . Well, crazy. We're gonna laugh about this later, right?"

"Heck, Irvin," I managed a shaky smile. "I'm laughing about it now. Very quietly. On the inside."

Prue had calmed down and stopped screaming, and now was shaking her head repeatedly and muttering under her breath. "Just a friggin' possum. Just a friggin' possum."

"That was the biggest possum I've ever seen in my life!" I amended, hoping to make her feel better.

"I can't believe it friggin' attacked you!" She opened the back door and brought the cats in, giving them some canned food in a bowl. "I'm sorry. I feel so stupid!"

"So do I," I assured her, and Irvin shook his head in agreement. We were all feeling much more sober by the time animal control arrived. They set live traps under the house, and Irvin found a piece of plywood in the garage that Prue nailed over the hole in the closet.

"I'm taking my cats and staying at my mom's until that thing is trapped!"

The animal control officer came over with the cop who had helped me off the floor. "You need to go to the Emergency Room right away," I was directed without hesitation. "We won't know until we can contain and quarantine the animal if it's rabid, but you should start rabies treatment immediately."

"Rabies treatment? You think I have rabies? The bite didn't look that bad." At least, I really hoped it wasn't. Now that I was thinking about it, the back of my leg was starting to really hurt. I didn't want to look at it again.

"Opossums aren't the cleanest animals, ma'am. Even a scratch can carry the risk of serious infection, and while they don't usually carry rabies, there's no cure for it. You need to be vaccinated right away." If the animal control officer was trying to scare me, he was out of luck. I'd been scared pee-less already. I didn't have anything even close to fear left in me.

"I'll take her to the hospital, Officer," Irvin promised quietly. "This was all my fault."

"No, it wasn't, Irvin!" I gave him a chuck on the shoulder. "You didn't sic the possum on me or anything. It's no one's fault!"

There was a sudden burst of laughter from the other officer, and I realized he was holding the video camera that had been on the bathroom shelf where it captured the whole event. "That's confidential investigative material!" I tried to warn, but it was too late. The cops and the animal control officer had gathered around the tiny screen and Prue and Irvin joined them. I could hear my voice say I was going to turn on the water. That was followed by groans of disgust as we reacted to the smell.

Then there was the screaming and the growling and the scrabbling and the pounding . . . and all of them, cops and animal control and Irvin Zettlemeyer, were laughing. I held out my hand. "Okay! That's it! Give me that camera!"

The nice cop managed to stop laughing first, wiping his eyes with the back of his hand. "I'm sorry, ma'am, but that's YouTube worthy! You should see it!"

"I don't want to see it." I sulked. I was cold and wet and my arm really hurt. "I just want to go home and put on dry clothes."

Prue managed to stop laughing and came over to give me a hug. "Kam, I promise that Irvin and I look even more stupid than you do. We ran like sissy brats and just left you! I shut the door in your face. Oh, god . . . it's terrible! I'm sorry!"

Irvin wiped his glasses on his shirttail, looking chagrined. "She's right. I look like a Muppet or something, running and waving my arms."

The animal control officer spoke reassuringly. "Actually, this video would make an important educational tool. You dealt very well with being attacked by a wild animal. I'm surprised it didn't roll over and play possum- pretend it was dead-when you hit it on the head with that piece of equipment."

"The EMF detector? It's not heavy. It probably just pissed him off. I just didn't have time to think of grabbing something heavier."

Prue suddenly appeared at my elbow, pushing a stack of dry clothes into my hands. "Here. Take these. They're probably really big for you, but they're the smallest things I have. You can change in my bedroom. Here's a plastic bag for your wet things."

I gratefully made my escape and stripped off my wet clothes. The t-shirt was a black v-neck that read "Big Girl" and the black cargo-style pants were two sizes too big for me, but they were dry. It was a little awkward trying to change with one arm, but I was already bleeding through the towel wrapped around my wound. Stripping off my soaked jeans, I peeled the torn denim away from my leg and scrutinized it. There were two deep marks that looked more like scratches than bite marks, but they were clearly from teeth. Great. I was going to get rabies. I stuffed my wet clothes into the bag and fluffed a hand through my curls, but there was no avoiding that I looked pretty much like a drowned Q-tip in a black t-shirt.

By the time I emerged, Irvin had gathered up all of my gear. I took the animal control officer's card and promised that I would look at the video but cautioned that my paranormal investigations were strictly confidential. Unless all three of us agreed to release it for educational purposes, I wouldn't turn over the video.

"She means it." A new voice came from the doorway, and I felt sudden tears spring to my eyes. "She's a legal expert, and she doesn't compromise her clients."

"Hey, D.B.?" The nice cop smiled in welcome, but his voice was confused. "What brings you down here? This isn't your jurisdiction."

Detective Ron Brittle smiled warmly at me. "I was on my way back from a stake-out at the bar on Reed, and heard Kami's name on the scanner."

I couldn't help it. I burst into tears. It wasn't the first time Ron had seen me at my worst, but I was hoping that the last time would be the only time. I mean, Ron knew what a messy screw-up I was, but he didn't need to see it first-hand. Even worse, just the sound of his familiar voice somehow made everything seem safer. Safe enough to cry, at least.

Irvin cleared his throat quietly. "Hi, D. B."

"Hey, Zettlemeyer. How's it going?"

"We were attacked by a possibly rabid possum," Irvin mumbled. "So, you know, not so great."

"Oh, come on. You two took down a serial killer. What's a little opossum compared to that?" Ron's joshing smile faded as his gaze took in my bloody, towel-wrapped arm. He pointed towards the door, all no-nonsense cop. "Right. Kam? Get in my car. You're going to the hospital." Ron didn't waste any time.

"Wait? This is the girl who survived the trunk-girl killer? They're the ones who caught him?" The cops were suddenly staring at me with respect. Instead of stopping my tears, it made them come faster.

"Yeah, but that video wasn't nearly as funny." I tried to joke, but I was pretty much done trying to be amusing.

"You're a legend, lady." Nice cop gave me a warm smile and thrust out his hand. I took it and he gave me a strong, comforting handshake. "Very pleased to meet you."

"She's pleased to meet you, too." Ron gently stepped in and steered me towards the door. "If you need anything more from her, you can call me, okay? Come on, Kam. Let's get you out of here."

"Wait! My gear. My car!"

Irvin waved in a shoo-ing motion. "I'll finish packing up all of your stuff and Prue and I can bring it to your office tomorrow, along with your truck, okay?"

I handed him my keys. It was so easy to think of Irvin as just a flaky nerd with a hyperactive imagination, but he really was a good guy. "I'd hug you, but I'd get blood all over you."

"No worries." He waved me off, and I turned to leave, but suddenly remembered Evrett. No way was I leaving him here alone with Prue's cats and an attack possum. Poor Evrett. Just once, I should try to take him somewhere nice. I pulled his velvet bag out of my duffle and headed for Ron's car. Not because I was eager to get to the ER, but I couldn't wait to get out of Prue's house.

IT WAS AFTER TWO IN THE MORNING when we arrived at the emergency room. It was unfortunately busy for the wee hours of a Tuesday morning, but when Ron flashed his badge and combined the words animal attack and rabies, I was ushered in immediately.

I squeezed my eyes shut tight and answered every question they asked as they cleaned my arm and leg. They determined that I had indeed been bitten, and I would need rabies immunoglobulin, which they injected directly into my leg near the bite, and rabies vaccine, which they gave me the first injection of in my arm. I would need four more injections spread out over the next two weeks, which they gave me a schedule for. I was so tired that as much as I wanted to protest, I couldn't find the will. And I really didn't want rabies.

The doctor gave me a course of full spectrum antibiotics to cut any bacterial infection from the claw marks on my arm and told me to take some Tylenol for the pain.

"Those scratches are deep enough that they may scar," the doctor, a bright-eyed woman with short black hair and gentle hands, explained to me. "But we can't stitch it. If the animal actually turns out to have rabies, then stitching can increase risk. You'll need to change the dressing every day. If you can't do it yourself, you can come back here and someone can do it for you."

Ron was waiting when I walked out. I had to sign the releases for the treatment.

"You want me to call your mom?" he asked as we walked back to his car.

"No, I don't want to wake her up."

"You shouldn't be alone."

"I'm exhausted, Ron. I just want to sleep."

"I know, but I think you need something else first." He pulled out of the lot and turned towards downtown. It took several minutes for me to figure out that we weren't headed back to my office. And I was just too tired and worn out to care. It was the first time I'd ever ridden in the front seat of his unmarked police car. That was trust. I guess I could afford to give him a little trust in return.

FIVE MINUTES LATER, I REALIZED HE WAS pulling into the parking lot of the all-night pancake house. "Two waffle and bacon specials," Ron told the waitress before she'd even seated us.

"Sure thing, D.B.," she answered with a cheerful smile. I realized that he must come here a lot in the wee hours after long investigations.

"And hot chocolate. We've had rough days." He gestured to my gauze-wrapped arm.

I wasn't hungry. I was in pain. I was exhausted. I sat down across from Ron in a window booth, and the waitress delivered glasses of ice water. The first sip stuck in my throat, and I felt like I would choke. Oh no! I did have rabies! No, that was silly. Rabies symptoms took days or even weeks to appear. I took another sip, and that one went down easily. Before I knew it, my glass was empty.

My waffle and bacon arrived, and I took a cautious nibble. Then I realized that I'd never tasted anything so delicious in my entire life. It was the best waffle in existence. It was the best waffle ever in the history of waffles! I inhaled every bite. And the bacon . . . Okay, it wasn't the organic applewood-smoked artisan bacon that my mother's friend who owns a smokehouse in Napa makes, but it was darn good.

Ron made small talk here and there. "So, how are things at Reese's? Any more problems from her ex?"

"Not yet. I doubt he's gone for good though."

"I tried to run down his current location, but according to Port Authority, he never re-entered the country from Costa Rica." Ron shrugged. "He must have snuck across the border or something."

That bothered me. "That doesn't make sense. Unless he's doing something illegal, why sneak back in?"

"That's the hundred-dollar question, isn't it," Ron answered. "What about Reese?"

"We've been trying to come up with ways to pull in extra business to offset what we'll lose to the new coffeeshop." I shrugged. "I think we should line up some events, book signings and that kind of thing."

"Call your brother," Ron advised as he poured syrup over his waffle.

"Kenny? Why?"

Ron stared at me for a moment, then blinked. "You really don't know?"

"Know what? Last time I talked to Kenny was Mom's birthday, and all he talked about was Mz. Wan." After his legal fiasco, he started dating his lawyer. And it was no wonder. She was stunningly beautiful, and she had to be a darn good lawyer because she'd gotten him out of his last scrape with a clean record.

"Seriously? You don't know?"

"Know what?! I thought last time you saw him, you were arresting him!"

Ron laughed. "Bygones be bygones. He was in the wrong place at the wrong time, is all."

"And let my car get stolen and dumped in the reservoir."

"It's not like he dumped it there himself," Ron chided. "Anyway, he sold that comic book series he's been working on and it went crazy viral. He's signed for a full series, and they're talking about a video game and movie rights. He's practically famous in the comic book community. There are whole websites dedicated to his work."

No freakin' way. Had I fallen through some hole in reality? "We're talking about my loser brother who went to Burning Man with some guy named Snake? That brother?"

"I can't believe you didn't know. He just did a signing at the mall, and they had to call in extra security. It was a mob." Ron was laughing at me.

"Wait. How do you know all this?"

"I follow him on Twitter. Duh."

Duh. I'd just been duh'd by a major crimes detective. "Let me get this straight. You follow my loser brother? The one you arrested?"

"Nooooo. I follow your famous comic book artist brother who was acquitted of all charges." Ron grinned at me, and I found myself grinning back. He was quite handsome when he smiled like that.

"Fair enough."

"Anyway, he has a huge network. He'll be an asset to the café."

Kenny? Doing a signing at Reese's? I'd suggested Writer Rick to Reese, before. Writer Rick was an afternoon regular at Reese's, an author of adventure novels about a top team of jewel thieves who got into all kinds of predicaments. He was a Reese's fixture, and it made sense to host a signing for him, but I hadn't even known about Kenny. Well, he still owed me for my Kia, didn't he? I could convince him to do a signing, I was sure of it. "Why not? He owes me a favor or two."

Before I realized it, I'd scarfed down my entire breakfast and licked the last bits of chocolate sprinkles from around the edge of my hot-chocolate cup.

"Are you feeling a little better?"

I nodded. "I didn't realize I was even hungry."

"Stress and pain do that." He'd taken a more leisurely approach to his breakfast but finished the last bite of his waffle before eying me seriously across the table. "I'm going to suggest something, and I don't want you to take it the wrong way."

"I always take everything the wrong way, Ron."

"Okay." He paused, tasting the air for a moment before coming out with it. "You need sleep, and you shouldn't be alone. I'm offering to let you sleep at my place. The spare bedroom is comfortable, and I just made the bed up for Casey. She's supposed to be here on Wednesday."

His sister, a clothing sales representative, stayed with him during her business trips to the Bay Area. There were worse places to stay than Ron's spare room, but I wasn't ready to do that. "Right now, I think I could sleep in the back of the car. But I really just want to go home. Thanks for the thought, though."

"At least let me take you to your mom's."

"Oh no! Do *not* make me explain to my mother why I might have rabies!" I rejected that immediately. "Besides, Hoover is alone at the office."

"Okay," he sighed. "I give in. Let's get you back to your sofa."

CHAPTER 6

———

Tuesday Morning

SPRING SUNLIGHT STREAMING THROUGH the high set window woke me and I blinked into the familiar surrounds of the back office. Hoover was curled up on my chest, his deep trademark purr vibrating against me. My arm throbbed and my back and knee ached as I gently rolled him off before he suffocated me. I hurt all over, and my mouth felt like it was full of cotton balls. Ugh. What the heck? Had I been hit by a truck? A kind of smallish one, maybe? Then memory flooded back, along with the knowledge that I'd been attacked by a possum and possibly exposed to rabies, and then I'd eaten bacon and waffles and gone to bed without brushing my teeth. I was also still wearing Prue's black "Big Girl" T-shirt. Well, I was having a banner week, wasn't I? And it was only Tuesday.

I wrapped my bandages in plastic wrap to keep them dry and took a quick shower, getting my hair just wet enough to tame down the curls. I pulled on a pair of soft cotton shorts and a loose v-neck t-shirt that left my injured leg and arm free before gently returning Evrett's helmet to his armor. "Thanks, Evrett. You're my hero."

The office phone rang and I grabbed it. "White Legal Services. This is Kami."

"Kami, it's Jack."

Sudden warmth raced through my heart. Jack. Jack Austen, ex-fiance, sort-of-boyfriend, and, coincidentally, my accountant. *Chill, Kami. He's probably calling about your tax filing.* My heart didn't listen and started beating wildly. I tried to swallow it down and managed to produce a casual, "Hey, what's up?"

His warm voice was soft and did nothing to slow down my crazy heartbeat. "I have a dilemma I'm hoping you can help me with."

Jack needed *my* help? My heart screamed, "*Yes! Yes! Yes! Anything!*" I took a deep breath and answered with all the calm I could muster. "What kind of dilemma?"

"I had plans with Adam for Sunday night, but he has an emergency business trip," Jack left a long pause, before finishing in a rush. "So, I have an extra ticket to the Sharks game and I don't want to go alone, so I thought maybe, if you don't have anything else going on, you could come with me. Or you could just meet me there, if you want . . . Or not. I just thought maybe . . ."

"I'd love to," I interrupted. A Shark's game. Like our first date. My heart screamed, "*Told you so!*" I tried to keep my voice steady. "I haven't been to the Shark Tank in forever. Do you want to pick me up here at the office?"

I heard Jack laugh and it made me smile. I loved his laugh. We set a time and hung up. I didn't realize until afterwards that I probably should have told him about the opossum/demon attack. Eh, Jack knew me well enough to know I was pretty much feral with or without rabies. Jack knew me too well, which was why our relationship was complicated. What I didn't know was where my Sharks jersey was, and I had a bad feeling it was in Kenny's closet. Or on his floor or under his bed or wherever else he kept things I gave him.

I JAYWALKED ACROSS THE STREET TO REESE'S with my cellphone pressed to my ear. "Kenny?"

"Yo. Is this the sister? I didn't know I still I had one."

"Oh. stop it." He knew exactly how to push my buttons. Joke's on him. I know my little brother's buttons too, but I didn't dare push them today. "I need your help."

"Oh, so that's how it is. You don't need me until you need me."

"That doesn't even make any sense."

"Yeah, it does. You want me, you call. Otherwise, you're like the silent sister I never wished I had." He was sticking his tongue out at me over the phone. Don't ask me how I know these things. I've had Kenny as my brother his entire life.

"Look, it's not for me. It's for Reese."

"Reese? Double-chocolate-mocha-extra-whip-with-coconut-syrup-on-top Reese?"

I didn't know how Kenny drank so many of those without succumbing to diabetes. I guess his sour side just outweighs the sweetness. "That Reese. Someone's opening a new, trendy café down the street, and she's having trouble with the competition. I know it's short notice, but their grand opening is tomorrow. Can you help?"

"What do you need?"

Did he really just agree to help and ask what I needed? "Who are you, and what have you done with my brother?"

"I'm his evil twin. I killed him and hid him under your floorboards."

I was fairly sure he was joking. My office building had a concrete floor, not floorboards. "Great. He was a pain in the butt. What I need is this . . ." I took a few moments to outline my plan.

"You're right, it's short notice, but I can swing it. I have tomorrow afternoon free. I'll call my publicity guy and get the books overnighted."

My brother had a publicity guy? I really didn't know what to say, so I just said, "Wow, thank you!"

"Sure. I love Reese's," Kenny finished, "I'll see you tomorrow."

"Hey, wait a sec . . ." I held him up. "Did I give you my Shark's jersey? Can I borrow it back?"

"Uh, yah. Sure." Kenny didn't ask what I wanted it for. I wasn't sure why he was being so nice, but I thanked him again before I hung up and swept into Reese's.

WHEN I WALKED IN THE DOOR OF THE COFFEE SHOP, the phone was ringing, but Reese ignored it, met my eye, and waved me to the far end of the counter. Uh oh. I knew that look.

She thrust a flyer into my hand. "Do you know anything about this?"

It was a half-page flyer, the kind you could whip up with any office printing software, printed out in black and white on a standard laser-jet printer. It read Reese's Café in large Comic Sans font at the top, and below that, in a totally different font, "Best coffee! Come and Try!" Under the advertising statement, there was a badly photoshopped picture of a monkey with a coffee cup upside down on its head like a hat. The monkey was wearing a T-shirt with the address and phone number of the coffee shop on it. I glanced it over then met Reese's eye in horror. "This is totally tacky. Where did it come from?"

The phone was still ringing and Max finally picked it up, muttered a few words and hung up again.

"They've been calling all morning," Reese groaned. "Apparently someone plastered them all over the windshields of all the cars in the BART parking lot. And the hospital, too."

"But I don't think that's even legal."

"It's not." Reese groaned. "We're going to get fined for this. It doesn't even have our logo on it."

"It obviously wasn't done by anyone actually working for the coffeeshop," I agreed. "No logo, no catchphrase. And they misspelled Marin Street in the address. It has to be someone who meant well but didn't know what they were doing. A customer, maybe? One of the cab drivers? The hospital and BART are both popular pick-up and drop-off."

Reese glanced around the café, taking in the mid-morning clientele, mostly businesspeople meeting over coffee to discuss work. "I just can't imagine any of the regulars doing this."

"Well, if you get fined, we'll fight it, but the first step is to be proactive. That will give us the upper hand." I pulled out my cellphone and called Ron. It was an abuse of our friendship, and I apologized as soon as he answered, but after I explained the situation, he gave me a set of numbers to call and file complaints with, including the hospital security and BART police.

"And you're doing okay?" Ron asked before I could ring off.

"I'm a little bruised from falling in the tub and my leg hurts, but I'm fine. No sign of rabies yet."

"Not really something to joke about, you know," Ron chided with a small chuckle.

As I hung up, Reese was staring at me, taking in my bandaged arm for the first time. I wished I'd put on a sweatshirt. "Did you just say rabies!?"

"Uh, yeah. The demon in Cherryland turned out to be a possum living under the house. We had a confrontation, and, well, it exorcised me."

"Opossums don't usually carry rabies," Max interjected. "Their body temperature is too low to support the virus."

"It was the rare just-in-case situation that the animal control people were concerned about, because they aren't usually aggressive—Possums, I mean, not animal control—so they wanted me to get vaccinated anyway," I explained tiredly. "Can I please have a bagel with egg salad and an orange smoothie?"

Max got my breakfast, and Reese went in back with the list of numbers Ron gave me to start doing damage control. Bagel and smoothie in hand, I scooted back across to the office. Hoover met me at the door, running around my legs and sniffing hopefully at my bagel. "Not a chance, buddy."

He jumped up on my desk and waved his tail, knowing he'd win me over in the end and get a taste of egg salad. I pulled up the café website, added links to Kenny's surprisingly beautiful professional website, and put up a banner announcing his appearance at Reese's. As I was busy updating all the social media links, I heard Morri's key in the back door of the office. Hoover cast a lingering glance at my bagel, and then dashed to meet his best friend.

"Well, hello, my hairless herald of hearty humming!" I heard Morri exclaim and a moment later he appeared in the hallway with Hoover riding on his shoulder.

"The letter h today, is it?" I grinned at Morri, but his eyes had already narrowed.

"What's happened to your arm?"

"Wild animal attack," I said casually, hoping he'd take it for a joke.

"Really? Hmmm." He drew Hoover off his shoulder and settled him back on my desk with plentiful pets for the spoiled beast. "I trust if it was my business, you'd tell me."

"More Father Joe's business, really," I admitted. "I wish I'd realized it was a rogue opossum and not a demon infestation. I owe him a box of Mrs. Morri's cookies for calling the cops when I didn't check in on time."

Now Morri's grizzled head was cocked, and he was frowning. "You went alone?"

"Oh, no, of course not. I had Irvin with me." I said as cheerily as I could muster.

Morri's glasses were pushed up onto his forehead as he rubbed his eyes with the knuckles of his index fingers. "Believe it or not, I just don't want to know. I worry about you too much as it is. But that's not what I came down here for." He reached into his pocket and handed me a flash drive. "Here, see what you can do with these. The San Amoro newspaper took three of my best, including one of Hoover. The article will go live on Friday, but it won't be in the printed version until next Monday."

"That's great! It's better than I could have hoped for." I plugged in the flash drive and downloaded several gigabytes of images. Morri had come through in spades with pictures of the Reese's Coffeeshop van, smashingly good candid shots of Reese, Max and Tobiana all hard at work in the café, and mouthwatering images of the food and drinks on offer. He'd also taken portrait shots of some of the customers. Before I could even finish looking through the photos, he handed me a typed page full of quick quotes taken from Reese's loyal customers, aka the taxi-cab crowd, to add to the social media pages.

The quotes were inspiring, and the photos were nothing short of gallery art quality, even to my untrained eye. "You've still got it, Morri. You should make a coffee table book out of these!"

The worry fell away from his expression, and I saw a rare glint in his eye. "I pitched a couple of versions to some of my stringer connections. If we're lucky, we'll manage to get something in the

Chronicle and the Tribune as well. I also sent a pitch to AP business about small business competition in close-knit suburbs. We'll see if they bite."

"You're really enjoying this, aren't you?"

"Well, it's not war reporting or anything, but it's important. This is the kind of struggle we face in our neighborhoods. Bombs don't fall every day, but economic challenges do."

I realized he was so excited he hadn't used a word that started with h at all. "We have my brother coming to do a signing tomorrow. Can you cover that event, too?"

He grinned. "I shall be there with bells on!" Then he paused. "Your brother? Kenny?"

"That's the only brother I've got. His art has gotten famous lately, I guess." I tried not to sound proud, but Morri saw through it.

"Good for Kenny. He's a bit of a wild one, isn't he?" Morri waved and headed back upstairs to his office, probably planning to reach out to more of his publishing connections. I finished my bagel, giving the last bit of egg white to Hoover, and was working on posting videos when I got a text from Ron.

"Check Twitter."

Check Twitter? I opened Twitter and immediately saw what he was talking about. Kenny had Tweeted his impromptu appearance, and his followers had started sharing. Not dozens of shares. Hundreds. There were over two hundred shares and almost five hundred likes. Before I could panic, I saw that Kenny's friend Hoser (a real gentleman despite his nickname) had retweeted and shared it to Facebook, both on his personal account and on his band's page. The band's page included a picture from one of Kenny's comic books of his main character hunched in a café with a cup of coffee. That post was also garnering a lot of attention.

I belatedly realized that I somehow managed to forget that Hoser's Steampunk blues western band, SteamTrails, had a good-sized following, but soon it was obvious that his fans were retweeting, as well. Great! And that gave me another idea. I messaged Hoser directly. "What's your band doing Saturday afternoon? Want a surprise gig to help Reese out?"

"We are booked Saturday. We can do Friday, though. Let me check with the rest of the band to be certain." Hoser's texting was as prim and dated as his actual speech. How quaint. For one of my brother's friends, Hoser was adorable.

Within the hour, I had SteamTrails booked for a show on Friday afternoon with a five-dollar-a-head cover charge. I threw down a handful of my collected Reese's gift cards as prizes for a steampunk costume contest. Before I knew it, those posts had been reposted to the Bay Area Steampunk Facebook page.

Within minutes, Ron Brittle had reposted the events to the San Amoro Public Service board. As soon as that share happened, Reginald Burroughs, my lawyer and one of my ten Facebook friends, posted it to the Oslo and Burrough's social networks. The shares and likes skyrocketed from there. The blitz had begun.

With Kenny and SteamTrails booked, the schedule had a gap on Thursday and I thought we needed to make a splash there as well. I sent a Facebook message to Writer Rick. How many local authors could he pull together for a mass surprise event in under forty-eight hours? I explained that Reese was struggling in the face of the new café down the street and we needed to bring in new customers. I sweetened the deal by offering that all authors would receive a free coffee drink and pastry. Writer Rick posted to his local writer group and within an hour we had six authors, ranging in genre from romance to action-adventure and science fiction, committed to an impromptu book fair. I started the tweet blasting and Facebook sharing, and watched as the authors shared it with their networks.

I couldn't believe it was really that easy! I didn't quite trust it. I called Twila and warned her about what I'd done.

"I'm seeing it," she answered. "I had to turn off social media alerts on my phone! Anyway, I'll call in the reinforcements and we'll be ready for tomorrow."

Before I could answer, my attention was torn away by yelling voices outside.

CHAPTER 7

————

Tuesday Afternoon

SMACK DAB IN THE MIDDLE OF MARIN STREET, Reese in her brown apron was toe-to-toe with Wyatt in his green apron, and both were yelling like it was some kind of competition. I caught snippets of their blistering confrontation as I pulled on my worn sneakers and tugged my denim jacket over my bandaged arm.

"I have a permit!" Wyatt was insisting, his hands waving in the air.

"Not for my lot!" That was Reese. "You can't park that here!"

"Well, pardon me! I didn't realize you owned the street!"

I overturned my office chair sprinting for the door. I leapt between Reese and Wyatt with my arms outstretched to hold them at bay. When you're barely five feet tall, planting yourself between two dragons is probably not the best plan. I managed to pray to whatever gods might exist that they didn't rend me limb from limb. "Hey! Hey! What's the problem?"

"That . . . thing! In front of my shop!" Reese threw her arm out to point so violently that I was concerned she'd dislocate her shoulder. "He's got to move it. Now!"

"You're crazy." Wyatt twirled a finger at his temple. "I have a downtown parking permit that specifies I can park in any spot."

I looked across the street and saw a forest green Subaru wagon with Café Fantastique vinyl door-clings sitting in the reserved parking in front of Reese's.

"Both of you just calm down." I tried to keep my voice even and reasonable. "You're going to end up arrested if you don't chill out." Chill out? I cringed. I sounded like my mother. They both stopped yelling and stared at me.

"Just whose side are you on?" Reese's voice was somewhere between a pit bull's bark and Darth Vader's growl. If I didn't defuse this, it was going to go badly for everyone but mostly for me.

"What business is it of yours anyway?" Wyatt snapped at me.

I gulped in a deep breath. "Okay, at least you're yelling at me instead of at each other. Wyatt? You gotta know that it's not neighborly to park your business car right in front of Reese's. C'mon, we all have to get along here, and screaming matches in the street aren't going to solve anything." I gestured down the mostly empty street. "There's a dozen spots open between there and here."

Wyatt stood over me with his arms crossed.

"You have your own parking lot . . ."

"We need that for customers!" He cut me off with a sharp bark.

"Great. Reese? Go get your van and park it in that empty spot by the entrance right where their customers will have to pass it to get into the lot. You have a permit, so it's perfectly legal."

"Oh, no way!" Wyatt took a step, but I planted my palm against his chest. If he pushed at all, I'd go over like a one-legged plant stand, but I had to hope he wouldn't push. If he did, Reese would likely take it as an assault on me and do some real damage. Women like Reese don't put up with men pushing women around.

"Then move your car," I told him impatiently. "Seriously, if you want to play dirty, Reese can play just as hard. Just . . . egads, grow the hell up, both of you! Like it or not we're all stuck on this block with each other."

Reese looked both smug and angry at the same time.

Wyatt looked frustrated, but I could see something in his gaze that said I'd won. "Fine! I'll move my car. But if I see her ugly van down here, I'm calling a tow truck."

"Do that and your little *Fantastique* car will become one busted ass P.O.S." Reese retorted.

"Hey! No more threats. No more screaming. Both of you walk away." Neither of them moved. They both stayed within inches of my outspread hands, glaring at each other. I fluttered my fingers in a 'go on, shoo' movement. The doors of other businesses were starting to open, and people were pausing on the sidewalk. "Off with you both! Go on, before anyone else sees you behaving like toddlers in the middle of the street."

Finally, Wyatt dropped his arms to his sides and Reese turned around and headed back towards the café. I knew she'd have words for me later, but I didn't care.

I lowered my voice, all trace of authority gone from it. "Wyatt? Why on earth would you park your car right in front of Reese's?"

He turned away and his voice was so low I almost didn't hear him mutter, "I didn't."

"You . . . wait . . . what?" I ran after him and planted myself in his path. "What do you mean you *didn't*?"

"I did not park my car in front of Reese's." Wyatt's face was flushed but his eyes were no longer wide with fury. "I parked it over there!" His finger jabbed towards Café Fantastique, "At the curb in front of the shop. Then I went inside and started working on paperwork in the office. I swear, Kami, I didn't park it there."

"Why didn't you tell Reese that?"

"She didn't give me a chance! And I'm surprised that you did, frankly. It sounds crazy, I know, but I parked it right there next to Fantastique. I was going to move it around to the back alley after Grady got here." He ran his hand wearily through his hair. "What the hell is going on around here?"

Baffled didn't begin to describe my feelings. "I don't know, but I don't think ghosts can drive cars."

"What about push them? I mean, I've heard of this town where if you park on the railroad tracks, ghosts of people who died on the tracks push the car off."

"That's an old urban tale and it's been disproven. They did a land survey and discovered that the ground is slanted there. Cars naturally roll off the tracks, but the lay of the land creates an optical illusion that makes it look like the ground is flat. Besides, we don't have any railroad tracks, and even if we did, it would take a hell of a lot of energy to push a car from here to there. I don't know what spirit, *human* spirit at least, could do it." I sighed, wondering how I could avoid getting more involved with Café Fantastique's mess. I didn't want to solve Wyatt's problems. I wanted to solve Reese's. "Who else has keys to the café car?"

"No one. I have one set. We bought it used. I keep meaning to have another set made but haven't gotten around to it."

"And where do you keep the keys?"

"In the desk drawer in the office. I was sitting right there."

I finally gave up. "I have no idea what's going on around here, but it might be best to keep all of your keys on your person for a while. There is only one thing I can tell you. Since it wasn't a ghost, it's not really my problem. Please, just avoid Reese for a while, or maybe forever. She's doing her best to make the most of the situation, and you should, too."

Wyatt just nodded, and I could see he didn't relish the idea of drawing Reese's ire any further.

I turned away at that and walked back to my office with my head up and my shoulders square. As soon as I was inside with the door firmly at my back, I started laughing and I laughed until I was sitting on the floor out of breath. When I finally looked up, Hoover was perched on the bookshelf, staring at me with his head cocked and his tail twitching as if judging my lack of dignity. "You eat spiders off the floor," I reminded him as I caught my breath. I gathered myself together and tried to put the whole incident out of my mind, but the question remained. If I believed Wyatt—and I did—who really moved the car?

I HEADED ACROSS TO REESE'S AND FOUND HER in her little closet-sized office, rather violently counting out the till for Max. I leveled a stare across the counter at her. "Well, that went well."

"I just can't believe his nerve!"

"He told me he didn't park the car there."

Reese threw a handful of dimes into the cash register with a resounding clatter. Roughly half of them scattered into the nickel and quarter sections. "That lying, crazy sonofa . . ."

"Whoa. Whoa now." I held up both hands, and Max ducked under Reese's arm to take the cash drawer before all his change ended up on the floor. "I'll tell you one thing. I believe him. I think someone pulled a not-so-funny prank on Wyatt, maybe his uncle or the partner. Wyatt needs the café to succeed, and I don't think he'd risk pissing you off."

"He pissed me off when he opened that place."

"Reese, you have better prices, better food, and better service. Did you know they're cutting costs by not hiring help? Grady and Wyatt are doing everything themselves. They won't be able to keep the kind of hours you do. And . . ." I glanced around to make sure that the taxi drivers were all intent on their muffins and coffee before continuing in hushed tones. "Guess what? Those 'home-made' baked goods signs on their windows?" I paused for effect, deepening my voice conspiratorially. "It's a *lie*, Reese. They have whole shelves in their stockroom full of cake mix."

"Mix?" Reese stared, completely nonplussed.

"Mix. And generic mix at that. Nothing fancy, organic, or gluten free about it. Now, don't go sharing that around, but I'll bet you anything that your cinnamon-raisin marble coffee cake would kill anything of theirs in a taste-test any day of the week."

"Wait . . ." Reese stood slowly and crossed her arms. "Just how do you know that?"

"Uh," Oops. "I . . . uh . . . saw it."

"You. Went. To. Café. Fantastique."

If she'd had a knife instead of the afternoon cash deposit, I might have been afraid. I had never heard of anyone being killed by a handful of cash. Though, on second thought, it wasn't the tool that mattered, it was who wielded it, and the wielder in this case was Reese. A gulp choked my throat. "Ugh. I did. They hired me to look into something for them."

"You took work from them? Kami!" I don't think my own brother had ever managed to make my name sound more like an epithet than Reese did in that moment. "You . . . you . . . *traitor!*"

"A traitor who reports back is called a *spy*, Reese." I held up both hands in surrender. Her eyes were still narrowed murderously, but she lowered the cash. I breathed a little easier. "Believe me, they're serving cookies made with cheap soy shortening and their coffee bean is the same as yours is. They can't hold a candle to you."

"Yeah, well, that's not up to me to decide. It's for the customers to figure out. They open officially tomorrow and after that, my clients are gonna head down the street. I'm finished." She wrapped the cash in a rubber band and dropped it into the safe. "Time to pack it in and get a day job."

"Um, Reese . . ." I started to say, but she fired me such a sharp look that I hesitated. Thankfully, at that very moment Twila arrived. She came into the office to hang her jacket and fetch her apron and I grabbed her arm and pulled her beside me. "Twila has something to tell you!"

Reese looked back and forth and waggled her finger at us. "Alright, Tweedledee and Tweedledum. Just what did you two do? It's all over your faces. You guilty as hell, ladies, so fess up."

Twila moved a half-step closer to me. If we were going down, we were going down together. She pulled out her phone and opened it to the Reese's Coffeeshop Facebook page. Reese stared at it for a second.

"What the heck am I lookin' at? Where did those pictures come from?" She pointed to the event listing. "What's that?"

"That is your updated Facebook page, and this is the famous comic book author who is going to be here tomorrow afternoon signing books," I said. "Morri took the photos and gathered the quotes from patrons. Twila and Mallory did the video shorts for TikTok and the rest."

"What?"

Twila took over. "Tomorrow's event already has over five hundred likes. And we've got Writer Rick and his pals coming on Thursday, and a steampunk event on Friday. Café Fantastique's grand opening week is gonna suck beans!"

"Non-organic, over-roasted, bitter beans," I added, feeling tough just saying it.

Reese's arms dropped to her sides, and she just stood there, staring at us in disbelief.

"So, you'd better get baking," I warned Reese. "Comic book fans love cookies." I pointed towards the kitchen. "Seriously. You just keep doing what you do best, and you'll have all your regulars back in a week, plus a pile of new customers."

Reese nodded, her tense shoulders easing slightly. "Yeah, I probably shouldn't have lost my temper at that guy, but when I saw their car right smack in front of my door with that ugly green logo— What's that supposed to be, anyway? An earthworm?—I just lost it."

"I think it's supposed to be a coffee bean. I don't know why it has eyes, though."

"It's kinda creepy," Twila confirmed.

I continued, "Just . . . as your legal consult, promise me you won't lose it anymore. In public, at least?"

"Girl, you know I sure as hell can't promise that!" She headed back to the kitchen, squeezing past Sasha, who was carrying a tray of fresh, hot scones to add to the case. Halfway through the door, she turned back. "How many are coming tomorrow?"

Twila shrugged. "Hard to say. Likes don't always equal attendance, but I guess Kenneth's pretty popular. We'll be ready. I already called in reinforcements."

The inviting scents of cherry and almond drifted from Sasha's tray and my nose perked in what I was fairly sure was a perfect imitation of Hoover. "Man, do I need a scone! I deserve a scone."

Twila pointed towards the front. "No, you need to be making signs. The windows need doing, and flyers for events need to be delivered to every business on the street. I already emailed you the flyer templates."

I OBEDIENTLY RAN BACK TO THE OFFICE and grabbed my paints and stencils. By the time I was done, Reese's front windows had two new lines of text. The side right of the door read "Fresh Cookies, Muffins, and Cakes", and the left side stated, "Baked from Scratch Daily."

WHEN I STEPPED BACK INTO THE CAFÉ to check my work, the phone was ringing. Max grabbed it with a despondent, "Reese's Coffee and More, can I help you?"

There was a long moment of silence, and then Max looked around, confused, "I . . . Uh . . . Just a sec . . ." He covered the receiver and waved at us. "It's a journalist from Bay Area Prime wanting to know if they can interview Kenny White after his event? What event?"

"Tell them, yes, absolutely!" I called out.

"Yes, absolutely." Max said dutifully into the phone. After he hung up, he gave me a worried look. "Kenny White is coming here? Are you sure?"

"My brother owes me multiple favors, Max. And we get business, he gets business, and all it costs Reese is a double mocha with whipped cream and coconut syrup."

I saw light dawn in Max's eyes. "Wait. No way. CoconoMocha Kenny is *Apocalypse Starshine* Kenny White? Seriously? Oh, man. Oh wow! I had no idea!" Max was gushing like a twelve-year-old schoolgirl, not an appealing look on a twenty-two-year-old, six-foot-three barista. "That's so awesome! Why didn't you tell me?"

"Yeah, well, I don't like to talk about him," I grumbled in reply, leaving out that I hadn't even known until last night that my brother was the guy who wrote Apocalypse Starshine.

CHAPTER 8

Tuesday Night

I'D JUST GOTTEN BACK TO MY OFFICE and settled into my chair when Prue pulled up in my little pickup, trailed by Irvin Zettlemeyer in his car. Irvin came in with my duffle bag and set it on my desk.

"How are you? Are you okay?"

I smiled faintly. "I'm a little sore and tired, but I'm okay. How's Prue holding up?"

"Now that she knows it was just a possum, she's fine." Irvin glanced out the window to where Prue was waiting by his car. "She's talking about adopting the demon if he's cleared in quarantine but not eligible for re-release."

"Adopting the demon?" I stammered helplessly for a moment. "Is she insane?"

Irvin smiled dreamily, and it was the most genuine head-over-heels-in-love smile I've ever seen in my entire life. "Yeah, she is. But who am I to judge?"

He handed me a check for the investigation fee and waved. "I owe you way more than this, for what happened."

"What happened wasn't your fault," I said. "But now that you mention it, if you want to help, if you could share some of the events we're holding at Reese's over the next few days on social media, that would be great."

"Done." He glanced over the flyer I had just printed out. "Oh! SteamTrails is playing this weekend? Only a fiver cover charge? I know a few people who would love that."

When did I start to really like Irvin? "Thanks. I appreciate it."

"If you're going to the concert, I'll see you there!" He jogged out the door before I could tell him that if I was at the concert, I'd probably be in the kitchen or working the espresso machines.

I settled down with my laptop and started going over the evidence from the night before. Hoover weaved around my screen and arms, begging for pets as I synced the two video feeds with the voice-recorder and settled in for an hour of listening and watching. There wasn't much to see or hear. There was just video of darkened rooms with no movement and no noise other than the audible voices of Wyatt, Grady, Thomas, and myself punctuated by the periodic crash of the ice-machine. The two times I thought I saw something on the video, I paused to screen-cap the images and use my image manipulation program to blow up and clarify them. They both proved to be nothing more than dust floating close to the lenses. I still had two more hours of evidence to review and was close to giving up when I saw something in the dark shadows of the feed from the camera that had been pointed at the office. It looked, just briefly, as if the clean tile floor of the office darkened slightly right in front of the desk, like a stain slowly spread across the floor. Then it was gone.

I backed the video up twice to study it. The entire event took less than five seconds, and you had to be watching closely. A dozen possibilities circulated through my mind. Had one of us passed near the desk and cast a shadow? Had a passing car or flying bird blocked out the ambient light that filtered through the thin blinds over the office window? Had the camera lens refocused in the darkness, leaving the impression of a shadow? Was there something in the office that could move and cast a shadow, like an unstable lampshade or hanging ornamentation of some sort?

Sherlock Holmes had this great idea about eliminating the impossible, so that's where I always started with any investigation.

I honestly hadn't seen any evidence of haunting in the café. This was the first hint I'd even gotten that something might be amiss. I pulled up the other videos and the audio and synced them up again. The video from the dining room confirmed what the conversation on the audio told me: all four of us had been in the dining room at a central table when the shadow occurred. No one had been in the office, or even in the backroom. No cars passed outside while we were there, though a delivery truck had lumbered past a few minutes after.

I picked up my phone and the business card Wyatt had given me.

"Café Fantastique, how may I help you?"

"Wyatt? It's Kami. Hey, I had a . . ."

Wyatt cut me off. "How did that sound? I'm vacillating between that greeting and 'Thank you for calling Café Fantastique' and I can't decide. What do you think?"

"I think you answered the phone, which is more than I can say for most establishments these days. Personally, I like starting with thank you, though." I rushed forward before he could interrupt me again. "Which is why I wanted to say thank you for trusting me with your investigation the other night. Would it be possible for me to swing by to confirm a few things?"

"Oh, man . . ." Wyatt paused. "I'm sorry, it's absolutely insane in here. I have interviews for employees all evening, and I still have to finish setting up the dining room for tomorrow. The cabinet installers left sawdust all over everything, and I just don't have a spare second for anything else."

"No worries," I reassured him quickly. "It's probably nothing. I've been through most of the recordings we took and everything is fine."

"So, no ghost?"

"No ghost that I can see. There's one little weird shadow on the tape and I wanted to check something with the lighting, but it can wait until things have settled down. I really don't think you have anything supernatural going on."

"Thomas and Grady will be happy to hear that," Wyatt sounded distracted.

I signed off. "Good luck getting ready for opening!"

"Thanks, we need it. I don't suppose you'd consider helping out tomorrow, just a bit?" His voice was pleading.

"Sorry. I told you upfront where my loyalties lie. But I really do wish you success tomorrow." Mostly because I knew we could beat anything Café Fantastique had to offer.

IT WAS ALMOST TIME FOR MY ANTIBIOTICS, and I was supposed to take them with food. I put down the ghost hunting work, picked up my class homework, and headed back to Reese's. Twila fixed me a turkey sandwich and an iced tea, and I headed upstairs to my favorite table.

"Kam?" A familiar voice greeted. I looked up to see Ron standing at the top of the stairs.

I gave him a puzzled look. "Shouldn't you be working?"

"I'm just grabbing some early dinner." He waved a hand towards the counter. "May I dine with you?"

I glanced around suspiciously. "Where's Dorkbrains?"

"*Dortman* is with the DA prepping for a trial that starts next week." He emphasized Dortman's name to remind me that I'd promised to try to stop doing that. "Come on, Kam. I have to work with the guy. And he is a good cop."

I didn't answer that. Instead, I closed my laptop and waved him to the chair across from me. With a chagrined smile, I handed him the weird monkey flyer that I'd called him about earlier. It seemed like ages ago. "Sorry to bother you earlier. I wasn't sure who to call, but I knew we had to move fast. Thanks for your help. I know you deal with major crimes, not petty stuff like this."

"It seems like they were trying to do Reese a favor, but failed completely." Ron studied the ugly flyer for another second before turning it upside down. "That monkey is staring at me. Are you sure it's not an employee of the cafe trying to help?"

I glanced around the café. Jill was making Ron's sandwich. Twila was behind the counter, pulling espresso for a couple of women in yoga clothes. Sasha was cleaning the toaster oven before the after-work crowd hit. Reese was on the phone. Tobiana, a retiree who had filled in shifts at Reese's since before the days when I worked there, was refilling the cream and milk carafes. I thought about the kitchen staff and weekend crew. "No. Not a chance. None of these guys would make a move like this without Reese's blessing. You know this gang as well as I do. We're all loyal to Reese."

"We?" Ron raised an eyebrow at me.

"We." I confirmed. "I still fill in shifts from time to time. I'm loyal."

"Even with a new coffee shop opening down the street?"

"Especially with a new shop opening." I changed the subject as Jill delivered a bagel topped with smoked turkey and melting Gouda cheese to Ron. I had to resist the temptation to snag a bite. "The new owners seem nice enough, but I'm not jumping ship."

Ron took a bite of his food and smiled as he chewed. "Me either. This is really good."

There were a few moments of silence as we both enjoyed our dinner together. Uh oh. Was this a date? It couldn't be a date if it wasn't planned, could it? I mean, if it was a date, someone had to ask someone else out, right? I found myself watching the shifting grey-blue of his eyes and the way his jaw moved when he chewed. He was freshly shaved, his short dark hair swept back from his receding hairline. His suit was conservative grey with a dark blue tie that set off his eyes. Realizing I was staring, I hurried to start a conversation. "So, how have you been?"

"I'm okay. Still struggling with evidence in that burglary chain. That's why I'm down here again today. I'm canvasing businesses. Someone must know something, but no one wants to come forward. Whoever is doing it seems to know how to get in and what to take, but the businesses are so random. Why hit the dog groomer's when the watch repair place is just two doors down and has far more valuable stuff? They went in the upper-story window of Steeds Antiques and took some valuable platters but skipped the jewelry store across the street."

"I hate to think it, but could it be gang related?" Most of the gang activity was centralized north of us in Oakland or south of us in San Jose, but it wasn't unusual to have random crimes associated with them in the mid-East Bay. "Some kind of initiation ritual for new members or something?"

"Could be, but it doesn't seem organized enough for that." Ron started to say something, then apparently thought better of it. Confidential investigation information had to remain confidential, after all. "What about you? How are those bites healing?"

"My leg hurts, but I don't know how much is the bite and how much is that immunoglobin injection," I grumbled. "Honestly, I'm mostly just tired, but that could be from being up all night. Early bedtime for me tonight, I think."

"I envy you your freedom. The new captain has us accounting for every minute of every day. I can't even stake out a suspect without signed permission." Ron gathered up his own mess. "Speaking of which, I'm already behind schedule today, so I better get back to it. For some reason, I overslept this morning."

"Hey, thanks for looking out for me last night. I hate to admit it, but I needed the help." Before I could be any more vulnerable, I continued with, "Are you coming to Kenny's signing tomorrow?"

"I already have signed copies from him." He grinned wickedly. "I think your brother likes me better than you do."

And then he fled the scene faster than a thug with a stolen diamond.

CHAPTER 9

Wednesday

I WOKE TO HOOVER CURLED AGAINST ME, purring softly and I gently stroked his ears. I treasured these little moments of cuddle time, just the two of us alone on the old leather sofa, the yellow crocheted afghan wrapped around us. It seemed all too soon that the alarm-tone on my cellphone rang out, and I gently set the cat aside to fetch my antibiotics and some Tylenol. I showered, changed the dressings on my wounds, and went to find some breakfast. I bumped straight into Morri and Mallory.

"Good morning, gentlemen!" I greeted before I followed their line of sight down the street. There was a line from the corner of our building all the way down the sidewalk to Café Fantastique. Even from our side-on vantage point, I could see that their dining room was full. My heart sank. "Oh, that's not good."

"I daresay it's a disaster," Morri agreed, his wizened face puckered in a frown. As we stood there in solidarity, someone in a battered hooptie-mobile of a Cadillac pulled half-way into the alleyway that led to the narrow parking spaces behind 542 Marin Ave, blocking in my pickup and Mallory's sedan.

"Welp, so much for the neighborhood," Mallory muttered under his breath.

"Oh! He did not just do that!" I ran to the alley, waving my arms at the sign that led to our little parking lot. "Hey! Get your ugly piece of junk out of my alley! Does it say free parking there? No. It doesn't! What part of *private* don't you understand?"

The driver of the car turned, flipped me an obscene gesture, and got in line for the new café. White hot fury boiled behind my eyes. This was war. I pulled out my phone and called city towing. Private parking meant private parking, and this jerk was blocking the alley. I made sure to speak loudly enough that the guy could hear me. "Hi! This is White Legal Services, and I need an illegal park towed out of my private parking, please."

"You callin' a tow? Seriously?" The man came back, got in his Caddy, and pulled out, circling around the block.

"I hope he's headed to hell," I told Morri and Mallory.

Mallory had a smug grin on his face. "I wish, but he's probably headed to the public parking on Main."

"Well, I'm headed to Reese's. My brother is signing this afternoon, and I want it to be awesome for both him and for Reese." It was the least I could do for either of them.

FOR TEN IN THE MORNING, REESE'S COFFEE and More was dead. There were a handful of taxi drivers by the window, and a few of the business-morning regulars at the counter, but easily three-quarters of the seats were empty. Reese was behind the counter, rearranging pastries to make room for a fresh stack of cookies. Her face was a study in depression.

"Are you ready for this afternoon?"

She shrugged. "Does it matter? Look at this place. It's as bad as a funeral home in here. Might as well just carve my tombstone and dig the grave."

"Give me a cup of your Arabica Bold and an apple bagel with cream-cheese. Then I'll get to work."

"You're abandoning me? Can't you work over here today? People driving by will see all the empty tables and wonder what's wrong with us!"

"And what's right with *them*?" I flicked my hand in the general direction of Café Fantastique. "Don't sweat it. They'll come back when they realize those guys are all hype and no substance. And yes, I'm working here today, but I need food first."

While I hastily ate and chugged down my coffee in the corner, I rewrote the daily specials chalkboard, renaming old sandwich specials with names from Kenny's comic books. I wasn't sure how good a match the characters were to the menu items, but I thought it looked good when I was done.

Twila breezed in as I was finishing up and she ran in back to grab her apron before rushing back to my table. "Omigod," she hissed to me, "Your original post on Kenny's signing has over four hundred shares! The Facebook events page has hundreds in the attending list! Where are we going to put them all?"

Four hundred? I'd hoped for forty, maybe fifty. I glanced around the café. We had seating for forty, but . . . four hundred? So maybe we'd have a line out the door, too? Would that be a bad thing? Hopefully, all of them would buy something, but even if they didn't, planting the café in their subconscious as a good place to be would help tip the scales.

I jumped up, hung the specials board, and went to get my own apron.

"You two are acting like something's actually gonna happen," Reese grumped. "No one is coming in here. I'm gonna end up taking all these cookies to the homeless shelter or somethin.'"

"You," I pointed at her, "are going to go in back, lose that apron, put your hair down, and show me the hard-core, serious business-woman that you are."

"Oh, I am, am I? And since when are you the boss?"

I grinned at her. "You're the boss. You should look the part."

She huffed, but headed for the office.

A harried looking man in an ill-fitted black suit jacket over a blue T-shirt and jeans hastened through the door. His bleach-blond hair was short and spiky, and he had a healthy but lean uncomfortable look about him.

"Can we help you?" Twila asked. He stopped, his eyes popping a little as he took in the willowy night manager. Under her apron, she wore a cute mid-thigh dress with short sleeves. It had an almost

1950's look to it, but somehow seemed to cling to her frame in a way most guys would find highly appealing.

"I'm Willy Royce? I'm publicity manager with Blackline Comics Publishing? The Badge-man called and told me he needed two-hundred copies delivered here? How do you want to do this?"

Twila snapped into action and dealt with the practical side of the book signing thing. I'd totally forgotten we were going to need books, and how did it work? Did we pay for the books? Did they buy them directly from the publisher? Kenny at least had thought to get the books here. Maybe I owed him more of an apology than I thought. Could it be the brat had grown up and I'd somehow missed it?

In the storeroom under a pile of boxes of napkins, I dug out the small folding table and the portable register that Reese used for special events, like the annual San Amoro Wine and Art Faire. At the counter, I broke up some cookies and brownies into little sample cups while Max brewed up some Special Sumatra Single Origin coffee for the same purpose. Willy Royce had brought pro-motional posters featuring Kenny's name in big, red 'KAPOW' style letters over blown-up frames from his comics. I helped him hang them in the front window and at the front counter. Morri appeared with his camera and started taking publicity shots for the website. The whole place looked and smelled festive and fan-tastic. Score one for Reese's.

I was just starting to wonder what had happened to Reese when she reappeared, drawing gasps from staff and patrons alike. Her black hair, normally tied up in a braid at the back of her head, was down and fell in waves around her shoulders. She was still wearing her brown t-shirt, but her brown work pants were replaced with sleek, chocolaty pinstriped pants and she'd topped it with a matching designer jacket. Her makeup was perfect, from the smokey haze of eyeshadow to the prim, conservative lipstick she wore. She stepped in front of me and turned in a circle. "Is this acceptable?"

"You look amazing, boss," was all I could say.

"You look fantastic," Twila enthused before taking Reese's arm and introducing her to Willy Royce, who was already muttering about doing more events at the coffee shop in the future.

We were all heads down making the final preparations when Reese's awed voice caught our attention.

"Well, getta load of that."

I looked up to see Kenny walking through the door.

No, *sauntering* through the door. He was sauntering. He was clean-shaven with his long, wavy blond hair pulled back into a tidy ponytail that fell in ringlets at the back of his neck. And he had Jenni Li Wan on his arm. She was wearing a slim mini-dress in a classic comic book print fabric, and her long black hair, which I'd only ever seen done up in a bun for court, flowed down her back in loose sections interspersed with tiny braids full of brightly colored ribbons that matched the colors in her dress. The competent defense attorney was nowhere to be seen. The quiet, thoughtful potential sister-in-law was replaced with . . . a comic book geek girl? "Oh gawd. Kenny, what did you do? You broke Li!"

She burst into a singsong of giggles.

"What?" Kenny looked her up and down and for the first time I noticed that he was wearing pressed black slacks with matching belt, a grey button-down collarless shirt, and a sleek black dress jacket that hung from his straight frame with GQ quality. You see, the flat-chested, flat-stomached, no buttocks, no hips, and square shoulders that look completely boy-town on my five-foot-something girl frame work extremely well on Kenny's six-foot-one-inch man frame. It was a big joke (and sometimes less of a joking matter) between us that he got the beauty and I got the brains. I hadn't seen him get cleaned up like this since his court date, but even then there'd been a school-boy uniform look to his suit. His current wear put him solidly in the style column of *Entertainment Weekly*. He finished studying Li and looked back at me. "I didn't break her. I just added to her repertoire."

Repertoire? Where did Kenny Knucklehead even learn that word? I came forward and gave him a quick hug. "You look amazing, Ken. I'm so proud of you." And where the hell had those words come from? "Thank you so much for doing this."

"Yeah, well, anything for Reese." Kenny smiled at Reese who was approaching with the previously mentioned double-mocha-extra-chocolate-extra-whipped-cream-with-coconut syrup-on-top.

"They're starting to show up." Willy Royce suddenly waved his hands, and I glanced out the window to see a disorderly mob gathering on the sidewalk. "Places, everyone, and I'll get them lined up. As soon as the clock hits two, I'll let them in."

I took advantage of the ensuing scramble to buy a copy of the three comics that were available. I started to say, 'Hey, bro,' but stopped, struck again by the handsome young professional artist/author who was my kid brother. It was time to play on his field and show some respect. "Hey, Badge-man, can you sign these for me?"

He didn't miss a beat. "It'll cost you a brownie."

"The brownie is on the house," Reese interjected, sliding one out of the case and handing it over to me. She glanced out the window where the line was queuing up, at least thirty strong and growing, and a relieved smile came across her face. "Kenny, I gotta say, kid, you done good."

"It's all down to you, Reese."

I stopped and looked between him and Reese. Reese was my muse, my can-of-whoop-your-ass-if-you-don't-get-it-moving, my inspiration when I'd run out. I had no idea how many more people she shared her unique brand of inspiration with. I looked at Twila, but she shrugged at me.

Kenny cleared his throat as he realized everyone was staring at him. Li leaned over and squeezed his hand. "I was in here late one night, drawing, and you asked what I was working on. It was late, just a few other customers, so I showed you, and you said, 'That's real talent, kid. You don't ever let go of that, and don't let anyone tell you different.' You believed in me when no one else did."

No one else, including me. What kind of big sister was I? "Ken, I'm sorry."

"Yeah, me, too." But he didn't look at me. His eyes were on Reese. She stood in the middle of the store for a second, then suddenly swooped in and hugged Kenny so hard that she rumpled his shirt. When she let go of him, she turned and went back into the kitchen without saying a word. And then the clock pointed at two and Willy Royce opened the doors.

I headed through the kitchen door, cradling my freshly signed copies of Apocalypse Starshine. I needed to make it up to Kenny, but how? How did one erase years of having a lazy slob of a brother? I didn't know. Once when we were kids, my brother broke my favorite toy. Our mother, who still wears the world she dressed in as a kid growing up on a commune in the seventies, told me to love my own brother as my own heart. I'd pinned him down and written "Brat" on his forehead in permanent marker. Maybe I'd left that mark on my own heart. I'd forgotten how to love him. Even when they pulled my car out of the reservoir with a dead body in the trunk, and I'd known through the core of my entire being that I couldn't imagine a world without my kid brother in it, I still hadn't remembered to love him as my own heart. I didn't know how someone made up for that.

Unfortunately, there was no time to think about that now. There were bins of salads to make, sandwich fillings to prep, and muffins to pop in and out of ovens. Only when Max gave me the thumbs up to let me know there was enough did I hang up my apron and sneak out the back door of the café.

I paused on the doorstep of my office and glanced back at the line of people waiting to meet Kenny White, creator of Apocalypse Starshine, and wondered if pride could be a little bit of a substitute for love.

I was so tired I didn't even look at my computer before I crashed on the sofa in the back office for a nap.

This time, it was the warning whoop of a police siren that woke me. Shaking off the yellow afghan, I stumbled out the front door to find two cop cars parked in front of Reese's. Oh no. I grabbed my phone and limped across the street where Reese was huddled talking to one of the officers.

Twila was standing in the doorway of the coffee shop. She caught sight of me and waved me over, instantly accusing, "Where did you sneak off to?"

"I needed a nap. Why?" I glanced around, but everything looked okay inside the café. The comic book crowd was mostly gone, though several tables were still taken up by obvious Apocalypse Starshine fans. "What happened? Everything looked good when I left."

Twila shook her head. "It was awesome at first. We had to hold people back at the door so that we didn't break fire code. Your brother is the bomb! Instead of any kind of reading, he and his girlfriend . . . she is his girlfriend, right? . . . acted out scenes. The fans loved it. We sold out of muffins. We blew our monthly sales totals out of the water in the first hour."

"First? It was only supposed to go an hour." I glanced at my phone. It was almost seven.

"Three hours. They ended up doing three shows to accommodate everyone who showed up, but then they just kept coming and making him sign." Twila made a face. "We ran out of cheesecake and pear tarts, and there was nearly a riot over the last chocolate chip scone. Finally, they ran out of books, so that Willy guy called a halt to it and gave everyone vouchers for first-in-line at his next signing."

"Oh, gee. But sales were good?"

"Yah, they were . . ."

"So what's wrong? Why are the cops here?"

"Tivon showed up."

I groaned. "Reese didn't kill him, did she?"

"No, but he tried to take over the show! You know, pulling his big Oakland DJ act, telling everyone what to do. He didn't seem to realize that he's been out of the scene so long no one knows who he is anymore."

"I'm surprised Reese didn't kill him!"

"He was insane, screaming how he loved Reese, calling her his baby, and saying he was only trying to help her in her time of need." Twila waved towards the police cars. "He only left when I called the cops."

"Oh gawd." I groaned and buried my face in my hands, but something Twila said piqued my interest. "Wait. He said he was trying to help her? You don't suppose he was behind those stupid flyers at the BART station, do you?"

"He might have been, but I'm not sure Tivon even knows how to use a computer, let alone spell anything." Twila poured me a cappuccino in a to-go cup and snapped a lid on it. "Sorry, we're out of clean cappuccino cups. Anyway, I hope Writer Rick doesn't bring in that kind of crowd tomorrow."

"I'll get my apron and start running dishes," I promised. I hadn't even checked the results of my content spamming since Kenny's event had started. "I don't know how many people even saw the post about the authors."

Twila held up her smartphone. "Word is spreading. A lot of the authors and publishers have what they call street teams, and they leap into action, sharing tweets and whatnot. It's the same thing for bands, by the way."

I cringed, realizing that Hoser's band probably had the entire Bay Area steampunk fan community as its street team. "Did you tell Reese about the half-off steamed drinks deal for those in costume on Friday?"

Twila shook her head. "Nope. Not going to until the sales numbers are in. I'll pull out the spare steamer unit tonight, the one we use for the street fair, and run it through a cleaning cycle so we'll be ready for the fans."

"Well, I'll be around to help with the signing tomorrow, I promise. No bailing."

"I hope so because if Tivon shows again, I'm going to need help holding Reese back."

"The dude needs to take a hint."

"The dude needs to go back to Costa Rica or wherever." Twila agreed.

"And Reese needs to get a restraining order," I said hopefully. "We can file that first thing in the morning."

Reese came back in just as I said that and nodded. "The police report should help. I'm just sorry he took off before they could arrest him. I'd sleep better knowing he's not lurking around somewhere."

"As soon as I'm done helping clean up, I'll get order of protection paperwork ready to take down to the courthouse first thing in the morning," I told Reese, but added the usual caveat, "It can take

up to forty-eight hours for the judge to sign the temporary order—
IF the judge signs the order—so be extra careful in the meantime.
Make sure everyone on the staff knows he's blacklisted."

WHEN THE DISHES WERE DONE AND THE COUNTERS wiped down,
I left Twila to finish locking up and headed back to the office. In
the file room, I had to dig through a few boxes to find the copies
of Reese's divorce paperwork. I still hadn't gotten back the filing
cabinets taken in the great Juliet Hanford raid, and even though
I appeared to be winning the legal battle over the inheritance she
had stolen, I didn't expect to get those beautiful oak and brass filing cabinets back anytime soon. It took a little while to find the
right set of boxes, but once I did, my own filing system had the
paperwork in my hand in no time.

Charles Hanford was no slouch of a lawyer. The divorce documents were concrete. I couldn't see a single loophole that Tivon
could exploit. I rolled off a copy of the documents, and then wrote
up an order of protection filing to deliver to Reese first thing in the
morning, though I didn't hold up much hope a judge would sign it.
Tivon was a snake and a slimeball, but he didn't seem dangerous.
I was more worried about Reese doing something unwarranted in
the violence department. I'd never seen her so riled up.

CHAPTER 10

---※---

Thursday Morning

EARLY THURSDAY MORNING, I WOKE BEFORE dawn, my body finally seeming to gotten enough rest. I changed my dressings and was pleased to see that the angry red swelling around the scratches on my arm was gone and my leg looked far better than it felt. Stupid demon opossum. Reese's wasn't open yet, so I used my key to go in the back door. Reese was in the office, working on the books. She was back in her café clothes, complete with apron and braided hair.

"Yesterday was crazy," she said with a sigh and shake of her head. "I can't believe you guys pulled that off for me. We made more sales than we normally do in two weeks."

"And Writer Rick is coming today with his friends," I reminded her with a smile. I handed her the neat manilla folder I'd put together with the restraining order papers. "The courthouse opens at eight am, and you need to have these filed ASAP."

Reese glanced at the clock. It was just before 7 am. "I need to open the shop."

"I'll open. I still remember how. And Max will be here in a minute, right? We've got this."

She nodded. "Okay. I'll be back as soon as I can."

There's a rhythm to working in a restaurant, a pattern that can be soothing. The morning customers were the usual taxi drivers and businesspeople on their way to work. Max and I fell into the old regular pattern as I took orders and pulled pastries, and he managed the drink station. Only when Sasha and Tobiana came in at ten did I feel okay leaving them to their work and heading back to the office, promising to return after lunch to help set up for the author event.

BACK IN THE OFFICE, I TURNED AROUND my own open sign and settled at my desk to catch up on my classwork reading. I hadn't gotten very far beforewhen the bell on the door chimed.

I glanced up, then smiled. "Hi, Ron. What's up?"

Ron Brittle was standing in the doorway, and behind him was Detective Dortman. "Do you have a moment, Kami?"

Uh oh. "I take it you didn't just stop by to say hi?"

Ron exchanged glances with Dortman and neither of them spoke for a prolonged moment.

Finally, Dortman spoke up. "Um, Kami . . . There's no easy way to say this . . ."

"Oh my god. What?" I felt a sinking sensation at Dortman's very tone. The man simply didn't do concerned. He did bad cop, and not much else. He was being nice, and if he was being nice . . . I felt a stab of panic that generated somewhere around where they jabbed a huge needle full of rabies vaccine into me. "It really did have rabies, didn't it? I have rabies? I'm dying?"

"Rabies? What?" Dortman shot Ron a confused look. "What rabies?"

"The possum? That bit me . . . had rabies?" I sank back into my chair. Rabies didn't have a cure. I was going to start running a fever, then I'd stop being able to swallow, and then . . . The room started to spin.

"No, Kami! Calm down." Ron stepped forward and handed me the cup of coffee in his hand. "It's not the possum. They may not know whether it has rabies for a week or so. But you're taking the vaccine. You're fine. You won't get it." He glanced over at his partner. "She had a tangle with a wild animal Monday and ended up in the ER. She's still healing. I doubt she could have done it."

"Done what?" A new realization started to dawn on me. I was a suspect? In what?

"Her prints already came back from the system." Dortman narrowed his eyes at me, his 'ugly Doberman' stare.

"I've also been working almost continuously at Reese's." I explained, my brain slowly starting to wrap around what they were saying. "Now, what fingerprints are you talking about?"

"We should be doing this down at the station." Dortman muttered.

I held my tongue but shot him a look that suggested that Dortman could go back to the station and stay there indefinitely, preferably in a small cell with a large biker dude named Bare Bear. The coffee Ron handed me was Reese's Arabica Medium Roast, straight. I took a sip, and then another, my brain coming fully online. They ran my fingerprints for something. What? Something at Reese's? I reined in my obstreperous streak and decided that being agreeable was my best course of action. "Sure, we can do this at the station." I pulled out my cellphone and started scrolling through my contacts. "Just let me call Oslo and Burroughs so my lawyer can meet me there."

Reginald Burroughs was God's answer to ugly Doberman detectives. And Dortman knew that from experience.

"I don't think that will be necessary." Ron shook his head, and I was almost willing to forgive him for handing me straight black coffee. "We just need to clear you as a suspect."

"Suspect in what crime?" I might not be a full-fledged lawyer yet, but I knew my rights.

"As I started to say before you leapt to the worst conclusion . . ." Ron had to know me well enough by now to know that's how I work. Think the worst and the best will surprise you. ". . . I'm sorry to tell you this way, but Wyatt Halden was found dead at Café Fantastique this morning."

Wyatt was dead? I spent some time trying to wrap my head around it, gave up and blindly downed the rest of Ron's coffee. I needed more caffeine and maybe a hot shower and a donut to even start figuring this out. "Wyatt? Are you sure?"

"Is there any reason we would find your prints in Café Fantastique?" Dortman asked.

"You ran crime scene prints already?"

"It's ongoing, but yours are easy to identify. You have those burn scars from working ovens at the coffeeshop." It was true. I did have burn scars on both thumbs and my right forefinger from hot baking trays, but it was hard to wrap my head around Dortman remembering that fact. Then again, this wasn't the first time they'd had to run my prints in relation to a crime, was it? What was this? The third time? "Grady Halden found the body this morning."

Uncle Grady found the body. "Is he okay?"

"Who?"

"Grady? I mean . . . finding his nephew like that. Poor Grady. He's sweet."

"Grady Halden isn't your concern right now." Dortman settled on a stool across the desk from me. "I'm going to ask again. Any reason your prints would be there?"

"Absolutely. My prints are probably all over everything in there. And I can show you exactly why . . ." I pushed up from my desk and started towards the back office. "I have it all on video camera."

"You what? Why?" Both Dortman and Ron were staring at me suspiciously.

"It's not like that!" What did they think I was? Some kind of spy? Well, okay, I was a spy, but the surveillance had all been legal. "I was doing some paranormal research for them. They thought the café was haunted."

"Haunted?" Dortman laughed, then suddenly stopped. "Wait. Is that why you asked me about the old robbery?"

Ron just stood there with his arms crossed. He was in major crimes mode, unreadable.

I sighed and stared at my sore, wounded arm and the messy bandage job I'd done on it. "Yes, that's why I talked to you. Whenever there's been a violent death, there's a possibility of a confused or trapped spirit."

Dortman shook his head in disbelief. "You're crazy."

"That's been well established already." I waved my bandaged arm in his direction. "I have the rabid opossum bite to prove it. Wanna see?"

"Kami, I don't think that's helping." Ron's voice was calm, but amusement roiled behind his blue eyes.

I shrugged, feigning innocence. "Not my fault. I'm crazy. And I have rabies."

"You don't have rabies!" Ron was becoming a little less calm.

"You don't know that. You won't know that for days, and by then, I could have bitten you already. Then you'd have rabies, too."

"It's rabies. Not zombiism."

"Zombiism isn't even a thing."

"Shut up, both of you!" Dortman slammed his thick fist on my little folding desk, causing it to shudder. Evrett's gauntlet slipped a fraction of an inch on his sword hilt. "Can we be serious for two goddam seconds? A man is dead."

Wyatt. *Wyatt* was dead.

"You're right. I'm sorry." Contrition never tasted so bitter. "I like Wyatt. I like . . . *liked* . . . him a lot or I would never have agreed to set foot in that stupid café at all." I felt pressure behind my eyes, but I blinked it back ruthlessly. "I'll turn over all the video and images from the investigation if you think it will help. Technically, it's under a non-disclosure agreement, but since the assignee of the agreement is deceased, I don't think it matters. The video will show that, yes, I was in Café Fantastique. In fact, I was in pretty much every area of the café on Monday night." Monday night, and it was now Thursday. "When did he die?"

"We'll know more after the coroner is finished." Dortman was surprisingly forthcoming. "He was last seen by his partner doing paperwork after closing last night . . ."

"I was helping Twila close Reese's café last night. After that, I was here. Alone." Which meant I didn't have an alibi, except for Hoover, and that cat would lie to anyone if they offered him fried chicken or a cheeseburger. "By partner, do you mean Grady? Or Thomas?"

"Thomas . . ." Dortman stopped suddenly, eyeing me as he

remembered who he was discussing the case with. He took a swig of his coffee and looked back to Ron, cutting me out of the conversation. "He was found in the office. I tell ya, I got a bit of deja vu walking in there. He was right about where the kid was shot during the hostage robbery."

I felt a shiver down my spine. "Right in front of the desk, facing the wall safe?"

"Different desk than back then, but yeah. How'd you know?" Dortman shifted his cop-stare back to me, but I couldn't exactly mention that I had video of a shadow on the floor.

I shook my head, throwing some chaff and redirecting with bafflement. "Creepy, isn't it? You getting called to a death in the same place? I'm sorry, Dortman, that's gotta be hard."

"Yeah, well. I've been doing this a long time. San Amoro isn't a big town, and weird stuff happens."

Weird Stuff Happens. I was going to put that on a t-shirt and make it my motto.

"What about your former boss, Reese Calhoun?"

I feigned stupidity. "What about her? She's awesome."

Dortman didn't miss a beat. "She was none-too-fond of the new café, was she? Competition in her neighborhood? She's been the only coffee shop down here for going on ten years."

I went from baffled to pissed off in point-two seconds flat. "Café Fantastique couldn't provide serious competition for Reese's, even if they did serve cookies made with real butter. Reese has the neighborhood behind her. She's already held one successful event this week, with another one scheduled for this afternoon. She made enough yesterday to float the café for a month if she has to. Café Fantastique had a line out their door yesterday, but I'm sure they didn't come close to Reese's. And they had to make a thousand over projection to break even for the day."

"And you know this how?" Dortman was making notes in his notebook. Ron was keeping his mouth shut, letting his partner lead. Probably wise since personal involvement can taint the investigation. I tried not to take it personally.

"Wyatt said so. He said he was afraid they wouldn't make

enough money to even cover their costs. He'd sunk everything he had into the café." And now he was dead.

"Did you tell Reese Calhoun any of this?"

I hadn't. "No. I did tell her that Café Fantastique's supposed 'organic, fair trade' coffee beans are exactly the same coffee that she buys, from the same supplier. I may also have mentioned that they don't make their snickerdoodles with real butter."

"What does that have to do with anything?"

"I'm not sure, really." I wanted to cross my arms, but my scratched up bandaged arm prevented that. I followed the train of thought aloud. "Café Fantastique wanted to be the hot new eco-friendly café in town, but they weren't the all-organic, GMO-free service they were advertising themselves to be. They had to cut costs and were using bulk coffee beans, cheap cake mixes, and low-quality ingredients. Maybe someone had a problem with that."

"Did you?"

I met Dortman's gaze with raised eyebrows. "Yeah, I did. They use soybean shortening to make their snickerdoodles. That's not a snickerdoodle. It's a *snickerdon'tle*. And it's disgusting. Marin Street clientele are mostly white-collar workers, but we're still a hard-working neighborhood. If someone is going to pay four bucks for a cookie, they expect it to taste good."

Dortman cleared his throat. "Are you suggesting that Wyatt Halden was killed over a cookie?"

"No, not exactly." I sighed. "I'm sorry, Detective. It's been a long week. Let me try to make more sense." I gathered my thoughts and started over. "They advertise as fancy organic and fair trade, but from what I saw, most of their ingredients weren't organic, or fair trade. They were just industry standard generic restaurant supply. Their advertising was all lies. Wyatt mentioned that they were in debt over the remodel and equipment, so my guess is that they were trying to cut costs by using chain-supply coffee beans, and the like. What if they had organic suppliers lined up but bailed on them? Or their backers found out they weren't what they advertised? Could they have pissed someone off badly enough to want to kill Wyatt?"

Dortman sighed. "Possible, yeah, but I haven't seen long shots like that since the Raiders last made the playoffs."

"The Raiders haven't made the playoffs in forever. And they went to Las Vegas, so they don't count."

"Precisely." Dortman intercepted my pass and kept the ball. He continued casually, "I have a witness who saw Reese arguing with Wyatt yesterday morning."

"It was the day before yesterday. I'm a witness to that, too." I admitted. "I broke it up, settled everything down. It was no big deal. Someone played a stupid prank and parked Wyatt's car in front of Reese's door."

"A prank?" Ron's eyebrows went up.

"Wyatt said he didn't do it, and I believe him." I shrugged. "I was about to chalk the haunting in the café up to a prank, too, but there was one thing that I wanted to check out. If you pull my phone records, you'll see the call to the café where I talked to Wyatt about it."

"A *thing*?"

I sighed. My paranormal research work was supposed to be confidential, but if it helped find whoever killed Wyatt . . . Wait a minute. Dortman hadn't used the word murdered, had he? "How did Wyatt die?"

"We'll know more after the coroner report."

Doberman. I smiled in what I hoped was an ingenuous manner. "I liked Wyatt a lot. I just can't see anyone wanting to kill him. Maybe it was natural causes? Or an accident?"

"Miss White . . ." Dortman didn't smile, but Ron did. I took comfort in that. "I'm asking the questions."

"Really? I hadn't noticed. I thought we were just having a friendly chat over coffee . . ."

"Why don't we just review your evidence?" Ron interjected. He was using his official detective voice, but there was still a hint of a smile behind his eyes.

Hoover came in and stretched his front paws up to Ron's thigh, begging to be picked up. Ron declined, even though he still bent down and pet him. "Sorry, cat. I'm working."

"Are you sure that thing isn't a possum?" Dortman asked, and I realized it was the first time he'd ever met the hairless Sphynx cat.

"Opossums don't purr." I scooped Hoover up and took him to the file room, where I opened a fresh can of his favorite wet food. He twisted around my legs, purring and singing until I put his dish down.

With Hoover satisfied for the moment, I extracted the memory cards containing the café investigation footage from the safe and returned to the front office. "I have copies of everything on my laptop, but once I make the copies, I keep the originals from each job in their own file in the safe," I explained for Dortman's benefit. "No one can get to them except for me. They can't be tampered with or accidentally copied over or erased."

"Exactly what did you see that you wanted to check out further?"

So Ron was going to home in on that, was he? Well, he asked for it. I connected my laptop to the large monitor and pulled up the video. "I'll show you. Most of the time, in these situations, when you spot something unusual in a picture or hear something strange on a recording, it's not hard to find a logical explanation."

"Like rabid opossums?" Ron asked with a smile.

"Yes, Detective. Like rabid opossums." I tried not to sigh. I found the time-coded place on the video and directed their attention to it. "If I find logical explanations, my work is done. If I can't answer the evidence with an explanation, then there's something more going on."

"Ghosts and ghoulies." Dortman rolled his eyes.

"Watch . . ." I ran the recording in regular speed, the shadow appearing on the floor and then fading away again. "See that? Now I'll slow it down . . ."

The shadow spread, slowly, like a spilled liquid, then faded away.

"I've matched it up with the timestamps on the rest of the videos, and we were all in the dining room of the café when this happened. There were no cars passing, and even if there were, that office window faces the back parking lot. The kitchen area was dark, with no movement." I backed up the recording then pulled up the time-stamped kitchen and dining room recordings to play beside it. It clearly showed me, Grady, Thomas, and Wyatt, all sitting around a table with our backs to it, looking into the shadows. Wyatt was facing the camera, his eyes alert in the darkness. So young and alive. How could he be gone? I felt sick and put my head down.

"Man, you okay?" Ron's voice snapped me back and I looked up at him, then followed his gaze to Dortman. Dortman was normally a ruddy-looking guy, kind of puffy and reddish in the way that guys who eat too much and drink too much and don't do enough yoga look. But even in the warmth of my sun-drenched front office, he was seriously pale.

He didn't take his eyes off the screen, and his usual bravado drained away from his voice, leaving it faint as he asked, "Kami, may I please see that video again?"

I backed it up and reran it in slow motion.

"Hell," he grunted.

"I'm going to go out on a limb here and say that's where the body of the robbery victim was lying ten years ago?" I asked quietly. Phantom stains were my area of expertise. Or one of them, anyway. "Listen, Detective, don't leap to conclusions here. There could be a thousand explanations for that shadow. Some kind of security lighting, or there was some kind of light from the computer." I didn't mention that the power had been shut off. "Or there's a ceiling vent that lets in streetlight, or . . . I don't know what else. But always look for the physical explanation before leaping to the metaphysical."

I felt awkward and strained, trying to comfort Detective Dortman, but the man was obviously shaken. After a long silence, he finally nodded. "Yeah, you're right. It's just weird as hell."

"Kind of like *that* is weird as hell?" Ron pointed at my screen.

While I'd been busy backing up and re-running the office footage, the kitchen and dining footage had continued to run. Specifically, the dining room footage of me sneaking back into the kitchen to put on Evrett's helmet. I felt a hot flush rush over my cheeks. "Oh, that. That's not what it looks like."

"You know, Cheshire was almost named the Medieval Knight Killer because of that helmet. The press heard you say 'trunk girl' and I guess that had a better ring to it." Dortman looked around him and, I think for the first time, noticed Evrett standing in the corner. "That the thing?"

"It's Fourteenth Century French," I evaded the trunk girl comment. Ron had been irritated by that phrase since I'd first said it to him, and right now, I needed Ron on my side. "It belonged to a crusader."

One who died on his way to the Crusades. An experience he'd felt necessary to share with me through a vividly unpleasant dream one night. I didn't feel it necessary to tell them that.

Ron sighed. "Do I even want to know why you're wearing it around that place in the middle of the night?"

"It wasn't the middle of the night. It was around ten, which, technically, is barely after prime-time television." They were both staring at me. I wasn't getting out of this easily. "Okay. I'm going to tell you both a secret, and you have to swear on your badges that you will keep it."

Ron nodded. Dortman looked cagey.

"Promise," I insisted.

"As long as it doesn't have anything to do with the investigation or interfere with police business in any way, then yes." Dortman grumbled. "I swear."

"Ron?"

"What? You tell me all kinds of stuff. I haven't blabbed yet, have I?" I could see genuine curiosity behind his eyes.

"It's not just my secret," I warned, "and if it gets out, then I'm going to have serious problems. The pack up, sell my building, and move to Calcutta kind of problem. Do you understand what I'm saying?"

"Look, Kam, if you'd rather not . . ." Ron's words drifted off, almost like a warning. Was he afraid I was going to say something incriminating?

"You saw the video. I know what it looks like. Here's the thing. That suit of armor comes with the crusader that wore it. His name is Evrett. And the night I was kidnapped by Dillon Cheshire, that helmet let me see the spirits of his other victims. When Dillon took the helmet away from me and put it on, he saw them, too. That's how I managed to escape. I don't know why. I don't know how. And honestly, sometimes, I'm not even sure that it really happened. I was drugged, I was woozy. Maybe I imagined the whole thing. But I think that somehow, because Evrett is between life and death, he can help me see through the veil."

They were both staring at me as though I'd lost my marbles.

"If I put it on right now, would I see ghosts?" Dortman's voice was thick with disbelief, and possibly verging on hilarity.

"No. There are no ghosts here except Evrett, and you can't see him through his own connecting object. Besides, the helmet wouldn't fit you. It's too small."

"But you think you see ghosts when you put it on?"

"Only if there are ghosts to see, or who want to be seen. I don't know for sure. I figured it out by accident, and I've only had a few opportunities to test it."

Dortman was looking between me and Evrett with shadowed eyes, but Ron was shaking his head. "And do I even want to know what you saw in the kitchen of the café?"

"Yeah. I'm sure you really do." I looked him right in the eye, willing my gaze to bore into his bright stare. "I didn't see anything. No ghosts. No lights. No shadows. No voices. No *nothing*. I even asked Evrett if he saw anyone, but he didn't respond. Ron, the only piece of evidence that I came up with to bear out any hint of a haunting in Café Fantastique is that shadow on the floor."

"And what do you think that shadow is?"

"I told you. I don't know. And I don't make guesses. I would need to go back in under the same atmospheric conditions and test out what could have caused it."

"What if it was a ghost?" Those were the last words I expected out of Dortman's mouth. The guy was seriously shaken up. "Could you see it with that helmet? Talk to it?"

"Probably not, no," I admitted. "If that shadow really is haunting related, my impression is that it's a residual."

"A whada?" asked Dortman.

"Residual. A piece of energy or memory left behind. Residuals aren't ghosts so much as they are imprints of events, old memories that stick to a location. They can be imprints left from positive things, good times, like phantom music from empty ballrooms, or they can be tragic, like the stains of blood from a murder. Ever wonder why there are so many supposedly haunted theaters, even when no death ever occurred at the location?"

"I saw a TV show about that once," Dortman admitted. "Sounds of footsteps and music in theaters that are leftover remnants of old performances."

"Exactly." I smiled, impressed with Dortman's knowledge. "There's nothing there to see except old memories that replay. Evrett can only help where the haunting is a spirit, an intelligent haunt. He can't call up residual energy on command any more than you or I can."

"Right. Well." Dortman looked to Ron. "I've seen enough to know she's telling the truth. I don't think she's our murderer."

"So, Wyatt *was* murdered?" I pounced on that sliver of information about of what had happened to Wyatt, but I was too tired to be clever about it and Dortman instantly returned to his parrot statement.

"We'll know more after the coroner report."

"Kami, can you make copies of the investigation video for us? You can leave out the helmet thing and the shadow thing. The important thing to establish is who was in the cafe with you that night and what areas of the shop you were in. Everything you touched for fingerprint elimination." Ron pointed to the screen again, and I nodded.

"Sure." I copied the video of the walk-through that I took with the handheld camera, as well as the rest of the footage, cut it all to a thumb-drive and handed it to Dortman, a small gesture to show I was trusting him.

He nodded as he took it. "Thank you for your cooperation."

They started to leave, but I didn't know how to keep my big mouth shut. "Detective Dortman? What happened that night, the night of the hostage robbery?"

He stopped walking and then looked back over his shoulder at me, his hand on the door-latch. There was an emptiness in his gaze that sent a chill through me. "Let sleeping dogs lie, Miss White."

Dortman turned away and continued walking without looking back. Ron gave me a small half-smile. "Don't forget to take your meds."

"I won't." I hesitated and our eyes met. "Thanks again for looking after me the other night."

"You'd do the same for me." His eyes twinkled for a second. "Do me a favor and try to stay out of trouble until this case is solved, okay?"

"I always *try* to stay out of trouble!" I groaned, offended. "It just comes along and slops itself all over me."

I could hear his laughter trail back to me as the door swung closed.

CHAPTER 11

Thursday Afternoon

As SOON AS BRITTLE AND DORTMAN were gone, I went to the door and looked out. There was a single police cruiser and Ron's unmarked down by Café Fantastique, but nothing else. I headed up to the empty office on the second floor and climbed out onto the fire escape. From there, I could see down into the café's parking lot. The coroners van and the crime lab van were both there, and people were standing around the back door. Law enforcement was doing a good job keeping things on the downlow at lunchtime on a weekday. Unfortunately, it was so low key that even my good spy position on the fire escape revealed nothing.

My phone rang and I glanced at the caller ID before answering. "What's up, Twila?" I asked. I leaned as far over the fire escape rail as I could, but still couldn't see anythnng interesting at Café Fantastique.

"Have you seen the Facebook page?"

"No, I've been kinda busy. Let me run downstairs . . ."

"Downstairs? Where are you?"

"Fire escape. Don't ask, I can't tell you." I ran back down to my office and logged into the coffee shop Facebook page. It had gone crazy. Someone had shared it to the taxi-driver's league and the local pet-grooming clinic, and from there it escalated. Overnight, the followers had jumped from a couple hundred to over a thousand. There were nearly a hundred new messages on the wall from Kenny's followers, all talking about what a great time they'd had. Writer Rick's book-signing event had almost eight hundred likes, with dozens of shares. "Holy cow."

"Holy cow is right!" Twila could be heard shuffling things around in the background. "I'm dropping off the kiddo at my mom's and I'll be right over to help set up. How are we going to handle eight-hundred people?"

"Take it easy," I said with a casualness I didn't feel. "Far more people share and like than actually show up to these things. Writer Rick has a loyal following, and so do a few of the other authors, but we'll be lucky if we get thirty or forty. Relax."

"*You* can relax," Twila barked back. "Reese can't fire *you* if this goes pear-shaped."

"Oh, believe me. She can fire me. Out of a cannon."

Twila laughed before she hung up, and I got dressed to head to Reese's.

AT THE COFFEE SHOP, REESE WAS NOWHERE to be seen. Max was at the espresso machines and Tobiana was running dishes and tidying up after the lunch crowd. Sasha was at the front counter with colored cards and felt pens.

"Kam! Look! I had an idea . . ." She was writing as fast she could, leaving black and red felt-pen marks on the counter around the pastry cards. "See what you think!"

"Killer Cream Cupcakes," I read out loud. "Tango Mango Muffins. Bullseye Chocolate Chips. Lemon Love Cookies . . ."

"Get it? They're all plays off the titles of the books of the authors who are coming." Sasha beamed at me and pointed to the case.

The white frosted tops of the killer cream cupcakes were decorated with black and silver icing in the shape of tiny daggers and pistols. The lemon "love" cookies were heart-shaped instead of their usual plain round shape. Bullseye chocolate chip cookies were decorated with little red frosting bullseyes with a chocolate chip in the middle. It was the kind of thing my mother would have come up with, if she ever read a murder mystery. "I love it. It's brilliant."

"Oh, thanks. I was afraid I was going overboard. And Max is putting up some special meals like you did yesterday."

My comic inspired menu was gone, replaced with the "Rick Royce Rage: Pastrami on Rye with Pepperjack Cheese" and "Vineyard Romance: Wine cured goat cheese on toasted wheat bagel with heirloom tomatoes". Max was working on another author related special below that, but I was too impressed to finish reading. "You guys have been working your tails off. But I'm not sure it matters anymore."

Sasha's gaze followed my pointed stare out the window towards Café Fantastique. "Yeah, they aren't even open yet. I wonder what's going on. I hope Health and Safety shut them down."

"I wish it was that simple," I replied without explaining. "Where's Reese? I sent her to the courthouse this morning."

Sasha shrugged. "Max said you opened this morning. Maybe she's getting her hair done for today's event. I heard she got dressed up yesterday."

"Well, we've got this, with or without her. What can I do to help?" For the next hour, I rearranged chairs and tables, set up an author reading area on the second floor, and put together a sample tray with tasting size cups of Sumatra Pale Roast and bowls filled with nibble-sized pieces of chocolate chip and lemon love cookies.

Writer Rick arrived, a hand truck laden with boxes of books in tow. The adventure writer's tired grey eyes lit up when he saw his name on the specials board in front of his favorite sandwich. "I have a special? Really?"

Max grinned. "It's just what you usually order. Maybe if this works, I can talk Reese into making it a permanent special."

That wasn't fair. I practically lived at the coffee shop, and I didn't have my own special.

Twila raced in and took over the cash register as more authors showed up. There were books to lay out, chairs and pens to fetch, and free drinks to make. The impromptu schedule had the readings set upstairs, with each author having half an hour to talk, read excerpts, and answer questions. The usual Thursday customers wandered in, snagged their usual tables and their usual food and drinks, but they stayed for the authors, buying books and chatting, even after the coffeeshop was crowded with newcomers seeking their favorite authors.

It quickly descended into a kind of controlled chaos. Twila managed the register and Tobiana took over serving, I was behind the counter with Max, madly serving up bullseyes and hearts and killer cream cupcakes while he had all three espresso systems running full blast. I didn't realize how much readers love their coffee. By the time the last author finished talking and the lines at the signing tables had petered out, I was nearly dead on my feet. My hand throbbed from flexing the tongs around so many pastries. I'd been working at a desk for too long, I guess. I'd once been Reese's chief sandwich-maker. Now I couldn't even get through an afternoon at the pastry counter without my feet aching.

"How'd we do?" I asked Twila as I passed with the last bus-tray full of dirty plates. She was running the sales totals on the register, and I paused to look.

"Very well. You know, I don't think we had half the people we had yesterday for your brother's event, but apparently book people eat and drink more than comic people." Twila looked around. "Where is Reese?"

I was starting to get a sinking feeling. "I'm sure she'll be back soon. She was excited about this when I saw her this morning."

"I tried her cellphone, but it's off," Max said. He looked as tired as I felt.

"Maybe she's trying to get an emergency injunction from a judge for the restraining order. She'd have to turn her phone off in court." I said hopefully. "I'm just glad Tivon didn't show up again today."

By the time I'd helped clean up and put the café back to rights for the evening dessert and discussion customers, I was practically crawling. I needed a long nap and a hot shower. I walked back over to the office and fed a disgruntled Hoover. He'd been alone all day long . . . Well, I didn't know how alone. Hoover sometimes played with Evrett when I was neglecting him, and if he raised a ruckus he could usually get Morri to come downstairs and play. Now that I was home, he wanted food, cuddles, and playtime, not necessarily in that order. By the time he had wound down, it was nearly six.

I tried to nap while Hoover stood guard on the armrest and made sure my blonde frizzy curls didn't escape from my head. His help in this matter was limited to occasionally batting at them, followed by patting my head with his paw. So, not helpful at all. I couldn't sleep anyway. I kept thinking about Wyatt. The cops hadn't told me anything. Not that I'd expect them to, seeing as I was a suspect. I finally gave up and headed to the coffee shop for some dinner.

Down the street, Café Fantastique was completely dark. Only Ron's unmarked car remained parked a few spaces away from the café door, blending in with the rest of the downtown traffic. I was tempted to sneak down and look in the windows, but I didn't dare. Inside Reese's, Twila waved frantically with both hands.

"Detective Brittle just left!"

I didn't want to let on that I knew anything. "What did you tell him?"

"He asked who was working last night and this morning. He took copies of the timesheets." Twila lowered her voice. "He wanted to know when I last saw Reese."

"Wait," I felt a sinking feeling in my gut. "You mean she isn't back yet?"

"No. And she's not answering her phone. What's going on? Does this have anything to do with Fantastique being closed today? D.B. wouldn't tell me anything." Something in my expression must have given me away, and Twila gasped. "Oh god, is Reese okay? What happened?"

I glanced around at the customers. "Not here." Grabbing her sleeve, I towed her into the backroom where Sasha was just finishing putting up a batch of croissant dough to rise overnight. They both leaned close. "The cops already questioned me this morning.

One of the owners of the new café was found dead. They wouldn't tell me anything, except that my fingerprints were inside the café."

Twila jerked back from me. "What were you doing in Café Fantastique?"

"Spying," I explained shortly. "I was asked to do some legal work for them, and it gave me a chance to look around. Fortunately, they have all of it on video. Unfortunately, I don't have an alibi for between midnight and six this morning. And if we can't find Reese . . ."

"Then she's a suspect, too," Sasha groaned, rubbing her flour-coated hands on her apron. "She's been upset about the new place all week, and she's been pretty nasty about it."

"Reese is not a murderer," Twila stated firmly. "She's probably taking time to get herself together before turning up."

"Well, we can't speculate," I warned gently. "All we can do is keep the shop running just like we would if she was on vacation. We all know what to do." I put a bagel in the toaster for myself and pulled out the tub of egg salad. "I'm going to get some dinner, then I'll do the closing paperwork and prep the night deposit."

Twila nodded. "I'll do the drop on my way home. We just keep going."

Sasha nodded, then yawned. "I'll open tomorrow. I need to come in early to do the croissants anyway."

"Should we cancel the concert tomorrow?" I asked Twila, but she shook her head.

"Not until we know what's going on."

I took my dinner out to the dining room where I dug into my bagel with egg salad. I decreed it the best egg salad I'd ever had. Of course, I pretty much thought that every time I had Reese's egg salad. She bought pre-boiled, pre-peeled eggs, but the rest was her own recipe of celery, red onion, cracked black pepper, sea salt, and fresh dill and parsley with just a dab of her house-made mayo. It wasn't gooey or runny, nor was it dry and rubbery. And on a freshly toasted onion seed bagel, it was sheer heaven.

After eating, I felt far more human and bought a vanilla Greek yogurt with fresh fruit for dessert. I was just finishing eating when Dortman strolled into the café. His sweeping stare took in everyone there, including me, but he went straight to the counter and talked to Twila.

BEFORE I COULD FIND AN EXCUSE TO EAVESDROP, my phone buzzed and I looked down to see a text from Kenny. "call me NOW."

Oh, what now? Kenny never texted unless it was urgent. I was forced to leave dealing with Dortman to Twila's discretion and stepped outside to pull up my brother's number and call him back. "What's up?"

"Dad." Kenny's voice sounded small and far away.

"Dad? What about Dad?"

"Aren't you listening to the news? There's been a quake in Nepal, a bad one. There's avalanches, mudslides . . . thousands are dead."

In Nepal. How far did it reach into Sikkim? "The research facility?"

"It's okay, but Dad and his team were deep in the mountains doing field work. Professor Ling hasn't heard from them."

This was not what I needed right now. "Okay. Okay." I tried to process this latest disaster, sucking in air to keep calm. "You know it's not unusual for them to be out of touch . . ."

"They have satellite phones. Shouldn't those work?" There was real fear in my baby brother's voice. "Kami, I'm going to India."

"You what?" I could barely process that.

"My plane leaves in two hours. I wanted to ask if you would come with me."

Yes. I'm coming. Give me a minute to pack and I'll meet you at the airport. And leave Reese tangled up in a murder, and abandon my rabies treatment one injection in. Who knew what kind of treatment they had in India, but I knew that I'd rather be shot up with the stuff that would save me instead of the riskier vaccines that could cause brain damage and paralysis. And Reese was missing, and Wyatt . . . I couldn't. I felt tears spring to my eyes. "Kenny, I . . . I can't come with you."

"Dad is missing, Kam."

"I know. I know, but what can I do there? I'm a planner, a coordinator, a communicator. You're the one who leaps into action. You're the rescuer." Where had that come from? "I'm more help here. I can liaison from here for you. You'll be in the air for hours. If we're both on that flight, no one will be able to communicate."

Kenny was quiet for a moment and I could practically hear his brain churning as he tried to figure out how to debate with me. He couldn't have won a real debate with me even if he knew the vocabulary to try. His voice was miniscule and wishful when he spoke again. "I wish you'd come."

My heart hit rock bottom. My brother didn't need a collegiate-level vocabulary to smack me down. "I'm sorry, Ken. I had a medical thing come up. It's not serious, but I have to be here for treatment for fourteen days at the least. I can't come to India right now."

"A medical thing? That's not serious but is more important than finding our dad, who could be stranded or trapped in the Himalayan rainforest?" Kenny's voice was thick with emotion. "Are you being real right now?"

God, if I told him, he'd tell Mom and Mom would freak out. "Look, you can't tell Mom. You can't. Promise!"

"If she asks . . . I haven't told her yet that I'm leaving . . ."

"I'll tell her. Don't talk to her. Just get on the plane. I'm acting as your liaison, remember? I can be the liaison with Mom, too!"

I could hear him chewing his lower lip, but he finally said, "Okay, what is so important that you can't come find our father?"

"Rabies," I blurted out. "I was bitten by a wild animal, and there's a possibility that it has rabies, so I have to have injections."

"Rabies? You lying brat! If you don't want to come, just tell me! You don't have to make up some crap about having rabies. No wonder you don't want me to tell Mom." Kenny hung up on me.

Knowing that he wouldn't answer if I called, I texted him. "Ask D.B. if you don't believe me."

Leaving it at that, I turned to stumble back into the café and smacked right into the puffed out chest of Detective Dortman.

"You seen Reese today?" he growled.

"Not since early this morning. She hasn't come in." I muttered, unable to deal with him right at that moment. I didn't want to seem evasive, but I couldn't focus on Reese. "Sorry, Detective. I've had something come up . . . I can't chit-chat . . ."

"Something more important than murder?"

"One murder in a town directly adjacent to one of America's murder centers. It won't even make the six o'clock news on KRON4." I snarled. Maybe I was rabid after all. "My father is missing in an earthquake in Nepal. There are thousands of people dead. I'm sorry, but I can't care about your stupid murder right now."

I shoved past him back into the café, grabbed my books and latte, and fled back to my office, leaving him standing on the sidewalk staring dumbfounded after me. Inside my office, I locked the door and propped my laptop and cellphone on my desk. While scanning breaking news about the quake, I called the research station in the Sikkim Himalaya. It took three tries before I could get through, but I finally talked to Dad's partner. Professor Ling confirmed everything that Kenny had said. I gave him my phone number, email, and Twitter address and told him that Kenny was flying out within the hour and I would be liaison for the family.

Ling was worried, but his attitude was positive. We both agreed that my father and his field team were clever, resourceful, and very comfortable in the mountains. Chances were that something had happened to the satellite phones, possibly something as simple as an overload of the satellites from emergency communications over the quake.

When I'd done everything I could, including putting links on Twitter to rescue organizations that were establishing aid for the quake victims, I finally had to call Mom. Jaxine and I have a complicated relationship at the best of times, but I wasn't going to let Kenny tell lies about me before I had a chance to give her my side of the story.

"Sweetheart, I'm watching the quake coverage." Jaxine answered my call instantly. "Have you heard from your father?"

"No." I hesitated. They'd been divorced for ten years, but I knew she still loved him in her own way. Just as he still loved her in his way. Their ways just weren't very compatible. They were much happier with an entire ocean and half a continent between them. "Mom, I just got off the phone with Professor Ling. Dad and his team were out in the mountains. They haven't placed a sat-phone call since yesterday. But don't worry! You know Dad. He lives for that stupid forest. He knows it like the back of his hand. And his team is the best in the world."

"I know . . ."

She didn't sound like she knew.

"There's more. Kenny is flying out to India to help."

"That's my little boy. Always caring more about others than himself."

Wow. What kid was she talking about? Because that's not the kid I grew up with. "Okay. So, I can't go with Ken, but I'm going to act as communications liaison. If you have questions or information or anything, shoot them my way."

"Why aren't you going with him? You've spent as much time with your father in India as he has. More, even. You speak more Nepali and Sikkimese than he does, I'm sure."

"I can't go right now, Mom. One of my clients was murdered this morning. And I had a medical thing come up that requires that I don't travel."

"Oh! Are you sick? If you're contagious, you should be in bed. I'll bring you some soup later, after my organic gardening workshop. Do you have enough of my chamomile cinnamon tea? That's the best thing you can do for your immune system!"

Yeah. If my mother's chamomile tea could only cure rabies. "Sure, Mom, that sounds good. And I'm not contagious." Yet, at any rate.

I could tell her about the rabies exposure in person. She would be less likely to freak out, and I could get her to change my dressings. She was good at that kind of motherly thing. "Why don't you come by around nine this evening? We can have a chat after I close the coffee shop?"

"And light a candle for your father, if you haven't heard from him by then."

"That would be nice."

"Kami? Are you okay? You sound tired, sweetheart."

"I am tired, Mom. I need a nap." But the sight of Twila rushing towards my office, a wrapped bundle in her arms warned that I wasn't going to get one. "I'll talk to you later, okay?"

"Okay, angel. Get some rest. And drink some tea!"

MOM'S HERBAL TEAS. THE ANSWER TO EVERYTHING. I stood up and unlocked the door for Twila who rushed inside, dropped a black-plastic-bag-wrapped bundle on my desk and looked around wildly. "Kami! I didn't know what to do. You were the first person I thought of."

"Whoa. Okay. Didn't know what to do about what, exactly?"

"This!" She pulled open the trash bag and dumped the contents on my desk with a resounding thunk.

Lying on my desk, enveloped in a plastic take-out bag, was a Smith & Wesson 9mm. There was blood splattered on the barrel and the grip, along with a few hairs. Short, blonde hairs. Wyatt's?

"So, you put it on my desk because of course that's the first place it should go?"

"I found it under the dumpster behind the café! I thought if the cops find it there, they're going to think Reese . . . I mean, why would she? And where the hell would she get this? But why . . ."

"And now they're going to think we're obstructing justice. Twila! You can't just move evidence of a crime! That's bad! Did you touch it?"

"No! No, I picked it up with the plastic bag. Customers park back there all the time, even though they aren't supposed to. I couldn't just leave it on the ground, could I? I just locked up the shop and came straight here."

I picked up my phone and called Ron. He answered with a friendly, "Hey, Kam. How are you feeling?"

"Not so good. I'm pretty sure I have a murder weapon sitting on my desk. You better come over. And bring the Doberman." Hoover leaped to the top of the desk and started to move curiously towards the gun. I had to snatch him up under my injured arm, the motion firing raw pain up to my elbow.

I could hear Ron groan before he hung up. "Why do we still call it hanging up when all we do is push a stupid button on a screen?" I asked Twila, but she shrugged. "Never mind. The cops are on their way. They'll know what to do."

While we waited for the detectives to arrive, I pulled up the latest earthquake information again and scanned social media feeds for messages from other people in the Sikkim Himalaya region. Dad's research station was remote, and there was widespread destruction with thousands of lives endangered. It could be days or even weeks before any rescue attention could be spent on a handful of scientists in the rainforest. Twila asked what I was doing, and I was in the process of showing her maps of the epicenter of the quake and the comparative distance to Dad's research station when Dortman and Brittle arrived.

I UNLOCKED THE DOOR TO LET THEM IN, and Dortman instantly pulled out his camera and started taking pictures of the gun. "Ms. White? You want to tell me how you just happen to have the murder weapon?"

"I don't have it. It's just sitting there." I barked back. At Dortman's glare, I took a deep breath and continued as the law professional I pretended to be. "Twila brought it to me as her legal consultant. She found it behind Reese's Café and was afraid parking customers would find and take it. With the events we've been holding there are a lot of people coming and going." I pointed at the gun. "And now that I know it's actually the murder weapon, and that's really Wyatt's blood on it, I would seriously appreciate it if you would take it away to the station or the lab or wherever it needs to go."

"What's this?" Ron asked.

"I'm no gun expert, but it says Smith & Wesson on it," I growled before realizing that Ron was looking at my computer, not the murder weapon. I tried to keep my voice flat. "The quake in Nepal was near my father's research station in India. He was out in the field and hasn't reported in. He's missing. It's nothing to do with your case."

"God. Kam. I'm sorry." Ron was staring at me, but Dortman tapped his shoulder.

"Bag the gun and log the evidence." Dortman directed Ron. "I'll get someone from the crime lab down here to print her," he pointed to Twila, who looked kind of pale, "for elimination. After that, I want you to show me exactly where you found the gun."

"Neither of you leave. Stay right here with the door locked. Don't call anyone. Don't speak to anyone."

"Yeah, that's not happening." I told Dortman as I picked up my phone and called Reginald Burrough's direct number. "I'm calling my lawyer."

"I thought we were past that." Dortman frowned.

"That was before I had a murder weapon on my desk."

Reggie answered to the sounds of jazz music, and I knew he was at home, relaxing on his balcony with his partner, probably having a Thursday evening snack. As soon as I explained, he agreed to come. Reggie is a godsend. I do paralegal work for his firm from time to time, and he's handling the estate of my former boss, for whom I was the main beneficiary. He is my lawyer, but importantly, he was someone I considered a friend, and he was always there for me when I needed him. I trusted him, and I don't trust a lot of people.

While Twila and I waited, I made tea, my mother's chamomile cinnamon super-healing tea. I wasn't sure it could prevent rabies, but hey, it couldn't hurt, could it? Twila cradled her cup as though it was her best friend. Ron refused to touch his. He was in full detective mode and the fact that I'd called in my lawyer seemed to chafe at him. But he had his job to do, and I had mine, and right now my job was protecting myself and Twila.

REGGIE'S SLEEK RED TESLA HUMMED UP TO THE CURB, and he stepped out in a smoothly fluid motion. Reginald Burroughs was a tall and fit forty-something, with gorgeous black hair just turning silver at the temples, and a deep, penetrating gaze that could melt a jury with a glance or strike terror in the heart of a prosecuting attorney by turns. Tonight, he was wearing fitted black slacks belted with designer leather that matched his shoes and a soft grey button down. He looked like a model, not a lawyer.

"Ooh." Twila sucked in a breath as he swept around the front of his car and came to the door.

"Forget it, sweetie. He's married and we aren't his type anyway," I warned in a low voice before unlocking the door.

Reggie strolled in as though he owned the room, taking in the evidence bags on my desk containing the gun and the garbage bag the gun came in, then exchanged glances with Ron. But before he said anything, he took Hoover from my arms and cuddled the cat for a second. They had a bond stemming from a long-time friendship. Or at least from the grilled bacon-wrapped prawns that Reggie tended to serve at his barbecues.

"Hey, Hoover. You aren't a suspect, are you, good cat?" Originally from Wales, Reggie had a delicious accent worth melting over. Bay Area OUT magazine had named him most eligible gay bachelor two years running. He claimed he married Skylar just to break the winning streak. I was honored to call both him and his husband friends.

Hoover purred and rubbed Reggie's chin. If anything ever happened to me, like dying from rabies, Hoover was to go to Reggie. So was Evrett, who was Reggie's next stop. "Bonjour, Chevalier Evrett. You staying out of trouble?"

The armor was silent and still, which might have been because I had already outed him once today, or he just wasn't ready to talk in front of people. Or maybe he was just as tired as I felt.

"So, Kami? Twila? Tell me right now if Detective Brittle is going to find either of your prints on that gun?"

"Not a chance." I stated, holding up my hand. Unfortunately, that caused the sleeve of my denim jacket to slide down, exposing my bandage, which garnered a strange look from Reginald.

"And tell me that . . ." he pointed at my arm, and then back to the gun, ". . . has nothing to do with this?"

"It doesn't." Ron answered for me. "I was there for that damage. She's not a suspect. Not yet anyway, but if she's obstructing she could be."

"Are you obstructing, Kami?"

"No, of course I'm not! I called the cops the second Twila brought me the gun, I swear!"

"Twila Genae?" Reggie used her full name and gazed at Twila

with raised eyebrows, and I saw her get that wide-eyed dreamy look that he inspired all too often.

"I just put it in the bag. I used the take-out bag to pick it up, then put it in the trash bag so no one could see what I was carrying. I swear I didn't touch it with my hands at all." She paused and thought for a second, rubbing her palms together. "But my prints will be on the bags. I didn't think to fetch gloves."

"That's not the real problem." Ron warned Reggie. He pointed across the street. "They moved it from its original location."

"It was where customers might find it in the parking lot," Twila defended again.

"And we can't find Reese," Ron ignored Twila and kept his gaze on my lawyer.

That made my blood run cold. "What do you mean, you can't find Reese?"

"No one has seen her. Her house is locked up, no one at home. Her mother hasn't heard from her, and neither has anyone associated with the coffee shop."

"What? You didn't think you should tell me this?" I wasn't just offended. I was angry. Reese was my friend, my confidant, my muse. Heck, she was my personal chef. She couldn't just disappear!

Ron gestured to my computer screen where my Twitter feed was rolling through everything hash-tagged nepalquake. "I thought you had enough to be getting on with, ma'am."

"Don't ma'am me!" I slumped in my chair and hugged my sore arm.

"What time did you take your last dose of pain meds?" Ron checked his watch. "You're keeping up on your antibiotics, right?"

"I do have a mom, you know." He did know. He'd had to question her when Kenny was wanted for murder.

"Touché. Does she know?"

"About Dad? Or the rabies? Or about the murder?"

Reggie held up both hands and used his breathing trick. I hated it when he did that because I couldn't quite figure out how it worked. Somehow, Reggie would just breathe slowly and calmly, and the next thing you knew, you were breathing slowly and calmly, too. I'd seen him defuse robbers and carjackers, and even crying babies and unhappy hairless Sphynx cats with his magic. "Let's focus on what we can fix right now, okay? One thing at a time."

Dortman returned with a tech who fingerprinted Twila on the spot, then Reggie moderated a fairly quick question and answer session that didn't reveal anything we hadn't already told the detectives but made it clear that we hadn't held anything back, either.

At least the detectives had finally stopped pretending that they didn't know how Wyatt died. It seemed obvious to me. The gun had been fired, recently enough that it still smelled like fresh gunpowder, and the blood on it told me that the killer had somehow gotten close to Wyatt before they killed him. Why? What did Wyatt do to deserve that?

After Dortman and Reggie left with Twila and the tech to see where the gun was found, I reached for Ron's arm. "Sorry I was prickly. I'm just tired and stressed out."

"Yeah. I know." He stopped in the doorway, turning to look at me, then at Evrett. "Can I ask a favor?"

"What?" That was the last thing I expected. "What is it?"

"Look, I'm questioning my own sanity about this, but Dortman is the one who brought it up . . ." Ron hesitated, and I had to wave, urging him on. "If we get you and your magic helmet into Café Fantastique tonight, can you help us figure out the source of that shadow you recorded?"

It was the last thing I expected him to say. "Are you sure? I mean, ghosts can't exactly testify in court, or anything."

"I know I can trust you to keep a secret." Ron leaned over my desk, bracing himself on his fists. I could smell the warm, rich scent of his body heat laced with a manly deodorant. It was nice, but it didn't fill me with longing or anything. I guess I was broken in that department. Broken for anything that wasn't Jack Austin, my internal voice whispered. I told it to shut up.

"Yeah, of course you can."

"Something's not right about this situation with Café Fantastique. It's messing with Dortman's head It's strange . . ." Ron hesitated, his gaze shifting towards Evrett before he continued, "Something about that earlier case or something has him knotted up. I'm worried he's not all here. When I brought it up, he said maybe you're the only one who can figure it out."

"Ron," I paused, waiting for him to look at me as I scooted back from my desk. "You're talking about digging up something from the past. An ancient, closed cold case. When you ask the dead to talk, sometimes they don't say what you want to hear. Are you sure you want to go there?"

He straightened his shoulders and ran a hand through his brown short-cropped hair, his sharp stare boring into me. "Don't share this with anyone, not even your lawyer," he warned with a surprising intensity, especially since he knew I wouldn't promise anything of the sort. He waited for me to nod before he continued. "I think someone is framing Reese. I think she's in deep trouble. And I think it's all tied to that original robbery somehow. It's just a hunch. I don't have any evidence that even points that direction. Right now, the only evidence we do have points towards Reese Calhoun, and that evidence keeps piling up. You know me. I follow the evidence, not my gut." His eyes found mine. "You're the gut-instinct girl. But right now, my gut says this whole case is hinky as hell, and Reese is being framed. I'm inclined to listen to it."

"I have to go do the closing books for the coffeeshop," I said. His admission that he thought Reese might have been framed demonstrated Ron's trust in me, and there was no way I was going to reject that faith. "We're keeping the shop open for Reese, at least until we know what's going on. Twila and Sasha know as much about managing it as Reese does, so we're dividing the shop duties. At nine, Mom is coming by with soup and to change my bandages. I'd like to catch a shower before that, so it won't be a big deal if my dressings get wet. After that, I'm all yours."

Ron stopped in the doorway and looked back over his shoulder. "Are you?"

Was I? I felt a half-smile that I couldn't stop. "Ask me later."

He stepped out into the overcast afternoon without another word, but I thought I saw a smile on his face. Dang it. Why did I say that? As if life wasn't complicated enough!

CHAPTER 12

Thursday Night

I HELPED TWILA CLOSE THE CAFÉ. REGGIE HAD stuck around, sipping a smoothie, and scrolling idly on his phone. "In case Reese shows up, I want to be here."

"You're taking her case if she needs it?"

"Probably not me personally, but Oslo and Burroughs," he shrugged. I felt bad knowing that he was being kept from his husband on their night off, but I was also glad he was there. But Reese didn't show up. The café was quiet as a tomb as I put the cash drawers in the safe and Twila turned off the open sign and the lights. We stood around on the sidewalk for a few minutes after we locked the door. I was still hoping against hope that Reese would pull up and ask what we were all doin' standin' around like that. Finally, we all said goodnight, and went our separate ways,

I checked my messages the moment I was back in the office. Kenny's plane wasn't due to land for a long time, and there were no messages from Professor Ling, so I wrapped my gauze-wrapped limbs in plastic wrap and climbed into the hot shower that I'd desperately needed all day. Hoover sat on the toilet and serenaded me as I washed, his one-word, self-centered melody ringing in the small space, "Mmmeeeemeee meee meeee. Meee meee meeee meee meee!"

He didn't like being left alone and though his little kitty mind probably didn't remember why he was mad at me, he was still acting quite miffed.

"It's okay, Hoover," I crooned to him. "I'll be home tonight, and I won't leave you alone ever again. And guess what? Jaxine is coming over! You love Jaxine."

"Meemeee meee." Clearly, he thought he should go live with Jaxine.

Feeling clean at last, I scrubbed a towel through my short curls and, mindful that I would be on video investigating later that night, whisked some mousse through them to keep them unfrizzed. I dressed in my most comfortable old jeans and my old Golden State Warriors sweatshirt with the hole in the elbow and the spaghetti stain on the hem. The elastic on the sleeves was loose enough that I could push them easily up past my bandages. Then I put on the electrical tea kettle and turned on the front office light for Jaxine.

She arrived just after nine, her bright floral broomstick skirt swaying around her ankles and her matching orange and cream blouse fitting her still quite-fine body beautifully. I still wasn't sure how I ended up in a body with half of my mother's genes but not a drop of her graceful beauty. She was lugging a quart-sized crockpot wrapped in a towel and a fabric shopping bag filled with bowls and spoons and who knew what else. I had spoons, and bowls, but that was Jaxine all over. Never unprepared for anything.

The first words out of her mouth were, "Have you heard from Kenny?"

"His flight won't land until tomorrow. I messaged him online, but I don't know if his flight has Wi-Fi. Professor Ling promised to contact me as soon as there was news," I told her as I dragged my more comfortable chair from the back office to the front so that we could use my small portable folding desk as a table.

"And how is your class going?" She pulled a bundle of her special herbed whole-wheat rolls out of her shopping bag, the wafting scents of fresh-baked bread heavy with basil and sage causing my mouth to water. My bagel and yogurt had been a lifetime ago.

I wanted to say it was fine, but she'd managed to guilt me out of lying about my grades when I was about ten years old, and that old lesson still stuck. "I've barely been able to study. I squeaked an A out of my last paper, but I have a test next week and a ton of reading to do. I just can't concentrate."

"Oh, you'll get it. You're smart." She dismissed my academic troubles with her usual aplomb. In Mom's eyes, I was invincible in the classroom. Forget the fact that I had yet to actually finish grad school. I reached for a roll and that's when she noticed my arm for the first time. "What happened?"

"Just some bad scratches on my arm and leg. I was hoping you could help me change the dressing on it after we eat?"

"Of course. You should be drinking my clover green tea! If I'd known, I'd have brought you some." She gave me a careful look-over. "You look tired, but you don't really look too sick to travel. Are you sure you don't want to go to India? If it's a question of money, I can buy your ticket . . ."

"Mom, I can't go to India right now." I pretended to be very interested in my soup. Truthfully, I was extremely interested in the soup. It was chicken and rice, laden with peppers, onions, carrots, and Mom's homemade herb blend, and it was beyond delicious. I didn't want to spoil it with talking about rabies. I tried to make my tone as casual as possible. "It's no big deal, but I was bitten by a wild animal, and I have to have medical treatment for a couple of weeks."

"What were you doing playing with a wild animal? I've told you a thousand times how dangerous that is." That was Jaxine all over. All natural all the time. Save the trees. Save the oceans. Save the three-toed, purple-eyed tree frog. Nature was all-important, unless it was a danger to her children. Don't go hiking or surfing alone, don't eat wild berries or mushrooms, and never pet a wild animal. If you broke any of those rules, nature was just waiting to attack.

"I was helping a friend. The opossum was living under their floor."

"You know, there are professional people who can take care of that kind of thing." She ladled more soup into my bowl, even though I hadn't finished what I already had.

"Yeah, I know, but we didn't know it was a possum. It could

have been anything. They were hearing strange noises." I played the whole thing down. I wasn't going to tell my mother I was demon hunting. I didn't think even her open-minded hippiness could handle that. "Anyway, it's not a big deal. The scratches are far worse than the bite, but they have to quarantine the possum to make sure it's not sick, and I have to take some shots and pills and stuff to make sure I don't get anything it might have."

Jaxine's eyes narrowed in her patented mom stare, the one that pried out secrets. "You mean it might be rabid?"

"Animal control thinks that's a possibility." I shrugged as casually as I could. "I have to take the vaccine. But they don't usually carry rabies, so there's probably nothing to worry about."

She waved her spoon with a flip of her hand, a total lack of concern in the gesture. "Oh, of course there isn't. The rabies vaccine has come a long way since that time your dad got bitten by that squirrel. I hear you only have to have a few shots now, and they do it in your arm."

"Dad got bitten by a squirrel?" This was the first I'd ever heard of this. I paused. Not knowing where he was or what was happening to him was terrifying. Learning this tiny bit of his past, a scrape he survived, helped a bit.

"We were doing a plant survey in Big Sur back in college. This squirrel got into the tent while we were sleeping. I managed to crawl out, but your dad was trying to get the squirrel out of the tent, and it just went berserk! The tent collapsed and there was your dad, hopping around in the tent with just his arms sticking out the zippered windows, with this crazy squirrel running all over him! We had to cut the canvas away to get him out!" Mom started laughing and Hoover jumped up to see what was so funny. She scooped a piece of chicken out of her soup and waved on it to cool it before giving it to him. "Oh, I haven't thought about that in years! We really did have some fun times."

I didn't bother to remind her that Hoover wasn't supposed to beg for human food. At least she wasn't freaking out about the rabies thing. But I also felt a little bit disappointed. I guess at least part of me had been hoping for some sympathy. Hearing a story from when she and Dad had been happy together, though, warmed my heart and made me miss him even more. Seeming to sense my mood, she stopped laughing.

"I'm sure he'll be okay, Kam. He's resilient and resourceful. He always knows what to do."

"That's what I keep telling myself. They were out in the forest, and no one knows it better than Dad and his team."

"That's right." Jaxine smiled across the table at me.

"Do you still love him?" What on earth made me ask that stupid question. I knew the answer. Maybe I just needed to know that she was as afraid for him as I was.

"Your father? Of course. He's the father of my children. We had a good life together. We just couldn't stay together. He wanted his work, and I wanted my family."

Mom had come to grips with the divorce long before I did. The adolescent me didn't understand why my family had to be divided by an ocean. The teen-age me had been angry and hurt and hated leaving my friends to fly to India every summer. What teenager wants to go live in the rainforest in a humid, damp, spider-laden research station instead of surfing and going to movies? Now, those trips to visit Dad counted as a grand adventure and weirdly, I recalled them fondly. Time makes even giant jumping spiders and damp shoes lose their horror, I guess. And as an adult, I didn't quite know how to reconcile all those old feelings that still haunted me just as much as Evrett haunted my office.

"Kami, I hope you aren't using your father and our divorce as an excuse to avoid finding love of your own."

It seemed to come out of nowhere, and it struck me right in the chest. My body couldn't have taken any more abuse that day, but apparently my soul was a sucker for the free landing punch. "What? Why would you say that?"

"Jack told me you were going to a hockey game together." Mom's eyes were gleaming with hope. "You two used to go to games all the time. I just . . . I don't want you to be alone, sweetheart. You deserve more than . . . this." Her gaze took in the barren office. "Life has so much to offer you."

Jack. The game. Right.

I sighed. "Mom, don't get your hopes up for Jack and me. We're probably not getting back together."

"Oh, I know. But he's such a good guy."

It was always the same. "He is, but I blew it with him. Maybe he's giving me a second chance, but I don't want to rush anything."

And there was the issue of the detective who just asked if I was his. I shoved a bite of bread into my mouth.

"Uh oh. There's someone else, isn't there? Who is it?"

"It's not anything, just a little flirtation. Our professions aren't compatible at all."

That just made her more interested. "Who?"

"Do you remember Detective Ron Brittle?" Mom's soup splashed everywhere as her spoon dropped into the bowl and I winced.

"You're dating the fuzz who arrested your brother? Kami! How could you?"

"Oh, Mom. Kenny was acquitted. Anyway, at that point I would have arrested him, too! Or did you conveniently forget that he let my car get stolen?" The fact it had been stolen by a car thief who was then murdered and left in the trunk when the killer dumped it in a reservoir was all just a coincidence. "And we aren't dating! We have dessert at Reese's every so often and talk shop. He's nice. He even drove me to the hospital the other night and stayed with me while I was being treated."

"Oh." She seemed to consider this for a second and then waved her hand dismissively, "You know, Jack would have done that, too."

I somehow managed to resist slamming my head repeatedly into the desk. Probably because it would have spilled the soup. Time for a change of subject. "So, how was your organic gardening workshop?"

"Oh, great! We had about fifty people and we gave away thirty worm-kits. It was a big hit."

"Worm-kits?" I glanced at my soup. No, I didn't want to know about worm-kits. Not when I was eating. "Sounds like it was a good turn-out."

"So many people are giving up on the industrial farming machine. If we can get every household producing just ten to twenty percent of their own foodstuffs, that would cut commercial farming and pesticide use by millions of dollars."

That was my mother. We talked about gardening while we finished our soup and rolls with plenty of leftovers for my lunch. After Mom changed my dressings, she pulled out a white candle and a protective glass taper and set it in the window. Together, we struck the match and lit the wick. In the glowing candlelight, Mom intoned a little prayer. "Wherever you are, Davis, your family sends you our love. Come home to those who love you safe and sound."

Tears filled my eyes and refused to be blinked away.

"We light this candle of hope that you may find your way to safety." Mom put her arm around my shoulders and we stood and watched the flame glow for a time. Then she straightened and gathered her shopping bag. "I have Pilates class in the morning, but please message me if you hear anything. Come by tomorrow and get some clover tea. Oh, and don't forget to ice."

"Ice?"

"Your rabies injections," she answered casually. "They tend to swell and hurt. Icing helps."

"Oh. Right. Thanks."

I waved as she pulled away from the curb, then sat down to check my emails and Twitter feed. I was so busy looking for messages from Professor Ling or my father or my brother, that I almost missed an instant message on my personal Facebook account from the official Reese's Café Facebook account. I read it twice, but it made less sense the second time through. I picked up the phone to call the café, but a glance out the window showed that it was still dark, no sign of anyone around.

I started to type a return message a few times, but I couldn't figure out what to say. It was gone ten pm, and I spotted Detective Dortman's unmarked cruiser sliding up the street towards my building. Thinking fast, I typed out a quick and cryptic message and closed the screen before standing up to let the cops in.

CHAPTER 13

———◆———

"**A**RE YOU TWO SURE YOU WANT TO DO THIS?" I asked as I gathered my gear into my duffle bag. Ron and Dortman were standing in my office side by side, looking at me with anticipation. Ron looked pensive. Dortman looked haggard, his eyes shadowed with what I could only describe as fear. Just the idea of Dortman being afraid of anything frightened me.

I gave Hoover his food, promised to be back in an hour, and then I collected Evrett's head, stashing it in its velvet handbag.

"Pretty classy. I seem to remember when he was in Evidence all he had was a scarf." Ron probably meant it as a joke, but I was still steamed that my priceless antique had been in a filthy evidence locker for months. I'd finally had to use bullying combined with threats of insurance claims to get him returned.

"He's a prime example of fourteenth century blacksmithing. He deserves the best." There was a faint clank from Evrett's gauntlet, drawing both men's eyes. I might have bumped it with my hip when I turned, but I didn't think so. "You'll have to excuse him. He's a humble man. And he doesn't like being reminded of his age."

Dortman observed all this in silence. I didn't know what he was thinking, which was an oddity for my relationship with the man— Most of the time he was thinking of finding something to charge me with—but I was guessing that he wasn't comfortable with the whole ghost thing. I didn't blame him.

When my former boss bought Evrett and told me the armor was haunted, I thought it was a great joke. Until things started moving on their own or the armor would suddenly shift on its stand, or Hoover would curl and purr and stare at something or someone that I couldn't see. I finally had to accept that I was working with a ghost, albeit a very honorable and, for the most part, helpful one. We called in paranormal research group that Morri and Father Joe were involved with. They brought in a medium who asked Evrett if he wanted to move on, but Evrett said he hadn't completed his greatest mission. I'm a little concerned that he's still interested in liberating the Holy Land, but that's a touchy subject so I don't bring it up.

I shouldered my camera bag and looked for my headlamp before remembering that it had been a casualty of the demon attack. Ron asked if he could help, so I handed him my digital recorder and thermometer. "I haven't had a chance to swap out the memory cards in the other equipment, but we're just doing a debunk, not a full investigation, so I think this is all we need."

"What is that stuff?" Dortman eyed my gear like it was from another planet.

"Nothing you can't find at your local hardware store, for the most part."

"No Ouija boards or black candles?"

Instead of feeding into his fears, I merely held up the bag with Evrett's head. "If Evrett's coming, we won't need them."

As we walked—I mostly limped. The bite on my leg hurt—down the dark street to Café Fanastique, I was thinking about the message on my Facebook account. It didn't make any sense. I only hoped that my return message had been received. I debated telling Ron, but as it was, he'd have to tell Dortman and I'd find myself back in the obstruction of justice category as far as the older detective was concerned.

At the back door of the café, Dortman broke the crime scene tape seal, and produced a key to let us into the kitchen area.

I had to stop and catch my breath as the light came on. The previously pristine, inviting kitchen was a complete disaster. The cops had printed everything, and there was black dust on most of the surfaces. Grady's mixing bowls were on the floor by the sink, and other equipment had been shifted around. Looking through to the office, I could see that the cops had taken the store computer, and the desk was shoved to the side, probably to provide better access to Wyatt's body before they moved it. I didn't want to be disloyal to Reese, but my heart ached for Grady. This had been his dream and it had turned into a nightmare.

The kitchen light was on, but the rest of the shop was dark. I set down my laptop and pulled up the still pictures that I'd taken the night of the investigation. "Ideally, we should have everything exactly the way it was before, but I don't think that will be possible."

"Just do the best you can," Ron told me.

The blinds were already drawn, and the security system was off. I turned on the digital recorder, set it on a filing cabinet in the office where it would be out of the way, and slated the event. "Brittle, Dortman, and White in Café Fantastique, debunking shadow on office floor."

"Look for anything that could let light in or block it out. Anything with a reflective surface—like a mirror, shiny cabinet, that kind of thing—that could reflect light . . ." I groaned, looking at the cookbooks on the shelf that were all sideways now, and the shifted positions of the storage boxes. Equipment was shoved out of place. "Nothing in here is where it was. If it was a glossy book cover or something, we'll never figure it out."

Dortman was staring up above the desk. "Didn't you say light could get in through vents?"

There was what looked like a ventilation cover about two feet wide over the desk. "If it leads outside or to a vent on the roof, I think it's possible, but I'm a paralegal, not a construction worker."

"You have an electromagnetic detector?" Ron held it up with a raised eyebrow.

"That's legitimate paranormal research gear. Do you get a higher number around the vent?"

Ron flipped the switch and waved it as close to the ceiling as he could reach. "That's a negative."

Dortman looked around for a ladder, but Ron hopped up onto the desk. Wow, the guy was lithe, and pretty graceful. I wouldn't have expected that. He wriggled the vent back and forth and finally released it. He flashed his little light through but shrugged, "Looks like there's a drop ceiling, kind of a crawlspace up here. It's hard to see."

I grabbed my flashlight and climbed onto the desk. "Boost me up."

"Boost . . . ?" He looked a little doubtful.

"Boost me up there. Let's take a look." My bruised backside protested but I ignored the pain. Ron looked at Dortman, who shrugged.

"It's not crazier than anything else she's suggested."

Ron cupped his hands together for me to step into. I gave a little hop, grabbed the edge, and then, boost, I was up and climbing into a shallow crawlspace. "There's plywood . . . it's floored pretty solidly. There's insulation along the ceiling." The narrow beam of my handheld light flashed across something on the floor, something huddled and dark. "Ron? There's something up here . . ."

"What?"

I crawled across the floor, my flashlight making out other details. A plastic gallon jug, a small cardboard box . . . I moved closer to the lump. It didn't move. My heart moved to my throat. Was it . . . alive? Was it dead? I scooted closer.

"Kami? What is it? What are you doing?" Ron called.

I ignored him and sniffed the air. It smelled, but not of death. I was close enough that my flashlight made out details of the shape. Lumpy fabric.

"Kami?" Dortman's voice was impatient. "What's going on? Get back down here."

I reached out, stretching as far as I could while balancing on my toes so that I could leap back if needed. My fingers closed around thick cushiony canvas. It was just a sleeping bag, but there was something in it. I grabbed the hem between two fingers and flipped it back, keeping my flashlight tightly in fist. The beam darted wildly across the ceiling and wall before I aimed it back at the bag. Nothing there but a pillow.

As my heart slowed again, I realized the flashlight had illuminated something on the ceiling. A hatch. I pushed up to my knees and gave the thick metal handle a shove. It was a lot heavier than it looked, so I pressed my back to it and used my legs to push. Slowly the hatch rose. Soon, I was standing upright, my waist level with the roof of the café, half inside and half outside in the night chill.

"Kami! Get back down here!" Dortman barked, "Right now!"

"Coming, Dad!" I called back down. "You're going to love this."

"What is it?"

I looked around once more, then closed the hatch, crawled back, tossed my flashlight down to Ron, then grabbed the lip of the vent and dropped surprisingly neatly on the top of the desk, landing with a ten-point gymnast stance. "Now, why doesn't anyone film it when I do things like that? Why do they only catch things like being attacked by a possum?"

"Kam." Ron didn't look too appreciative of my attempt to keep them in suspense.

"Someone's been living up there. They've got a pee-bottle, a box of snacks and water, and a sleeping bag. And there's an unlocked roof hatch." I brushed dust off the knees of my jeans. "Someone has had full access to this building, at least since the remodel finished, if not before."

Dortman grabbed a chair, landed it on the desk, and climbed up to thrust his head and chest through the vent and shine his flashlight around. "Damn. We'll have to get the techs back here. They're gonna love this."

As he came back down, I took a deep breath. He wasn't going to love this part. "Unfortunately, even if someone was up there the night we did the investigation and had some kind of flashlight or something, there's still nothing that could cast that shadow on the floor from that angle." To prove my point, I stood on the desk and raised my arm through the opening, shining my light around the room. "There's nothing to cast the shadow. But it does explain a few other things. Like how someone could get the keys to Wyatt's car and move it without anyone knowing, and how heavy items of cookware could be moved around and turned on and off."

"But who would even want to?" Ron looked around the darkened café in bewilderment. "Nothing about this case makes any sense."

My mind strayed to the private message I'd received on Facebook, and for a second, I almost blurted out my suspicions, but I held my tongue. I didn't need Dortman on my back. Give me a possibly rabid bum-footed opossum any day of the week.

"Motive is the thing." Dortman mumbled. He was still flashing his light around the room, trying to figure out a way to cast a shadow on the floor. "We gotta look at who had the most to gain, and I think that's Reese Calhoun."

"Oh, please. Can you see Reese sleeping in a crawl space, playing pranks? I dunno if you know this, Dortman, but girls have a hard time peeing into gallon jugs." I couldn't help myself. I was tired, achy, and a little nauseous from the antibiotics. Or maybe the culprit was all of Mom's tea that she'd practically poured down my throat. Thanks, Mom. It might heal me if it didn't make me puke first. "Sorry, but this seems more personal. If you want to close out business competition, you either look for legal ways to shut them down or you simply out-competition them. Reese's Coffeeshop was doing both of those."

Ron gave me another of his now infamous raised-eyebrow stares. I thought it was cute when he did it to suspects. Well, to suspects that weren't me. "Kam? Were you looking for legal ways to shut them down?"

I smiled as sweetly as I could manage. It probably looked more like a grimace. "All I did was look at city ordinances and restaurant licensing requirements to see if there were grounds for a civil complaint, but I didn't find anything. We decided to focus on the out-competition angle."

"We?"

Okay, that stare was really looking less cute by the second. "*We*. Max, Twila, Sasha, Tobiana . . . and you. If you'll remember, getting Kenny to do a signing was *your* idea."

Dortman stopped flashing his light around. "If I didn't know you as well as I do, you'd be off the case, D.B."

"Oh, come on. None of us had anything to do with killing Wyatt!"

"But you're not exactly impartial, are you? You're loyal to Reese's Café, and there was a competition factor."

"I think your CD is scratched, Detective. It's skipping."

"I don't think anyone listens to CD's anymore, Kam." Ron finally cracked a smile.

"So, that collection of Rush discs in your glove compartment is what? Decorative?"

"Shut up, both of you." Dortman flipped off his flashlight and pointed at me. "Put on your magic helmet and tell me if you see anything."

"Put it on yourself," I retorted, unzipping the bag. The helmet was cold, very cold. "Um . . . Or not."

"You don't have to, Kam." Ron suddenly reassured me. "This isn't an official investigation. He can't order you to do anything."

Dortman's expression suggested that he might pull out his service weapon and murder us both in cold blood. I didn't think he'd risk his retirement, but who knew how he'd spin the story. Forced to defend himself after being attacked by a rabid paralegal?

"No, I'll do it." I held Evrett's helmet in my hands, the beautiful visored sallet collecting condensation from the warmth of my fingers against the supernaturally cold metal. "But first, I want the truth about something."

Dortman's head jerked up.

"What really happened the night of that robbery? If it's a closed case, then the files should be public record, but they aren't. Even the testimony from the plea bargain arrangement was closed. When I asked you, you said that the only victims that night were the hostages. What did you mean by that?"

Dortman was still, his eyes focused on the floor. "Let it go, Kami. It was a long time ago."

"It was in this building. If there are spirits stuck here from that incident, they won't see it as a long time ago." I wasn't going to back down this time. I gestured around me. "They're standing on a bridge, trapped by whatever happened to them. And if I'm going to look across that bridge, I want to know what I'm going to find."

"So you do have a spine, even when your special lawyer isn't here to back you up," grunted Dortman, but his voice didn't have its usual bite.

"Blame it on the rabies, I guess." I held up the helmet. "It's up to you, Detective."

Ron stepped between us suddenly, his palm raised. "Look, I don't want to sound skeptical or anything, but if he tells you what happened, it may influence what you tell us. It's like keeping witnesses separate in interrogation. And like you said, this may not work. You tried it once before."

"In the kitchen. Not the office. Though I did look this way through the visor."

"Try it." Ron reached out and put a hand on my shoulder. "I'll be right here. Just try it."

I really didn't want to know what I might see, but I nodded. "Okay, shut off the lights."

Dortman hadn't moved, but he raised his gaze from the spot in front of the desk and his eyes met mine, a silent appeal. Even Doberman dogs can make heart-rending puppy dog eyes when they want something, and I can't resist puppy dog eyes.

"Active spirits, what we call intelligent haunts, can feed off emotions. Even Evrett does it." I lifted the sallet, ice cold in my hands, to emphasize my point. "I suggest we all take a deep breath and focus on being calm and centered."

"Hipster yoga crap." But Dortman took a deep breath and exhaled slowly, and I saw his shoulders relax.

I switched on my modified K2 meter and the IR sensor and followed my own advice, taking a deep breath even though it did little to appease my apprehension. Cautiously, I donned Evrett's helmet. It was cold and close, cushioned by my short springy curls as I lowered it. The icy sensation was a little like dunking my head in a drink cooler—Doesn't every kid with a little brother end up with a cooler of ice water on their head at some point?—and I closed my eyes. When I opened them again, I was looking through the slits of the visor. I started to turn in a circle to take in my surroundings, but Ron started laughing.

"Don't make me hurt you."

"Please do." Dortman mumbled. "Assault on an officer of the law would make my night."

I thought he might be joking, but I didn't want to test that theory. The room was dark, everything turned off except for the walk-in refrigerator and the ice machine, same as the last time. "Is there anyone here?" I asked as I rotated slowly on my heel, the room appearing in chunky slats. Silence greeted me, but I could feel prickles rising along the hairs of my neck beneath the back of the helm's short gorget. I continued turning, trying not to look at Ron biting his lip to keep from sniggering. Dortman wasn't laughing. He seemed to have taken my call for calm seriously. "If there's someone here who needs to talk to us, you can use that device on the desk by lighting up the lights."

The K2 remained dark, and I was thankful for that. I turned a third time, and this time I saw it. A dark shadow spread slowly from the corner of the desk. "Are you guys seeing this?"

It was the first time I'd had someone there to confirm what I was seeing. Dillon Cheshire was the only other soul who had worn the helmet, and he was in a coma and couldn't tell what he saw.

"I don't see anything." Dortman gave me a confused look, and Ron shook his head but turned the video camera where I pointed, following my hand.

The shadow faded out, and then slowly repeated.

"This is just a residual." I explained with a shrug, the helmet weighing the movement. "Like a video of a memory playing over and over."

Gradually, I became aware of a faint light near my left elbow. It wasn't the shadowy waving figures I'd seen in Cheshire's torture chamber. This was just a soft glowing orb that rose and fell, brightening and then dimming again. "Oh! I can see you. Can you make the lights on the device light up?"

The illumination didn't move from my elbow.

"Kam? What are you seeing?" Ron's hand touched my shoulder.

"Just a light. Faint."

"Big? Small?"

"Rising and falling, like a lamp on a dimmer switch." I felt stronger analyzing what I was seeing. "Is there something you need us to know? Something you want to say? You can use the lights to talk to us. Light them up once for yes. Two for no."

The K2 remained dark, and I sighed, an echoing sound in the helmet. This was getting us nowhere. Suddenly the light grew brighter, and I felt a familiar icy sensation race up my spine to center on the back of the helmet. "Sir Evrett? Is that you?"

The lights on the K2 lit up full bore. I wasn't sure how I knew, but it was surge of certainty that carried over Dortman's stunned gasp. "That's Evrett. He's trying to help."

"Evrett? Is Wyatt here?" Wyatt's name caught in my throat. I hadn't really talked to anyone beyond life whom I had known when they were living. What if Wyatt was lost, hurt, and confused, and I couldn't find a way to help him?

The lights flashed twice. Not Wyatt. Thank you to all the powers that be. I wanted to ask about Wyatt, but I knew Evrett didn't know any more than I did about where the departed go or what they do. I could only hope Wyatt was at peace, wherever he was.

"Is there more than one spirit here?"

Two flashes.

"Do you know if they were young in life? Or old?"

The lights flashed three times, and there was a painfully cold press at the back of the helmet. "Evrett! Did you just head-slap me?" Head slapped by a ghost! That was all I needed.

"Yes or no questions only, Kam," Ron reminded me belatedly. "Like a polygraph test."

I didn't know what to ask. "Young?"

One flash. I looked to Dortman, but he was staring at the K2. "Watch the IR indicator, too. That will tell us if something, like your radio, is interfering with the results."

"It's dark." Dortman muttered. He fixed his attention back on the K2. "Is it JoJo Riceman?"

The lights blinked once.

"I'm sorry." At first, I thought he was apologizing to the ghost. Or to Evrett. But he continued with a grunt. "I'm sorry. I can't do this."

With those words, Detective Dortman cut tail and ran.

I heard the swinging door to the dining room creak, and then the bathroom door slam. A moment later, we could hear the sink running. I looked at Ron, but he grimaced and shook his head.

"Keep going."

I had no idea what to say next. JoJo. Who was JoJo Riceman? "JoJo? Is there something you need to tell us?

The lights blinked once.

"If you can say it loud enough, our equipment might hear it."

The orb had stopped rising and falling and was slowly fading.

"I don't think he has the energy, the strength."

The lights blinked once, and I knew that was Evrett. This was taking its toll on him, too. I only had one more idea, and it was a risky one, one nearly every serious paranormal investigator will tell you never to take. "Can you use my energy, Evrett? Can you use my strength to tell me what it is?"

The lights blinked once, and then there was cold, like a creeping breeze, chilly and dangerous, wisping over my arms, up my back, down into my unlaced running shoes. I instantly regretted my suggestion. The lights on the K2 blinked again, and then went dark. Thankfully, the painful cold receded as swiftly as it had come, and I welcomed the return of warmth with grateful relief. "Thank you, Evrett." I pulled off the helmet, and shook my head, feeling my smushed curls spring back to life. "I promise I'll take you back home soon, and I'll oil your beautiful helmet tomorrow. I'll polish all of you, in fact!"

"What was that?" Ron was staring at me. "Did you get any answers?"

"Go get Dortman and we'll listen to the playback on the recording together."

Ron looked like he was going to protest, but I was done playing Dortman's game, especially since he was too much of a chicken to stick around. "I'm sorry, Ron, but he's been hiding things from the start. He wanted me to do this for him, and then he bailed the second things got serious. I'm done being jerked around. Go get him or I'm leaving."

Ron didn't answer. He just nodded and left through the dining room door.

I CRADLED EVRETT'S HELMET IN MY ARMS as I went around and switched all of the lights back on. The metal was no longer cold, warming to room temperature as I held it. I dropped a grateful and loving kiss on the brow of the helmet before I tucked it back into its bag. While I waited for Ron and Dortman to return, I set up my laptop on the kitchen table and plugged in the recorder so that we could filter the results through my sound editing program if we needed to. I knew from my research with local groups that my luck with clear EVP recording was just that: Luck. Most EVPs were garbled or in tones barely at the edge of human hearing. Which made sense, since they were completely beyond human hearing without electronic intervention. I wished Dortman and Ron would return. I'd felt Evrett's protection wrapped around me like a blanket before, and without it, this place that had claimed at least three lives was just hella creepy. At least I knew Wyatt wasn't here, trapped in the void.

Ron finally came back with Dortman. The older detective looked like someone had held his head in the toilet. What was left of his hair was wet, as was his face and collar. I didn't look too closely at him, not wanting him to feel challenged or embarrassed. I pretended everything was normal. "Are we ready?"

Dortman nodded. I explained that we'd listen to the raw recording first, and if we couldn't understand it, we'd run it through the editing program and toy with the frequencies. "I don't want you to think I'm tampering with evidence."

"Wouldn't dream of it." There was something strained in Ron's voice. Well, it is a lot to take in the first time you talk to dead people.

I backed the recording up to where I'd allowed Evrett to use my energy. We could hear me make the request, loud and clear. What followed at first seemed unintelligible. Dortman growled, "Turn it up."

I turned it up, and this time it sounded like a voice. I could make out distinct syllables, but to my ears they didn't make sense. "I can try filtering it." I started to reach for my mouse, but Ron stopped me with a brush of his hand against my wrist.

"Play it again."

The stream of syllables came again and this time I recognized two sounds, but I didn't speak up. I wanted to know what the detectives thought they heard before I put in my two cents.

Ron was leaning close to the computer. "Can you slow it down? By, say, a quarter?"

"Okay . . ." I ran it through the sound program and slowed playback, the syllables coming more distinctly and with smoother resonance.

"Yeah." Ron smiled. "That makes sense."

"You can understand it?"

"Yes, can't you?"

Dortman and I looked at each other then back at Ron. "Okay, smarty-pants Detective. What do you hear?"

"Seriously? Geez, what did you guys take for your language requirement in school?"

"Spanish," I said. "It was the closest I could get to Latin."

Dortman grunted. "Didn't have to take foreign language. Took the department class on Spanish for law enforcement, though."

"It's French. I've been learning it for years. I want to go to France someday." Ron's smug tone was enough to make me want to smack him. "But this doesn't sound like modern French to me, more like something from old French literature. I think your knight didn't have time to translate."

That made perfect sense. Why hadn't I thought of that possible complication? Evrett had spoken in arcane French before. Only when Evrett spoke to me in my dream, or rather his dream, was it in English.

"Can you understand it?"

"Let me borrow your notebook." Ron listened a few more times, made a few notes, and pulled out his smart-phone and did some searches while Dortman and I stood there helplessly.

I hopped up onto the work-counter and rested my sore back against the wall.

"The first part says that they are sorry for the pain they caused." Ron paused. "I'm assuming that's JoJo saying he's sorry." Both of our gazes flicked to Dortman, but he was standing expressionless and cross-armed, so Ron kept going. "It was . . . it sounds like Tees? Teez? A name, at any rate. It was Tees's plan? No one was supposed to get hurt. Tees broke the rule. That's all there is."

Ron leveled his cop-stare at Dortman. "Buddy, I think it's high time you told us what the hell really happened here."

Silence filled the kitchen for what seemed like years before Dortman slowly started to speak. "I'd just got my detective's badge. I was the new kid on the block, always the first to get the crap jobs. We got the all-hands call. Drugstore robbery in progress, hostages taken." Dortman's expression was far away. He was somewhere in his memory, hands flexing as though on his steering wheel, pulling up in front of the drugstore. "You have to understand. The cartels were moving in back then. It was a big deal. A drugstore robbery meant they were after the hard stuff. It was a big deal The Commissioner was all for going in hard and fast, taking the perps down as fast as possible. SWAT was coming down from Oakland, but we got here first."

"It was a hot day. The front door was wide open, but there was no air conditioning. It was a sweatbox. This . . ." He waved his hand around the kitchen. ". . . was the actual pharmacy part of the drugstore. Where the sinks are now, there was a window, you know the kind of long wall window where you can see the pharmacist and watch them work. They had hostages, just five shoppers, everyday folk, but we didn't know. They had them over there, on the floor, where we couldn't see 'em. Four of us came through the door, my sup was in front, and there I was, rookie detective, in the rear. Why didn't we wait for SWAT?" He looked at Ron. "That's what you're thinkin', right? Why didn't we wait? Sounds stupid now, saying I was following orders, but yeah, that's what I did. Followed orders. Captain sent us in, and we went."

Ron was silent, but his hand was resting on the counter, and I could see his fingers flex towards his palm. He seemed aware of it and relaxed his hand again.

"We're not thinking anything," I reassured, "We just want to hear what happened."

"They started shooting first. And we shot back. My superior went down, and I started to fall back, but the other guys, they were charging in, so I went, too. To this day, it's all just a blur. Screaming hostages. Gunfire at close range. You know, when you take your accuracy tests, it's on the range with your ear guards on. You don't hear it. Not like that. Like canon fire from all directions."

"When it was done, we had two injured hostages, three injured cops, and one dead perp." Dortman's haunted gaze turned back to the office, and he swallowed a few times. "And one dead hostage. JoJo, the owner's son, in front of the safe."

"Was it friendly fire?" Ron's voice was deeply sympathetic and quiet in a way I hadn't heard from him before. He really was a good guy at the heart of things.

Dortman shook his head, his eyes still unfocused. "The forensics took days to sort out, but in the end, we could only come to one conclusion. It was an inside job. JoJo was mixed up with a gang. They were just stupid friggin' kids. They had the hostages facing the wall, but one of them could see the security mirror and witnessed the whole thing. The plan was to make it look like they took JoJo hostage and made him open the safe, but they hadn't planned on the store being busy or that there were shoppers that escaped and called the cops. It turned from a simple staged robbery to a full-blown hostage situation. When we started shooting back instead of retreating and waiting for a negotiator, they panicked and turned on each other. Thing is, that hostage always swore there were four guys. Four. We had two dead and one wounded and in custody. And Rubens never talked. He pled guilty to gain a reduced sentence, but he was already sick by the time he went to the state pen and didn't last a year. We called it good enough."

"Except for JoJo," I persisted. "Why is he still here, Detective?"

"Because we maintained that he was an innocent victim, even

though he was found with a gun in his hand and we had an injured cop with a matching bullet in his hip."

Ron's eyes widened. "You threw a case?"

"No, man. It's not like that." Dortman slumped forward, his body physically giving out at the lifting of the burden he'd carried so long, his palms resting on the black-dusted, stainless steel work-table. "I know it looks bad. It looks wrong. You gotta understand. That kid's parents lost their only son. They lost their boy that day. They were immigrants and they stood to lose everything they'd built. The insurance company would never have paid out for an inside job. What were we supposed to do?"

"So it became a story of armed robbers who kidnapped the son of the store owner and killed him when he didn't open the safe in time." Ron was rubbing his forehead and I felt sorry for them both; Ron who was seeing his partner in a new light, one he didn't like, and Dortman, who had carried an ugly secret for too long, and now had to live with the fact that JoJo's soul had been trapped in a vacant building for fifteen years.

"Looking at the situation now? From here, today?" I said slowly, "I don't see how I would have done anything differently."

"I've asked myself a thousand times if I could have done something different, but I don't know. I just don't know."

I couldn't answer that. "So, who was Tees or Teez or whatever?"

Dortman shrugged. "No clue. There was a bunch of factions running around back then, mostly wannabe imitators of the big gangs in Oakland. We think this was an outreach of one of those. Little punks running around making hitting convenience stores and gas stations into an initiation game. They wore bandanas and tats like badges back then, and every faction had their own play on them. We couldn't get any of the gangs to admit to knowing our perps, and like I said, Rubens never talked."

A creeping suspicion was growing in my mind and I never wanted to be wrong so badly in my entire life. "Detective? Was one of the tattoos three strands of barbed wire?" I leaned across Ron's body, carefully avoiding touching him, and appropriated my legal-pad and pen back to make a rough sketch. "Like this?"

Dortman studied it for a long moment, but I could tell the second he laid eyes on it that he recognized it. "Hell. Did your ghost show you this?"

"No. But I've seen it recently." I felt like crying. I opened the coffee shop website and scrolled down to the photo Morri had taken of Reese, side-on, smiling, her tattooed arm visible under the sleeve of her brown t-shirt. "Reese and her ex-husband, Tivon, each have that tattoo. Reese had hers turned into roses with thorned stems, but if you look closely you can still see the wire."

"And now she's missing and who knows where the hell her husband is?"

"*Ex*-husband," I reminded them coldly. I started packing up my gear. "The ex-husband that I sent her to get a restraining order against this morning. She never returned from the courthouse. So yes, she's missing, and her ex is out there somewhere. But even if he was the other robber back then, why would he be here now? Why kill Wyatt? None of that makes sense."

"The man isn't exactly stable," Ron reminded me, and Dortman nodded. The older man was starting to recover some of his color, but he still looked shaken.

"I'm scared for Reese," I admitted. "I keep hoping you'll find her. Even you arrest her, that's better than not knowing if Tivon has her."

"Tivon. Teev." Ron tapped the notes he'd made. "The EVP could have been Teev, not Teez."

"Tivon." I felt sick. "During the robbery, did he go out the back door, or maybe he already knew that roof hatch was there and used it to escape when the gunfire started." I slung my bag over my shoulder and headed for the door, but a sudden thought held me up. "Do you think he could be behind your break-ins? He would remember the neighborhood as it used to be, not the businesses that are here now."

"Explaining why he would hit strange places and just take what he could easily steal?" Ron shrugged. "It doesn't make sense, does it? I mean, the guy was supposedly loaded when he left the country."

Dortman grunted. "We're out of leads."

Guilt rippled in my gut and I cleared my throat. "Errmmm. Gentlemen? Promise not to arrest me?"

"No." Ron fingered the cuffs hooked to the back of his belt with a frown.

"Yes." Dortman interjected. "I promise not to arrest you. *Tonight*."

"And tomorrow?"

"Tomorrow's another day."

I glanced at the clock on the wall. "Tomorrow is only an hour away."

"Precisely." Dortman seemed disappointed that I'd realized that.

I pulled my laptop back out and opened my Facebook account. "I got a message right before you got here tonight. I answered it."

I could see there was new reply, and I glanced at Ron before I opened the string for them to read.

I'm fyn. dnot worry abt me

My reply read, "Reese? Is that you? Where are you?"

The final string read *strting Ovr*.

"I don't think Reese wrote those." Ron said it before I did, but it was Dortman who surprised me by completing the thought.

"She went to culinary school, has some education. I think she'd at least spell 'fine' right."

"I think so, too." I agreed, overwhelmed with gratitude that they believed me. "I think if she wanted me not to worry, she'd know this isn't the way to do it."

"Starting over." Ron read the last reply out loud a few times. "What does she mean? Is she running?"

"Maybe Tivon has her phone and is trying to make me believe think she's leaving the coffee shop and starting over somewhere else or something." I was getting a sinking gut feeling. "But she'd never leave like this."

"Unless she killed Wyatt Halden." Dortman's voice was low in the hushed space between us. "If Tivon knew about the roof hatch, it's possible she did, too."

"I thought we were past that." I closed my laptop and slid it back into its padded case. "Okay, I'm done here. I'll bill you gentlemen in a week or so."

"What? No, I don't think so." Ron started to step between me and the back door.

"Yeah. I'm just kidding about the bill. But this was supposed to be a freebie debunk, not a full investigation. I'm exhausted. I need sleep. I did what you wanted. And now, thanks to you," I glanced at Dortman, "I'm afraid my original job here just got a lot harder because I now I'm going to have to convince a grieving uncle and his partner the café is haunted and explain that the spirit of a kid who should have moved on years ago needs help now."

"Sorry. That wasn't the result that anybody wanted." Ron looked genuinely contrite, "But what I meant was, I don't think we're done here. I need your account information so I can get the IT department busy tracing that message. And then I need you tell me everything you know about Reese's past."

I smiled, but it felt stretched and ugly, and my face felt like stone. With my complexion under the kitchen's fluorescent lights, I probably looked like a death mask. "You can have my account information when you get a warrant, Ron." I saw the eager anticipation of an obstruction charge gleaming in Dortman's eye and it took me less than half a second to relent. "Oh, all right. Here." I jotted down my Facebook account id and password for him. "I'll bring my computer to the IT department tomorrow and show them myself. As far as Reese's past is concerned, you know what I know, probably more since she was your suspect and I'm sure you ran background checks."

"Is." Dortman corrected me. "Is a suspect. Everyone's a suspect until they're proven not to be."

"Which I have. So, goodnight, gentlemen. It's midday in Sikkim. I want to get back to my office and call my father's partner again. If we're done here?"

Ron sighed and nodded. "Hold up, though. I'll walk you back."

I WAITED IMPATIENTLY WHILE THEY TURNED things off, signed their names to the crime-scene notice on the door, and replaced the seal with a fresh one. It was chilly outside. A marine front had washed in off the Bay and the night had turned damp and close. I'd have to turn the furnace in the office on. I hated wasted power, but neither Hoover nor I were fond of the cold. That was April in the Bay Area for you.

"I know we're missing something, I just don't know what yet. Let's get some sleep and come at it fresh in the morning." Dortman was saying. "I'll call dispatch and have bulletins put out for Tareesa Calhoun and Tivon Shuman."

He walked back to his car and I could see him on the radio. Ron came with me back to the office and waited inside while I flipped on the lights and petted Hoover. "You sure you want to stay here tonight? If a killer can get into the café, who's to say he can't get in here?"

Ignoring Ron's question for the moment, I gingerly withdrew Evrett's head from his evening bag and returned him to his stand, straightening him gently. "Thank you, kind sir, for everything."

"Do you always talk to him?"

"I never know when he might be listening." I turned back to Ron. "But as to staying here, I'll be fine. This is my building. I know every in and out." I gestured at him to follow me and let him watch me open the heavy built-in safe and put the recording gear inside. Then I spun the tumblers. "The original copies are all here. I still have copies on the laptop. If for some reason, you need to get in, get a warrant and call Reggie. He has the copy of the combination in my will."

"You have a will?" I had the feeling that Ron had never really thought about having a will. After all, neither of us had kids, or much to leave.

"Reggie made me put it together after Charles died. I know we haven't talked about it much, but the estate I received was substantial. Some of the antiques are priceless. They're tied up in probate right now, but if something were to happen to me . . ."

Ron stopped in the arched doorway that led to the file room. "Are you planning on something happening to you?"

"No. Not at all! I just . . . it's better to be prepared, you know." I don't know if I ever mentioned this before, but I'm a terrible liar. Like, the worst. Reggie sometimes asks how I can ever hope to be a good lawyer without a poker face, but I'm just kinda hoping I can get by with being an honest lawyer.

I got the detective stare again, and then suddenly Ron stepped forward and gripped my shoulder, giving me a reassuring shake. "Is this about the rabies? Sweetie, you don't have rabies. That possum is just as healthy as you are, and as soon as you finish the treatments, you won't have anything to worry about."

I extricated myself with a bit more lingering than strictly necessary. "Yeah, I guess I'm just tired. It all just seems . . . you know . . . totally overwhelming. Things will look better in the morning, I'm sure."

"Sure they will," he echoed my tone as he stepped away from me. "Get some sleep."

CHAPTER 14

—◆—

Friday Morning

BEFORE TRYING TO GET ANYTHING RESEMBLING sleep, I called Dad's research station. It was easier to get through this time, but there was still no news from my father. Dr. Sing said that emergency services had their hands full, but the national park had sent a few rangers to help look. Missing American scientists weren't something the Indian government wanted to explain to anyone. "We sent up a drone earlier," Dr. Sing explained. "There doesn't seem to be much damage in the direction the team went. We will find them. Or they will come wandering back in a day or two, wondering if there is any cold beer."

Feeling slightly reassured, I blew out the candle in the window and joined Hoover on the sofa. I was exhausted, but I couldn't sleep. My eyes traced the shadows on the ceiling as the wind swayed the streetlamps and the occasional car drove slowly by. How could I sleep when Reese was missing and in danger? The police might think otherwise, but that was their job. Mine was to find Reese.

Hoover got annoyed with my restlessness and moved to his basket on the bookshelf to sleep. I tossed and turned for another few hours until the slow, grey light of dawn touched the window and I gave up. Kenny's plane would be landing in India soon, so I picked up my phone and checked my messages. I had been hoping he'd have Wi-Fi on the plane and would answer me, but I knew it was just as likely that he was trying to sleep on the flight to be rested when he landed.

The message supposedly from Reese was still up on my Facebook page. I was so tired that the letters swam in front of my eyes. Dortman said we were missing something, and I knew he was right. The text itself looked simple enough, but it didn't sound like Reese at all. Was there some kind of hidden meaning? Could it be some kind of code? Over it. Over what? The coffeeshop? Her divorce? Over something else? It. I.T.? A tech company? Over an IT company? My sleep deprived brain just couldn't make sense of it. I gave up and got dressed to help Sasha at the coffee shop.

Sasha already had things well in hand when I got there. The weekend croissants were already in the ovens, and the whole shop smelled of divinely baked, buttery breadstuffs. I took time to pull myself a latte and did a quick inventory to make sure we had enough stock for the weekend. Fortunately, when we'd run short during Kenny's event, Twila had placed a large order with the suppliers. I warned Sasha. "We're down to two gallons of almond milk. I hope that's enough. We promised half off steamed drinks tonight. Maybe we should cancel the concert . . ."

"SteamTrails already called to confirm first thing this morning. If we run out of almond milk, we run out. They can drink real milk or go with soy." Sasha was counting out the till for the morning. "I hadn't even heard of them, so I hope they're good. The lead singer had such a lovely voice on the phone."

Hoser did have a lovely speaking voice, it was true, but I'd never actually heard him sing. "Nice of them to call. But we should have canceled, what with Reese being missing and our competition shutting down."

"We already put out all of the advertising," Sasha reminded me.

I flipped the open sign on, and the usual weekday morning crowd started coming in. As I delivered drinks, I asked every taxi driver if they'd seen Reese or her car around town. The coffee shop van was still in the parking lot, so I'd assumed she'd taken her personal car, a distinctive green Kia Soul, to the courthouse. As each taxi and bus driver shook their head, I started to wonder if I'd assumed wrong. No one even remembered seeing her driving her personal car that week, and no one had given her a ride.

I was the only one who had been at the coffee shop early that morning when I sent Reese to the courthouse. Why hadn't I checked to see if she was in her car? If she drove the van to work, she might have taken a ride-share to the courthouse to avoid trying to find parking. As soon as Tobiana arrived, I promised her and Sasha that I'd be back to help with the concert, then I went to the office and dug around until I found Reese's home address.

THE MORNING CLOUD COVER HADN'T BURNED OFF YET, and it was cool and humid as I climbed into my little grey pickup and headed for Reese's house. My phone showed it was in a development of townhomes in a quiet suburb, backed into a cul-de-sac near the BART station. Driving into the neighborhood, all the houses looked identical. Tall three bedroom, two bath townhouses with single car garages, little driveways, and little lawns. Reese's lawn looked well kept, but so did all of the lawns. I wondered if it was an HOA that took care of the yards because I couldn't see Reese having time to mow the lawn or trim the tidy rosebush in front.

I pulled up, looked, looked again, and realized that Detective Brittle was standing on Reese's porch. I slipped my pickup into reverse and backed away. Not quickly enough, unfortunately, and Ron trotted off the porch and stopped me with a wave.

He came alongside and gestured for me to roll down the window.

"Hi," I said as the glass lowered enough to look him in the eye.

"Do I even want to know what you're doing here?"

"I'm looking for Reese," I told him flatly. "Same thing you're doing, right?"

"I'm serving a warrant, actually. We have two detectives going through the house right now."

That didn't sound good. "Have you found anything?"

"You know I'm not telling you, even if we did."

I opened my door, forcing Ron to back up as I stepped out, my tone pleading. "Okay, don't tell me what you found, but please, Ron, just tell me you didn't find Reese's body in there? It's okay to tell me what you *didn't* find, right?"

Sympathy reached his eyes and he shook his head tightly. "There's no one inside, dead or otherwise. Now, you should skedaddle before Dortman sees you and charges you with interference."

"I am not interfering!"

"Go home, Kami."

We stared at each other for a second, and I realized that was all I was going to get out of him. "I'll go, but not home. Can you just check one thing for me?"

Ron grimaced but sighed in acquiescence. "What do you want?"

"Is her Soul in the garage?"

Ron blinked. "How would I know that? You're the expert in the soul department."

Choking with laughter, it took me a few moments to clarify myself. "No, Ron! Not that kind of soul. Her green Kia Soul. I want to know if she was driving it when she went to the courthouse the other morning. The coffeeshop van is still in the back parking lot."

I saw light dawn in his eyes and he laughed, too, but then he sobered. "Crap."

"It is, isn't it?" My spirit plummeted. "That means either she drove the coffee shop van to work that morning, then took a rideshare or taxi to the courthouse. Or she went to the courthouse and drove the Soul back here, and then what? Abandoned her car? How does one go on the lam without a car, Ron?"

"Are you sure she was going to the courthouse that morning?"

"I sent her straight to the courthouse, so she could be there when the clerk opened. I stayed up late preparing the restraining order request. When she didn't show up back at work, I thought she might be trying to find a judge to do an emergency injunction."

"Hmm. Interesting." His face was expressionless.

"What? What's interesting?"

He shook his head. "Nothing." Now it was his turn to plead. "Please, Kami. Go home and let us work."

"Mmmkay. Will do."

"I mean it. Go home."

"I'm going." I got back in my pickup and cruised slowly down to the end of the cul-de-sac and rolled slowly past Reese's house on the way out. Ron stood on the porch with his arms crossed as I drove by. He stood and watched until I turned off the street.

I drove back to the office, but instead of parking in my rear lot, I pulled into Reese's coffee shop's private parking. After parking beside the brown van with the Reese's Coffee and More logo on the side, I ran around to the front door of the coffee shop and went through to the office. The spare key to the van was hanging on its hook. "Sasha? Has anyone taken the van out?"

"No," she answered as she dumped a tray full of dirty dishes into a bus-bin. "Next catering delivery is Sunday luncheon for the Baptist Ladies Auxiliary. Why?"

I grabbed the key and went out the back door. Why hadn't I thought to check the van sooner? I put the key in the driver's side lock and started to turn it but realized that it was already unlocked. My heart sank. I started to grab the doorhandle but stopped myself just in time, remembering not to put my prints on the latch. Instead, I cupped my hands to my forehead and looked through the glass. What I saw froze me in place as I tried to make sense of it.

The manila folder that I'd handed Reese that morning was on the passenger seat, tilted sideways, paperwork sliding over the vinyl seat. On the floor of the driver's side, Reese's good pinstriped suit jacket lay crumpled on the dirty floormat. An open sports drink bottle was lying sideways on the dashboard, and I could see where liquid had dripped across the dash and down the console.

I picked up my phone and started to call Ron but thought better of it. I had some making up to do with another detective. He answered with a gruff, "Dortman."

"Detective Dortman? It's Kami."

"Uh huh." He sounded distracted, probably going through Reese's underwear drawer or something.

"I'm at the coffeeshop, and seeing as Reese's car is in her garage
. . ."

"Uh huh." So Ron told him I'd been there.

"I checked the coffee shop van." The next set of words didn't want to come out, but I squeezed them past my tongue anyway. "It's not locked. The paperwork I gave her to take to the courthouse is still sitting on the seat, and her jacket is on the floor of the van. Her good pinstriped business jacket. It's designer. She would never leave it on the floor."

Now I had Dortman's interest. "Did you touch anything?"

At least I'd gotten one thing right. "I only looked through the window."

"Okay, don't touch anything. We'll be right there."

I slid the key out of the lock and returned it to my pocket. My mind was racing as I returned to the coffee shop. The paperwork meant she'd never left for the courthouse that morning. Someone, or something, had stopped her from driving away. What if it was Wyatt? Had she had another confrontation with him, one that ended with his death and her fleeing? I didn't think so. My gut said it was Tivon, and that Tivon still had her. But where was he?

"Kami?" Sasha called back to me. "Four fruit salads, please?"

Then there was no more time to think. Bagels, salads, pastries, sandwiches—the Rick Royce Special was still on the board—all had to be assembled and delivered. If I hadn't been so worried, it would have been kind of fun working with Sasha and Tobiana like I used to. Friday mornings used to be my favorite shift, and not just because it was the day Sasha baked all the croissants for the weekend.

News had started to spread about why Café Fantastique was closed, and all the locals were coming in just to gossip and ask if we knew what was going on. A lot of them asked where Reese was. "She's out," we all said over and over. "She's just out."

Out. Somewhere.

Ron and Dortman showed up with a tow-truck instead of a crime scene team. "We're taking it to the lot for the techs," Ron told me when I handed him the key.

"We need it back on Sunday for a catering job," I warned hopefully, but both detectives shook their heads at me.

"Cancel it. In fact, you should probably just shut down," Ron advised.

"We have a concert this evening. Too late to cancel," Sasha pointed to the signs on the windows.

"Well, you should probably plan on just closing after tonight," Ron suggested. I glanced at Sasha and she silently shook her head. I agreed with her completely.

"We'll take that under advisement, Detective," I said with as much sweetness as I could muster.

Tobiana handed each of them their favorite coffee drinks with a casual, "On the house. Go find our boss, please."

We stood in the window and watched the coffee shop van being towed away. It felt like an end to something.

CHAPTER 15

———

Friday Evening

DAVID HOSTNER, AKA HOSER, AND THE REST of the
SteamTrails band members arrived to set up at 5 pm sharp.
I had no idea what Steampunk Blues Western would sound like,
but they just kept bringing in more instruments, everything
from guitars and drums to banjos and accordions. Then customers started coming in, some in top hats and Victorian spats,
some in corsets and boots, and still others in vests with jaunty
bowlers perched on their heads. Some had goggles, some had
pocket watches, and a few had body modifications made of brass
gears. If I hadn't been so worried about other things, I might
have found it fascinating.

My own world was too messed up to consider dressing up in
costumes and pretending to be airship pirates or steam-driven
explorers. Despite that, I found myself caught up in the culture,
especially the language, a patter made up of gentlemanly faux-
English and bastardized turn-of-the-century lingo. I could even
appreciate the art of tea-dueling, even if that seemed like a messy
waste of perfectly good cookies. Good thing Reese wasn't there to
see just how many steamer drinks we gave away! I ran the espresso
machine nonstop for most of SteamTrails' two-hour performance,
done in three sets plus two encores, but my heart really wasn't

in it. Sasha called the order down the line, and I just whipped up whatever the customer wanted. It didn't take my mind off my troubles, but it let me zone out of them for a while.

"This is the best!" Max hollered at me over the rush of the milk steamer. "Those guys are awesome!"

They were pretty good, if you liked that kind of thing. They had kind of a blues rock sound with a hint of western lyricism. The more exotic instruments gave them an old-fashioned accent, and from time to time, the instruments went silent for impressive acapella barbershop quartet singing. For a five-dollar cover fee, customers could go up and listen, or they could hang out downstairs for free in what had turned into an impromptu Steampunk party. The party didn't seem to be slowing down even after the band had finished and packed up all their gear.

The band members joined the fans on the dining room floor and mingled, signing copies of their CDs as well as clothing items, cleavage, and just about anything else a Sharpie could be applied to. It was getting crazy.

"We've got to get them out of here," Sasha muttered to me. "It's nine!"

"What do we do? Yell, 'Go Home' at them? You'll start a riot! And some of those steam weapon things look a little dangerous."

"I've been up since five," she moaned. "I'm beat."

Max hopped up on the counter and waved his arms. With his best British accent he called out, "Ladies and Gentlemen! I appreciate that all are enjoying themselves, but the hour draws late. May I kindly suggest that you move this party to Magillies on Main? They're open until two! That's right. You don't have to go home, but you cannot stay here."

There were some grumblings and moanings, but they started to troupe towards the door.

"Nice work, Max."

"Should we call Magillies and warn them?" Twila asked in hushed tones as she pulled out the vacuum to deal with the literal fallout from the tea-dueling.

"Nah. Magillies will love it," I said offhandedly.

"F.Y.N.," Twila stated, "We made over twice what we did with the book signing yesterday."

F.Y.N. For your news, in our menu shorthand. Fyn. "Oh man. I'm an idiot!" I exclaimed. The strange message from Reese that had eluded me all day suddenly snapped into place, the letters becoming crystal clear in my mind. "Do you guys have this? I gotta go?"

Max nodded, "Sure. Everything okay?"

I could only shake my head as I dashed out the door and ran to my office.

REESE'S DIVORCE DECREE WAS STILL SITTING ON TOP of the box where I'd left it after making copies. I scanned through it quickly, then grabbed my laptop and headed for my desk, belatedly remembering that I'd promised Ron I'd drop my laptop at the crime lab. Too bad. If he wanted it, he should have taken it.

I pulled up the message. *I'm fyn. dnot worry abt me. strting Ovr.* I reread the messages, my heart pounding. The messages *had* been written by Reese, I was now sure of it. And it was a code half hashed from the coffee shop menu shorthand.

"Fyn" was shorthand for your news, and "dnot" wasn't a misspelling of don't. It was an abbreviation for a dine-out order, a takeout. She was telling me she had had been taken out, and "worry", the only word not abbreviated, was what she wanted me to do. The capital o in "Ovr" was intended to grab my attention and point to where she'd been taken. Her divorce papers only confirmed my suspicion. *Over It* was the name of the yacht Tivon had bought during their marriage. Tivon had a boat. That was how he'd returned to the United States without triggering port authority. He'd sailed from Costa Rica through Panama and up the west coast. Wherever that boat was, I'd find Reese. An old dog like Tivon didn't have that many tricks, the new boat probably had the same name, or at least a version of it.

Dortman could arrest me for withholding information, and Ron could hate me forever. If it meant finding Reese, then I didn't care. I carefully crafted a message to send back, praying that she would see it. "I'm Sorry Everything Ended."

I SEE. I see you, Reese. I hear you. I'm coming.

The problem was that there were literally dozens of marinas on the east side of San Francisco Bay, most of them up in Alameda.

"This would go faster if you just asked Ron for help." I wasn't sure if I was talking to myself, or just trying to justify what I was thinking. "But then he'd call Dortman and they'd storm the area with an entire squad, and it would be the pharmacy robbery all over. But what if you're right? You can't just go waltzing in and rescue her from Tivon."

I looked at Evrett, but he was still. Hoover was still asleep in his basket. I decided sensibly that I wouldn't go up against anyone. I'd just go check the closest marinas and if I found a boat with the word "over" in the name, I'd call the detectives for back-up. For a second, I was tempted to take Evrett's sword with me. It wasn't original to the suit of armor and didn't have a provenance, so I assumed that he wasn't attached to it the same way he was to, oh say, his head, but the old crusader had done enough for one night. And if I was going to keep stealing his sword for self-defense, I should at least take a fencing class or something.

I PLOTTED OUT THE FASTEST ROUTE TO CHECK OUT the the nearest marinas, changed the batteries in my flashlight, and checked the charge on my phone. I took my antibiotics and some more Tylenol and grabbed some trail mix to snack on while I drove. The salty peanuts were probably the most protein I'd eaten all day, and I wished I'd grabbed my to-go mug and filled it with the rest of Mom's tea. I settled for one of the water bottles I kept behind the seat. 880 was nearly empty at this time of night, and I made good time to Alameda. I figured Tivon had been gone too long to have a membership at any of the private marinas, so I started with the public marina.

I HAD TO PARK IN A PUBLIC PARKING AREA AWAY FROM the docks and when I got there, the gates to the dock ramp were locked. All I could do was walk up and down the waterside trying to read the names of the boats. The marina was well lit, but some of the boats were docked away from me, so I couldn't see their names. All the boats that looked big enough to sail through the Canal and up the coast were completely dark. If I had taken Reese captive, I sure as heck wouldn't turn the lights out on her, no matter how well I had her tied up. Wouldn't turn my back on her, either.

I gave up and walked back to my car, limping a little on my sore leg. The next marina on my list was the Bellina, and from what I knew from looking it up online, it was a little more hoity-toity than the Alameda public marina. I didn't know what kind of security they had, and it was likely that someone wandering around the docks at night would have the cops called on them. I was making contingency plans in my head and paying attention to where I was putting my feet in the shadowy parking lot when an all-too-familiar voice cut through my consciousness.

"So. Want to tell me what we're looking for?" Detective Ron Brittle was leaning on the hood of my pick-up. And he wasn't smiling.

"I'm thinking of buying a yacht when my inheritance comes through?"

"Beep. Wrong answer. Please try again."

"Hoover wanted fresh fish, so I was looking for a fishing charter."

"Kam. Come on. When they told me you'd blown out of the café right after the party, I knew something was up, so I followed you. You can't lie to me," he sighed, "and I'm starting to feel a little disappointed that you're even trying to. Seriously. Just tell me what's going on."

Something that felt a lot like guilt poked me in the gut. I pulled off my military cap and ran a hand through my curls. "So you can arrest Reese?"

"Are you helping her escape? Do you know where she is?"

"I have a hunch. That's all."

"And it's a boat."

"Maybe."

"No more games, Kam."

"No games!" I protested before clarifying. "I mean, *maybe* it's a boat! I think it might be, but I don't know for sure. If I saw it, if I found it, I was going to call you."

"Well, now you don't have to because I'm already here." Ron crossed his arms, and I felt that stab of guilt again.

"Will you tell Dortman?"

"I'm a good cop, Kam. I don't cover up the truth, no matter the circumstances."

"I'm sorry, Ron. That was unfair of me." I took a deep breath and explained what I should have called Ron about before ever leaving my office. "At first, I thought those Facebook messages were a hoax from Tivon, trying to frame Reese. It wasn't until I was working at the café tonight that I realized that the weird misspellings weren't misspellings at all. It was the shorthand code we use for customer tickets in the coffee shop. You know, like nb means no butter, and dnot means dine out. Reese used them as a code, deliberately making the messages look misspelled and uneducated to fool Tivon, using shorthand from the coffee shop. She sent it to me because she knew I would know the code. And that I would know that when Tivon went to Costa Rica, he left behind a yacht named 'Over It.' Reese sold it after the divorce was final. When she said 'starting over', and capitalized the O, I realized she must be referencing the Over It."

"How would he have gotten the yacht back?"

"I don't think he did. Tivon has attachment issues. He can't let go of things. That's why he's been stalking Reese. He got a new boat and named it the same thing, or something very similar."

Ron looked at his watch. "If we wait for morning, we can just call all the marinas . . ."

My response was choked with my own self-castigation. "It already took me too long to figure out those messages. He's had her all day. If we wait until morning that will just give him time to sail out of here with Reese. Or dump her body if she's not . . . not . . ." I couldn't finish the sentence.

"Or maybe she's been in on it the whole time," Ron suggested impassively, demonstrating that he was the true-blue detective investigating all angles. "How do you know she didn't have a change of heart? How do you know she didn't help kill Wyatt?"

I climbed into my pick-up and leaned over to shove the

passenger door open for Ron. "You don't believe that, or you wouldn't be here."

"I don't want to believe that you would lie to me and sneak around behind my back either, but just because I don't believe it, doesn't mean it's not true." Did I mention that one of the things I like about Ron is his blunt honesty? Sometimes, I don't like it all that much.

"You're right. I was afraid you'd shut me down, or not believe me." I glanced across the pickup as he slid into the passenger seat. "I'm sorry. I should have called you."

He didn't reply but gave a small nod "Okay, now that that's all sorted, what's the next marina on your list?"

"Bellina." I checked the GPS map on my phone and pulled out of the parking lot. "Is your car going to be okay there?"

"I'd actually prefer if we were in my car. It's faster." Ron glanced in the mirror to check his car, lonely in the nearly empty parking lot.

"It also looks exactly like an unmarked cop car, which it is. If we don't want to spook Tivon into running the second he sees us . . ."

"I get your point. He's probably seen my car all over this investigation," Ron conceded. "If we find him, if we see anything suspicious at all, I'll call for back-up."

When we arrived at Bellina, we had to park in a small visitor's lot. The marina had a guard post, and someone was on duty. I was glad I hadn't gone alone because Ron flashed his badge to get their attention before he explained what we were looking for. Despite a few shady looks in my direction and at my second-hand, slightly tattered pickup, the guard handed over a list of all the boats docked there.

"There's no Over anything here." Ron handed me the paper to check for myself. He used his phone to pull up Reese's bulletin picture. It was her driver's license photo and, like most ID photos, hardly looked like her. "Have you seen this woman, by any chance?"

The guard shook his head. "Nope. But to tell the truth, she looks like half the people over here."

"You mean Black?" Ron leveled a cold stare at the guard.

"Hell no." The guard reeled back, his expression horrified. "No! I mean, she's a woman! With boobs and hair. We got two kinds of people here. Women with boobs and hair, and men with no boobs and no hair. Nothin' really in between. You try over at the yacht club yet?"

"I thought they were a private club?"

He shrugged, rubbing a hand on the bill of his baseball cap. "Sure, but they have guests from other clubs, and over there, it's all about who you know, not what you sail."

We walked back to my pickup as I considered what the guard said. "Tivon was hot on the music scene in Oakland. He knew all kinds of people, but that was years ago. Do you think he stayed in touch with someone who would loan him their mooring?"

"I think that we're running out of marinas," Ron put on his seatbelt and pulled out his smart-phone. "I'll navigate. You drive."

I held my breath as I put the pick-up in gear and rolled out of the parking lot, but I was worried for nothing. Ron was an excellent navigator, always warning me well before a turn and never confusing his left with his right. I guess was just too used to Jaxine's navigation techniques in which "turn here" meant "turn on that street up there that you can't even see yet", and "take this exit" meant "take the exit we passed a mile back". With Ron, there was none of that. We arrived at the private yacht club, and I pulled up to the fancy gates. It was a vast complex and it took a few minutes to find the visitor parking near the office. "Now what?"

"Why don't you stay in the car?" He flung open the door and climbed out. I watched him head inside the building where he was soon engaged in a lively and somewhat argumentative conversation with the keenly dressed young man behind the desk. It was pretty clear that his badge was less welcome at the private venue. Who knew what kind of rich and famous people had yachts moored here? I imagined that Ron was going to hear a demand for a warrant any second.

I slipped out of the pickup, quietly pressing my door closed behind me and took advantage of the distraction inside the office to vault over the low concrete wall and onto the walkway that led to the boats. Some part of my mind was trying to remember the technical difference between a ship and a boat as I made my way down to the docks and stepped out onto the anti-slip causeway. Anything with *Over* in its name seemed like a tall order as I looked at the fifty or so yachts and cruisers docked at the marina.

Unlike the public marina, there was no easy way to see most of the boats without approaching them. But unlike the public marina, there weren't electronically locked gates everywhere. They assumed that if you had a keycard for the front gate, you were supposed to be here. It was easy to move up and down the rows of boats, bobbing along with the slight rocking of San Francisco Bay. I had no idea just how big of a boat I was looking for, but I assumed that the smaller ones closest to the shore weren't the sort that could sail up from Costa Rica. Also, if Tivon had Reese on that boat, he'd want her as far away from the other boats as he could. Reese's hollering when he'd come to the café had nearly caused me permanent hearing loss. If he was holding her against her will, heaven help his eardrums.

Still, if he was a guest at the marina, he might not have been able to pick a distant berth. He would have been stuck with whatever his friend or acquaintance could loan him. I stood still for a second in indecision, trying to decide which boats to check first. I'd have to be fast because Ron couldn't distract the night clerk forever. Or, the clerk couldn't distract the cop forever. Whichever it was, I didn't have much time. I hurried to the end of a long row of small yachts and started scanning names.

"Whatcha doin'?" The unfamiliar voice came low and soft to my right, and I answered before I turned with my planned lie on my tongue.

"Looking for my boyfriend's boa . . ."

I turned straight into a sucker punch that caught me on my cheekbone and I felt myself falling towards the water. I flung arms out and they arms windmilled helplessly for a second before a savage grip snapped around my scratched and bandaged arm. I heard a small splash off to my right as my phone was flung from my hand. Still reeling from the punch, I kicked weakly as my attacker swung me over his shoulder. I smelled cheap cologne and coconut rum. Tivon. Before I could scream, I was thrown down onto the rubberized matting of a yacht deck. Thankfully, the matting partially cushioned my head as it whacked into the deck. I rolled fast, catching the rail with my hand to pull myself up.

"RON!" I screamed his name as loudly as I could, but over the rippling of water, knocking of boats in their moorings, and distance between us, I couldn't know if he heard me. One scream was all I got. Tivon's hand clapped over my mouth, and I was dragged below deck.

I twisted my head to take in as much of my surroundings as possible as he pushed me down into a chair. To my inexperienced eyes, Tivon's boat was a fairly nice, tidy little yacht. He wrapped electrical tape over my mouth and around my head, effectively stifling anymore screaming, and managed to get my arms behind me and tape them to the chair. I don't stand much of a chance against strong breezes. I had no chance against a grown man, but what the heck, a girl's gotta try, right? I lashed out with both feet, hoping to maybe dislocate his knee or something, but he hopped back. "I don't know how you found us, but you better shut it."

Us. Was Reese really with him? As he went back above, I twisted and turned, hopping the small chair around. It was an aluminum deck chair with fabric weave forming the seat and back. I noted that the rest of the furnishing in the cabin was built-in fiberglass, with nothing loose to shift or fall in rough seas. Through the shadows, I could see through to the small bedroom. Sprawled on the bed as though she'd been tossed there, Reese looked like she was sleeping, her black braid trailing loose strands over the side of the bed. Oh, please let her be sleeping. Not dead. She couldn't be dead. I tried to say her name, but through the tape it came out, "Meeep!"

There was a pair of thuds from above deck and then a sudden hum as the boat's engines started up. Meep for real! He was leaving with us both and I had the sinking feeling, no pun intended, that the second we were away from shore, my deck chair and I would be going overboard. Possibly Reese, too, if she was still alive. But that also meant I had a window of opportunity. Tivon would need all of his attention to guide the boat out of the marina. He wouldn't have time to come and check on me.

I squirmed in the chair, testing the tape's strength. Electrical tape isn't like duct tape. Put duct tape on something and it stays put, sticky and strappy. Duct tape is what you tied hostages with, not electrical tape. Electrical tape stretches and bends. Maybe I could work it loose. Maybe if I was lucky I could twist . . . My right arm slid free with a raw bite of pain, and I felt my bandage pull away. What? The moron had not only tied me up with electrical tape, but he'd wrapped it around my gauze covered arm! The paper tape holding the gauze had come free and my arm had slipped right out. This was only my third kidnapping ever, but so far, Tivon just wasn't living up to standards.

With one arm free, it took me only seconds to get the rest of the tape off. *Sorry, chair.* It would have to go to the bottom of the Bay without me. I could feel the sway of the boat shift and knew that we were turning out of the dock. I hadn't seen what berth we were in, so I didn't know how far it was to the marina opening, but once he was out of the marina, our chances diminished exponentially the further we went out into the bay. I could only hope that Ron was watching and had called the Coast Guard patrol. "Reese?" I whispered her name as I reached the side of the bed. "Reese, wake up! It's Kami."

She was breathing, slowly and steadily, but she showed no signs of stirring. I reached out and touched her shoulder. "Please wake up, Reese!" She was warm, despite the chill air off the Bay, but the front of her shirt was damp, almost as if she was sweat soaked. Or had spilled something on herself. Or, I realized a little too slowly, someone had spilled something on her. Because he forced her to drink . . . I sniffed the stain on her shirt, but let's face it, I'm no chemist, and all I could smell on Reese's clothes was the familiar but faint scent of fresh-ground dark roast. I had to grab the edge of the bunk as the boat rocked into a hard right turn out of the berthing row. We were now in the main channel out of the marina. I was out of time.

I scrambled for my phone before remembering that it had been in my hand when Tivon surprised me. A light-speed search didn't turn up Reese's phone. Tivon must have taken it. It was probably with mine at the bottom of the marina, our little screens glowing blue text-icons at each other through the muddy water. The realization that there was no rescue coming spurred me into a plan. I was going to have to surprise him. I fantasized about pushing him overboard, but dismissed the idea immediately. With Reese, I might have stood a chance of overpowering Tivon, but without her help, I had to either get us both off the boat, or somehow alert Ron or the Coast Guard or maybe some other boats. Or someone. Anyone. A friendly porpoise, even!

Weapon. I needed a weapon. I started frantically searching drawers and cupboards as quietly as I could, trying to recall everything Grandpa Dan had taught me about boats and sailing. There was a lot of useless *pass on the port side, blow the horn coming into the channel, always put the lid back on the bait bucket* kind of stuff that might be good in a nautical emergency but not very useful in a kidnapping situation. Then I remembered him showing me the emergency kit and how to use the flare gun. All boats had to carry flare guns, floatation devices, and life-rafts.

Emergency kits were usually kept in the pilothouse, and I was pretty sure, as I felt the boat pick up speed, that's where Tivon was. I found rope, a kitchen knife, a chunk of stainless steel piping . . . was I playing Clue? The movement of the boat straightened out and I heard the engine gaining power. He was in the straight, headed for the open bay. "Reese! Please!" I shook her, probably a little harder than was warranted. After a second's hesitation, I took a bigger risk than letting Tivon throw me in the Bay—because at least in the Bay I had a small chance of survival—and smacked her lightly on the cheek. "Wake up!"

No luck. I was on my own.

I slipped out of the cabin, keeping low, which I guess isn't too hard when you're in the five-feet-tall category. Tivon was in the pilothouse, his back to me as he concentrated on driving between the lights of the navigation buoys. The wind had picked up, sweeping across the Bay and my light denim jacket was no match. I was trembling as I crept around the edge of the cabin. I cast my eyes back over the marina looking for some source of rescue, but we were no longer at an angle that could be seen from the main building, and I didn't see Ron running down the docks to rescue me.

I spotted the emergency kit strapped to the cabin wall and crept towards it. My fingers closed around the braces and I unsnapped them one by one, each click resounding through my cautious bones. Please don't let him hear. Please don't let him hear. The chant was silent but fervent. I didn't know who I was praying to, but whoever it was, I hoped they were listening.

The emergency flare gun kit had both handheld and pistol flares. Next time I saw Grandpa Dan, I owed him a huge hug and an ice cream cone. My plan crystallized in my mind, but I would have to move fast. The fired flares would make noise and shine brightly. They would catch attention, but I had no doubt that the second I fired it, Tivon would be on me. With fingers that felt like they were filled with jelly, I snapped a flare into the gun. Then I crept to the back of the boat, as close to the slowly receding marina and as far from Tivon as I could get. A last glance back at the cabin showed Tivon with his back to me, still focused on sailing. I held my breath, shut my eyes, pointed straight up, and pulled the trigger. CRACK! Bright orange glare lit the night!

It seemed to take forever to fumble the next flare into the gun and fire it. My hands were slick with sweat and my arms felt heavier than a full sack of French roast. With two flares glowing brightly over the yacht, I snapped the cap on one of the handheld smoke flares and pointed it in Tivon's direction. Orange smoke poured out, obscuring my view of the cabin, but hasty footsteps sounded over the crackling of the flare. Tivon's face appeared through the smoke, and there was no mistaking that he was pissed off.

I kept the handheld flare in my left hand, and with the right, aimed the flare gun at his chest. "Back off! Turn the boat around!"

You know those movies where the hero gets the gun, takes control of the situation, and the bad guy jumps overboard? If they ever turn my life into a movie, it won't be that kind of movie. Tivon rushed me like a linebacker and slammed me to the deck. The flare gun flew from my hand, slid across the deck and flipped over the edge into the water. I tried to thrust the smoke flare at him. If I couldn't burn him, I hoped the smoke would be enough to drive him off me, but he was faster and stronger and grabbed my wrist, holding the flare at bay.

His grip was ice cold and I was afraid my wrist would snap as he pinned it to the deck. With my right hand, I threw wild punches, hitting him in the ribs, the chest, and the face, anywhere I could connect. Orange sulfur smoke billowed around us, choking and blinding me, my lungs gasping for clean air. Then there was sudden distance between us. For a brilliant, sunset-glare-soaked second, I thought Tivon was backing off.

Then I realized I was falling.

San Francisco Bay runs between 50 and 60 degrees Fahrenheit, depending on season, and that grey-black water slapped me on the back with the power of a drenching ice-storm. I went under, my breath stalling painfully in my chest as I thrashed back to the surface. My face broke the surface and I immediately sucked in rank salty air. I hadn't been in the water in over a year, not since I quit surfing. But I was always a strong swimmer. Grandpa Dan's constant hounding about water safety rescued me for the second time that night. *Grab air whenever you can surface, don't leave oxygen to chance. Lighten your load if you can.* I kicked off my shoes and stripped off my jacket as I broke the surface, relying on my natural buoyance to help keep my head above water. *Look for safety. Swim to the nearest point of security.*

Tivon's yacht was speeding away, and I was being tossed in its wake like a piece of flotsam. Flotsam. That's what I was. And if I didn't get out of this water, I was going to be hypothermic drowning flotsam. The nearest point was the end of the marina pier, maybe thirty yards away, twenty if I was lucky. I gulped in more air and forced my frozen arms to paddle and legs to kick. I was already shivering, and I wasn't exactly in top form. The San Francisco Bay may look placid on still nights, but from inside, it was rolling and splashing, each ripple smacking me in the face as I struggled for the dock. I managed another deep breath and screamed, "Ron! Help!"

I had no idea where he was or if he could hear me, and the entire time, Tivon was getting further and further away. And he had Reese. Reese needed me. That thought alone propelled me forward, kicking harder than ever. I reached the end of the boat dock but I couldn't see a drop ladder anywhere. My shaking hands caught the edge of the dock, and I heaved as hard as I could, but the wood was slick and I went back in. Damn. "Help!" I reached again and this time my fingers found a crevice between the planks. My fingers squished into what was probably a build-up of seagull poop, and it took all my will to keep them there, digging and pulling with a fierce down-kick to propel my upper half out of the water and onto the dock. I was squirming the rest of me out of the water when I heard footsteps.

"Kami!" Ron was followed closely by the front desk guy. He grabbed my wrists and pulled me the rest of the way onto the dock. "What the hell?"

"Tivon! That boat! He's got Reese. She's unconscious. Drugged or something. I couldn't get her!" I was sprawled on the deck, babbling like an idiot, and every muscle was starting to shiver. "I couldn't get her to wake up and Tivon threw me overboard."

"I told you to stay in the car." But Ron had his phone out and so did the marina guy. He reached a hand down and helped me to my feet. Instead of rewarding the favor, I dripped water on his shoes.

"Oh. I thought you meant that as a suggestion." I tried to smile but my teeth were chattering. "As in, why don't I stay in the car? As opposed to, you know, not staying in the car . . ."

Ron shot me a glare but he was already on the phone with dispatch, notifying the Coast Guard. I kept my gaze focused on the departing boat, which suddenly went dark. "Where did it go?"

If it had sunk, if Tivon in his panic had crashed the boat . . .

"He's turned off the running lights." The marina guy said helpfully. "He's trying to evade detection."

"Oh, god." I glanced at Ron, "What if he throws Reese over?"

The marina guy instantly jumped into action, pointing us to

the end of the dock row. "The marina boat can outrun his, and it's sturdier."

Ron looked about to argue. He was out of his jurisdiction and had already notified the Coast Guard, but when our eyes met, I knew he was thinking what I was thinking. If Tivon threw Reese overboard, unconscious as she was, she would go under and never come back up. "Let's go."

Teeth chattering, soaked to the bone, I staggered after them and helped cast off the lines on the marina boat, a gunmetal silver civilian version of a Coast Guard emergency cutter with rescue-netting and tow rigs for helping stranded boats. Ron pointed at me. "You go back to the car, turn on the heater, and get warm."

I clambered onboard.

"I said . . ."

"I'm cold. Not deaf." I glared at him and the marina guy. The marina guy opened a supply chest and handed me a plastic envelope with an emergency blanket and poncho in it. Smart man.

"Get into the cockpit out of the wind," he advised as he started the engines. That was the best advice I'd heard all evening.

Hang on, Reese. We're coming.

The marina guy was an excellent pilot, and he went full throttle as soon as he was clear of the marina gateway. Ron turned on the monstrous spotlight on the helm and was scanning the water as we raced after Tivon's boat. I was still shivering, but the poncho and blanket helped. I didn't even want to think about what the filthy bay water was doing to the deep scratches in my arm and the bite on my leg. Blech. I was going to end up with some flesh-eating disease along with rabies.

The marina boat was wide and low, fast across the water. Time seemed to drag to a standstill, and even though I could hear the wind whipping against the polycarbonate windows of the cockpit, and see the waves churned up by our passing hull, it felt as though we were creeping on the black water. I refused to sit, instead clinging to the cockpit rail and staring out over the bay, watching the bright light sweep smoothly back and forth across the chopping water.

The Coast Guard made radio contact. They were coming out of Alameda Harbor, at least ten minutes behind us, and warned us not to make contact with the other vessel until they had arrived. "We're looking for a civilian that may be in the water," the marina guy told them coolly, but his eyes were focused on the dark shape ahead of us in the water, moving steadily towards San Francisco.

Setting down the radio handpiece, he shook his head angrily. "I knew that guy was trouble. I knew it."

"Tivon? How?"

"He was in Rubin Case's dock. Rubin said it was cool, that they were old friends, but he seemed reluctant. I shoulda known it was bad news. The guy kept making excuses about filing his registration. The only reason we didn't throw him out was that my dad is old friends with Rubin, and didn't want to make waves. Shoulda called the cops the first day he didn't file."

"I'm Kami, by the way."

"Yeah, I figured that was your name after the cop was yelling it."

"He was?" I must have missed that while I was busy almost drowning.

"Yeah. He was kind of pissed you didn't stay in the car." The guy gave me a lopsided smile. "He won't admit it, but he's definitely more worried than mad." He shifted sideways and offered me a handshake. "I'm Dreyven Lassen. My dad owns the marina. You can call me Drey."

"Nice to meet you, Drey." I shook his hand, surprised at how warm it was. Or maybe that was just how cold my hands were. "Thanks for your help in all this."

"So this guy kidnapped someone?"

"Yeah. He's got my friend on that boat, Reese Calhoun." And we were going to get her back. If I had to jump overboard and swim to that damn boat myself, we were going to get her back!

"Hopefully the Coast Guard can cut them off."

"I don't see how. Your boat is as fast as theirs, and they're behind us!"

Drey pointed up in the air, and I became aware of a slow, steady thrumming in the distance that swiftly became a roaring, echoing thudthudthud racing closer.

"That's how." Drey fired me a sideways grin, "The Guard doesn't mess around."

Blinking lights soared towards us from Angel Island and the Coast Guard helicopter dropped low to the water and hovered in front of us. Suddenly, the bay lit up in a giant pool of light, and directly in the center of that glowing white ripple was the *Over It*. And directly behind it, floating in the water, was something dark and brown.

Reese. Without hesitation, I threw off the blanket and poncho and dove straight from the prow of the marina boat. It occurred to me as I hit the ice-cold water for the second time that night that I was out of my mind, but I didn't care. I swam hard and fast and straight, and stronger than I ever had in any of Grandpa Dan's rescue drills. Somewhere behind me, Ron was shouting. And somewhere ahead of me, Tivon was yelling. I broke my gaze from the spot where I'd seen Reese, and glanced to the *Over It*. Tivon was screaming into the sky, and pointing a gun straight up at the helicopter. Did he think he was playing *Grand Theft Auto*?

I kept swimming, and I could hear the marina boat coming closer, moving alongside, but not so close as to catch me in their wake. I reached Reese, and nearly cried with relief when I found her face up and conscious. She was stretched out, bobbing on the churning water, her arms circling weakly, barely keeping her face above water. I scooped an arm around her chest and brought my body up under hers, supporting her weight as I back-treaded towards the marina boat.

Wake-waves splashed over our faces and for a second, Reese struggled in my arms and nearly pulled us both down. "Hold on, Reese! Hold on! Relax and let me carry you. Breathe when your mouth is clear." I chanted the advice Grandpa Dan had drilled into me so many times as I felt my own strength failing.

Then, on the back-stroke, my outstretched hand hit something solid and I realized it was a life buoy. I dragged Reese's arms to it, ducking under the towline, and that's when gunshots split the night. That moron Tivon was shooting at the heli . . . Styrofoam splintered across my face and the life-buoy jerked out of my numb, slick grasp! No. He was shooting at us.

Reese was totally out of it, gasping for air, her eyes wild. The spotlights of both the marina boat and the helicopter were directly on us, making us prime targets. I looped both of Reese's arms around the buoy and screamed, "Hold on! Don't let go!" as I waved to the rescue boat. I felt her being pulled out of my arms as they reeled her in. Another shot rang out and cut the water near me, followed by two more in sharp succession and I knew I was spotlighted, my yellow-blonde hair bobbing like a beacon right within shooting range. A clear target for Tivon's rage. I heard Ron yell, "Cut the lights! Cut the lights!"

I didn't think. I dove deep. Black ink water, black ink world. I was going to run out of air. I was going to freeze. I was going to . . . I broke the surface, sucked deep, and dove again.

When I came up again, I was only feet from the silver wall of the marina rescue boat and the spotlight was off. My mouth and nose were full of salt water, and I spluttered as I reached up and a strong hand wrapped around mine. Most days, I regret weighing approximately the same as a toothpick, but as Ron easily hauled me over the boat rail, I was thrilled.

"Reese! Where's Reese? Is she shot?"

"Coast Guard has her. The EMTs are taking care of her." Ron's tone told me that he didn't know any more than that. "Are you hit?"

"I don't think so. Fffreezzing thtthough."

Ron guided me into the cockpit and wrapped me back up in the poncho. The radio was blowing up with chatter, but I was shivering too much to listen. Now that I was out of it, the water seemed warmer than the breeze-tossed night air.

"Where's Tivon?"

Ron gestured, and I realized for the first time that his gun was in his hand. His lips were set in a grimace, and his usually bright eyes were dark and shadowed. "He's down. The Coast Guard is dropping a man to him now."

I glanced back over the black water, the helicopter's spotlight blistering to life once more. It was about a hundred yards between our boat and the *Over It*. A hundred yards on bouncing water. With a handgun. That was a hell of a shot. I glanced at the service weapon in Ron's hand, and then back at Ron's face. "You did that?"

"I didn't have a choice." His voice sounded empty and drained over the whipping East Bay winds.

CHAPTER 16

———— ❧ ————

Saturday Morning

IT TURNED OUT RON DIDN'T KILL TIVON, just wounded him. Good for Tivon, but bad for Ron. Turns out that you aren't supposed to shoot people outside of your jurisdiction. A small, wiry Alameda detective with a grudge against San Amoro PD stormed my sectioned-off cot in the ER and quizzed me for over an hour while the ER nurses struggled to get my body temperature regulated.

"I was in the water, being shot at. I didn't see much of anything, but if Detective Brittle used his weapon, it was to save lives." The tenth or eleventh time I repeated the words, with varying amounts of shivering and teeth-chattering, I finally resorted to asking one of the nurse's to call my lawyer.

I would have called him myself, but my phone was somewhere in the silty water under the marina. Only after Reginald Burroughs and Detective Dortman arrived and started mediating, getting the Coast Guard helicopter captain involved, did the Alameda detective start to believe me. Grudgingly, he had to agree that it sounded like a justifiable use of force. Finally, with the detective's demands sated and my body temperature riding at a low but safe 98.1, I was officially released by both the hospital and the cops, and allowed to go see Reese.

"I don't remember anything." For someone who had been kidnapped, drugged, and thrown in the Bay, Reese looked pretty darn good. Well, as good as one can look in a pale blue checker-print hospital gown. "You told me to go to the courthouse, and I got in the van to go. I was looking over the papers you gave me while the van warmed up, and that's all I remember."

"That's not surprising." Detective Dortman said. The Alameda detective remained silent, apparently knowing better than to mess with the Doberman. "Lab results says the bottle of sports drink on the van's dashboard was laced with Rohypnol and propofol."

"She always keeps drinks in the van," I confirmed. "She forgets to eat and drink and if no one reminds her."

"I drank it . . ." she muttered. "I thought it tasted stale . . ."

The Alameda detective rubbed his eyes. "So you were drugged, and this Tivon Shuman took you to his boat?"

"I can't believe Tivon did this. I mean, he's always been a little crazy, but I thought he was gone. Out of my life." Reese sighed and nestled deeper under the thin institutional blanket, careful to keep her IV'd arm clear.

The Alameda detective suggested that I wait outside, but there was no way I was moving an inch from Reese's side. Dortman didn't bother to suggest anything other than warning his counterpart unless they arrested me and hauled me away, I wasn't going to leave.

"She's a terrier, Alan. She won't budge." Dortman gave one of his patented hard-nose stares. "You can stay, but no interruptions, understood?"

I pulled my fingers over my lips in a zipper motion, then met his stare with a smile of gratitude. He returned it with a grudging half-smile, before turning his full attention to Reese. For half an hour, Reggie and the detectives yammered and coaxed and worked out the whole story. Reese relayed how she'd managed to wake up enough at one point to use her phone to message me in code. "I knew you'd get it."

I was ashamed to tell her how long it took me to figure it out.

"What do you know about the murder of Wyatt Halden?" Dortman asked.

Reese stared at him. "I'm sorry. I thought you just said Wyatt Halden was murdered?"

"You're telling me you don't know anything about it?"

"Detective," Reggie interrupted. "My client is invoking her right to remain silent at this time. She's in no condition to answer your questions. After she's released from the hospital and declared fit, we'll come in for a polygraph, okay?"

"And shouldn't Ron be here if you're going to ask about that? I mean, you both have the case, right?" I looked around. "Where is Ron, anyway?"

"He's with his union re . . ." The Alameda detective's words were cut off by the sudden shouting down the hall.

"Stop him!"

"Someone call security!"

"How is he even out of bed?"

"*Tareesa!* Tareesa, baby! I love you, *baby!*"

That last line was punctuated by a slam as the gown-clad, bandage-wrapped, crazy-eyed, wild-haired Tivon banged through the doorway from Critical Care and into the ER. "Where are you, baby?" He continued screaming her name as he ran down the hallway.

The Alameda detective moved to block him, and Reginald stepped back to block Reese from view.

"Baby! I just want you back. Say you love me!" His gown fell open and I buried my face in my hands to keep from giggling as the obviously pain-killer-happy, bare-arsed Tivon threw himself into the detective, eager to get to Reese. He had white gauze bandages wrapped around his upper chest and shoulder, starkly contrasting his dark skin, and he looked terrible. He'd ripped his IV out and blood trickled down his arm. He pleaded wildly as he struggled to get past the detective. "Just say you love me! I did it all for you, baby!"

Reese held up both hands, and gently pushed Reginald aside. Slowly, she pushed herself upright on the bed, gesturing for the others to be quiet. "Did what, Tivon? What did you do for me?"

The detective was still trying to wrestle him down to the floor. I was partly hopeful that he would taser him, but considering that

Tivon'd already been shot that night, it was probably better that he didn't. Dortman was standing close by but not interfering. His expression said he was enjoying the other detective's predicament a little too much.

"Everything! I rescued you!" Tears welled in his eyes. "I rescued your business. And this is how repay me?"

"You kidnapped me and threw me in the bay, honey." Reese's voice was quiet, low, and surprisingly considerate. I didn't know if the roofies were still working, or if she was just being uber polite in front of the cops. Nurses were starting to crowd in the doorway, one of them carrying a syringe, presumably full of sedative.

"Nooo . . . you . . I love you!" Tivon's eyes welled with tears even as he tried to squirm free of the detective. "I can't live without you!"

I couldn't help it. I started giggling. It was better than watching World Wrestling. The cop and the fugitive were scrabbling around on the floor, the detective trying to hold on to Tivon's arms, and Tivon's bare butt waving around as he fought to get free. You know that swallowing, gulping, hysterical giggling that happens when you know you shouldn't be laughing? I clamped both hands over my mouth. From Dortman's grin and his lack of interest in helping at all, I could only guess he was as amused as I was. I only managed to quell myself somewhat when I realized Ron was pushing through the crowd of hospital staff in the doorway. He was having a hard time getting through, and in the meantime, the situation on the floor was bordering on kinky soft porn. Reggie finally reached down and grabbed the detective, pulling him off Tivon, and then pinned Tivon with a foot in the back.

"Let 'im up, Reggie." Reese insisted, and slowly Reggie lifted his foot. She rolled her eyes, and I'd never been so happy to see her trademark smirk. "A man ain't got no dignity, rollin' around on the floor like an animal."

Tivon started to crawl to his knees, but it was obvious that he couldn't put any weight on his left arm. Reggie politely reached down, helped him up, and then propped him against the wall like a lopsided umbrella. Tivon lurched unsteadily towards Reese but

Dortman's arm snapped out and blocked him. There he stood, like a racehorse in a stall, leaning as close to Reese as he could get.

"Tivon? What the hell do you want from me?" Her tone said he was getting nothing, except possibly a punch in the teeth and a long stint in jail.

"Just want you to love me, baby. I love you. Just want you back is all." He paused, gulping for a second. "I did everything for you, Tareesa. Just for you."

"Uh huh." Reese had a look in her eyes, one I hadn't seen before, devious and cunning. Her gaze met Ron's over the crowd, and he slipped into the room behind Tivon. Her voice turned honey sweet as she met Tivon's gaze. "Okay, honey. Why don't you tell me just what all you've done for me lately?"

"Everything." Tivon looked a little bit deflated now that the adrenaline burst of energy had started to fade. His wild eyes glazed with pain. "I saw you workin' so hard in that dump, and I knew, with the right partners, I could give you so much more."

"The right partners?"

"We opened that new place, and I thought, once it was going, we could get rid of the Haldens and it'd just be you and me like the old days. Thomas'd be a silent partner, we wouldn't have to worry about him."

"You're the other half of Coffee Imports, Limited. You backed the opening of Café Fantastique." I tried to keep my tone even to not interrupt his spiel. It didn't matter. He didn't even hear me.

Reese's tone turned saccharine sweet. "You opened a new restaurant just for me?"

"Uh huh," he bobbed his head like a toddler who had just buttered his own toast. "I knew you wouldn't just leave your dump, though. You needed to know we were better, we were gonna be fantastic."

"And how were you going to do that, hon?" Reese strung him along, the detectives, lawyer, and a rather confused syringe-toting RN listening closely.

"I made those papers and put 'em everywhere. Silly stuff. Get people to think your shop was tryin' too hard." he stammered.

"I didn't know it was illegal to put that kinda stuff on cars now, though. We used to do that all the time back in the day."

"You made those *cute* fliers with the monkey on them?" Reese's fake appreciation was straining even my credulity, but the idiot seemed to be eating it up.

I glanced towards Ron. Was this kind of confession even legal? He gave me half-nod, so I had to guess that he'd Mirandized Tivon already. Even if they had, given his current state he could probably claim duress later, but there were an awful lot of eyewitnesses here.

"What else did you do?" Reese asked.

"I thought we'd do better," Tivon seemed to be melting into the wall, his good shoulder braced against the hand-sanitizer dispenser. His dilated eyes were focused on Reese's face with hungry desperation. "I needed to show we were successful, makin' lots of dough, more than you could earn at that old place. I did stuff at night to help us open sooner."

"And when that didn't . . ." Dortman shut up abruptly when Ron dug his elbow into his partner's side.

"But that didn't work, did it?" Reese asked with penultimate calm, and I realized she and Ron were playing a game of good cop, better cop, and letting Dortman and the Alameda detective play the bad and worse cops. Nice. I settled back on the stool and just watched.

"They thought it was haunted! Thought it had a ghost! Hilf'nlarious!" Tivon gave a high-pitched squeak of laughter before continuing, "I didn't mean that to happen, but it was funny, so I kept messin' with 'em. I thought once we were open and makin' money . . . but that didn't happen."

"What did happen, babe?" Reese asked softly, her voice low.

"We lost money. The big grand opening din't even break even. That idiot Wyatt was a screwup."

He was not! I wanted to scream, but held my tongue.

"He was always going on about budget this, budget that. Always waving those stupid spreadsheets around. Always complaining there was too much to do and we couldn't hire help, but every time I look around, he's on the computer or the phone. Stupid kid was a waste of space. Didn't want to pay for a full-page ad in the Tribune or get any radio advertising. All he got was the front page of the local rag. I knew needed to do somethin', get live music, hire a DJ, maybe get someone from the Giants or the Warriors. That kid said we couldn't afford it, kept talkin' about facetogram or tickertalk or somethin', whatever that is. I put my foot down, told him flat out I was the best club promoter in Oakland, I know how to advertise," Tivon's lips twisted in an ugly grimace. "You wanna know? You wanna know what he said to me?"

"What did he say, Tivon?" Reese encouraged, ever so calmly.

"He said *get outta my face*. Called me a washed-up has-been. A has-been!" The words practically spit from Tivon's mouth. "I couldn't let that stand. Couldn't let that kid ruin everything."

"No." Reese's voice was distant, and though she was making the effort to sound warm and inviting, repulsion flashed in her eyes. I reached out and squeezed her non-IV'd hand. "No, of course you couldn't," she continued. "And you did something about it? For me?"

"The gun was still up there. After all these years, it was right there where I left it. What was I s'posed to do? It was so easy." Tivon didn't even seem to know what he was saying. "Wyatt bent down to open the safe at the end of the day, and boom, there it was. All done. Just like back then."

Reese's eyes were dark, so dark, and the small hospital room was very still, despite the large number of people crowding around. Her tone was cool, cajoling. "Just like back when, Tivon?"

"Back when I wanted to marry you and you tol' me no rat-assed street boy was ever gonna marry you. So I got the money, didn't I? I set us up real good!"

"The drugstore robbery." She whispered the words, but Tivon was too lost in the past to acknowledge her.

"I took all those drugs and sold 'em, and the money, too. Didn't matter what was in the safe. We timed it so the tills hadn't been emptied from the days-take yet. I told you I'd do anything for you, anything . . . and without JJ and that moron Ruben takin' their share, it was all mine. It was ours! I did it all for you."

"I know you did, Tivon . . . I know you did." Reese collapsed back into the bed, her eyes blinking wearily. Ron stepped forward and nodded knowingly. They had everything they needed. Reese took a deep, shuddering breath. "Detectives? Please get this piece of shit out of my room and flush it away somewhere."

Ron and Dortman were only too happy to follow those directions, and the Alameda detective tagged along after them. The next moment, Reese's sister Jodi arrived, and we filled her in bit-by-bit. Eventually, Reggie reached over and touched my shoulder, "It's nearly dawn. Let's get you home."

I promised Reese that I'd see her tomorrow and let Reggie steer me down to the elevator and out to his car.

"How are you holding up?" he asked as he drove down 580 towards San Amoro, his beautiful, sleek Tesla barely making a hum as it rolled.

"I'm so tired I don't even know." I was carrying my wet clothes and shoes in a plastic bag that the hospital gave me. They'd also given me a T-shirt and sweatpants that said Oakland General on them, and a pair of flip-flops. But the sweatpants were long enough that I needed to roll them up, and the t-shirt was so big it seemed likely to swallow me whole. I curled up feeling warm and dry for the first time all night, and half-dozed until we pulled up in front of my office.

"Uh oh." The low warning in Reggie's voice shook me awake. "Looks like you've got trouble, kiddo."

Have I mentioned that I love it when Reggie calls me kiddo? Anyone else, I'd find it insulting, but when he does it, I feel safe and protected. But trouble didn't sound good, no matter what affectionate moniker came after it. I opened my eyes and saw a familiar silver BMW sitting in front of my office in the grey-shadowed dawn. As I got out of Reggie's car, Jack Austin stepped out of his.

Reggie got out but stayed on the driver's side, leaning casually on the roof of his car.

"Lawyer bringing you home before sunrise?" Jack said jauntily. "That doesn't look good."

"Neither does you waiting for me." I didn't mean to make it sound like a complaint. No one had waited up for me in a very long time.

"Kenny called me."

My heart stopped. My world stopped. Everything froze in place, and I could see everything suddenly in stark black and white relief. Jack's silver and chrome BMW, the wave of sandy blond hair across Jack's forehead, the shadow of the turret-like corner of my building outlined against the grey sky. "Kenny called you? Dad . . ."

"He said he couldn't reach you." Jack hesitated, waiting for me to explain why, but I couldn't. I just shook my head. My phone was gone, drowned in the bay. If I told Jack that, I'd have to explain what happened, and then he'd have questions. I couldn't deal with that right now. Jack continued softly, his bright blue eyes focusing on my face. "He wanted me to find you and tell you that your dad . . ."

My ears were ringing. If he said 'dead' . . . if he said 'dead' . . . "*Dad what,* Jack?"

"Was in a minor mudslide and he and his team are okay. They lost the Land Rover and all their gear, but Kenny and Dr. Ling found them on the trail. They'll all be safe and sound at the research station in . . ." Jack consulted his watch, mentally calculating time differences. "An hour or so, I think."

"You could have led with *safe*!" I gasped. Don't ask me what I was thinking because I don't think I had a single coherent thought when I threw myself into Jack's arms and hugged him as hard as I could, clinging to the best news I'd had in days.

Jack hugged me back.

And then he kissed me, and five years and a thousand heartbreaks were in that kiss.

My confusion around my feelings for Jack Austin was as much a part of me as breathing, but I didn't need it to make sense. I kissed him back.

CHAPTER 17

The Next Week

Aweek later, I was seated in the cafe with Reese in the quiet afternoon lull between the lunch crowd and the after-work crowd. "How are you feeling now, Reese?"

She'd taken a week off, but even when she was supposed to be on vacation, we could barely keep her out of the shop. Her dark eyes were guarded as she took in the coffee shop that she'd built into a successful business. "Guilty, to tell the truth. In the end, I owe this shop and everything, really, to that moron and the drugstore robbery. That poor family lost their son, their business, everything. I asked Reggie to try to find them. I want to apologize, make some kind of amends if I can."

"It isn't your fault, Reese. You didn't know."

"I should have seen it. I just didn't want to." Reese sighed. "I knew he was mixed up with some bad kids. I wanted to be the cool girl on the block, wanted to show I could run with the big dogs. I was just a stupid kid back then. He told me he brokered a big record deal for some friends, and I just believed him. I never asked."

"Like you said, you were kids."

"I was then. I should have known things never added up. I should have seen everything coming, the affair, the running away . . . all of it." She sighed and shook her head.

"Coulda, woulda, shoulda . . ." I quipped at her, teasing. "Someone told me that once. I can't remember who. Someone I worked for or something. Right here at this very table, I think."

She finally let out a small chuckle. "Yeah, okay." Reese took another look around the coffee shop and stretched her hands, cracking her knuckles. "What about you? How are you doing? D.B. said you dived into the bay in the middle of the night to save me. That's crazy."

"I'm crazy," I agreed. It seemed like a dream now, or a nightmare. "I'm doing okay. Nicky gets back from Hawaii tomorrow, and my dad is flying home with Kenny for a long visit."

"And Jack?"

"What about Jack? He's my accountant." I feigned innocence, but Reese's front window looked straight into my office, where Jack had been visiting almost every day. We'd taken walks in the park, dined at our favorite restaurant. We'd talked. A lot.

"Oh, I dunno. Just seems like you two have had a lot of *accounting* going on."

I couldn't help it. I was grinning, and probably looked like an idiot. "Yeah, lots of uh, you know, paperwork to take care of."

"Uh huh, I can tell." Reese grinned back. Then she brushed her hands together, her gaze thoughtful. "I can't believe how hard you all worked for me last week. You know, I was thinking . . ."

"Uh oh. What?"

"Well, Tivon was right that this place is getting a little shabby, a little aged. And there's a brand new, fully equipped, newly vacant café just down the street. Maybe it's time for a change of venue. Everything down there is all clean and new and shiny and . . ."

"Haunted," I interrupted.

"That was just Tivon screwin' around. He said so."

"No, Reese," I held up both palms to stall her. "You can ask Brittle and Dortman if you don't believe me. It's haunted."

"Really?"

"Really." I nodded.

Her eyes travelled around the dining room, as if seeing it for the first time. "Well, maybe we just need a new coat of paint. New chairs, too."

"Way more than we need a ghost," I agreed. Just then, I looked out the window in time to see Prue's car pull up and Irvin get out on the passenger side. He waved at me through the window, gesturing for me to come out.

"That guy is so weird." Reese stood up and headed back to work. I could hear her muttering as she walked away. "He scrapes the frosting off his carrot cake. Who does that?"

She was never going to let that go, was she? I stepped out onto the sidewalk just in time to see Prue come around the back of her car. She was holding one end of a leash. Slowly, the far end of the leash appeared from behind the tire of her car, attached to a limping, harness-wearing, wide-eyed opossum. I backed away. "Are you kidding me? I thought Irvin was joking when he said you wanted to adopt it! Just keep it away from me!"

Prue laughed. "Demon wanted to apologize in person. Here, he brought you this." She handed me a small bakery box."

"You're calling him Demon?"

"Yeah, he's a good little demon, aren't you?" She leaned down and scratched the top of his head. He made a little gaspy sound and rubbed his face on her hand. "That means he's happy."

"Prue . . ." I didn't quite know what to say. I opened the bakery box. It was from Morri's wife's cookie shop and was full of snickerdoodles that I knew were made with real butter. "Thanks for the cookies."

"Oh, you're welcome. We just wanted to say thank you and let you know that he has a clean bill of health. No rabies or anything else. His bad foot means that he's crippled for life, though. I couldn't bear the thought of having him put down or living the rest of his life in a tiny cage."

When she put it that way, I couldn't either. I took a cookie from the box and knelt down. "Hi, Demon. Wanna cookie?"

He watched me side-eyed for a moment, then gingerly took the cookie out of my hand and started munching on it, spraying crumbs everywhere. I stood back up and stepped away. "I guess that means we're friends?"

"It looks like it," Irvin said proudly. "He's a good demon."

"And your cats are okay with having him around?"

"I'm building him a big cage in the backyard with lots of room to play and roam. He's staying in the garage until it's finished." Prue explained. "But the cats don't seem to mind him, maybe because they knew he was under the house the whole time. They already knew his scent, I think."

I glanced towards my office. Hoover was in the front window, watching the proceedings with a twitching tail. He was not going to have anything to do with Demon. "You guys want coffee? I'm buying."

Irvin shook his head. "Still can't drink the stuff. We just wanted to stop by on our way home."

They loaded back into Prue's car and drove away, and I removed a cookie and took a bite as I watched them leave They were one crazy couple. I crossed the street to my office and started to open my door, but Mallory opened his door first and stuck his head out. Morri was with him and nodded approvingly at the box from Happy Cookie.

Mallory frowned. "Am I hallucinating? Was that a possum on a leash?"

"Mmmhmmm." I opened the cookie box and held it out to him. "They wanted to let me know I don't have rabies."

Mallory took a bite of cookie and shook his head. "This town just gets weirder every day."

"Weird stuff happens," I quoted Detective Dortman. "Could be worse."

Mallory pointed to the insurance sign in his window. "It could always be worse."

"Maybe you should add that to your window sign, Kami," Morri suggested. "Weird stuff happens but it could always be worse."

I looked at my window, taking in the list of tasks I did for a living, then I laughed. "No. I think I'm good. Maybe I should print t-shirts, though."

"Or write a book," Morri turned towards the alley. "I'm off home. Toodleloo!"

I waved, said goodnight to Mallory, and headed into my office.

Sitting at my desk, I propped my feet up. Hoover ran in and jumped onto my lap, begging for pets and possibly a cookie.

"What do you two think?" I asked aloud to the Crusader and the cat. "Should I write a book?"

Hoover knocked my computer mouse off the desk and Evrett's helm clanked. That was a definite no, then. I yawned. "Yeah. Let's just take a nap instead."

E.L. OAKES IS A WRITER OF MYSTERY and science fiction and author of the Kami White Para(normal)Legal series. She's a lover of books, coffee, cats, and gardening. When she's not at her computer, she can be spotted haunting the local coffee shops in search of the perfect mocha.

www.ingramcontent.com/pod-product-compliance
Lightning Source LLC
Chambersburg PA
CBHW011517100726
47899CB00010BD/3406